BRING ON THE LAW . . .

Harris raised the shotgun, earing back both hammers, and brought it to his shoulder. Thompson leveled his Colt, staring over the sights, and fired. Harris staggered, a starburst of blood dotting his shirt front, and tried to right the scattergun. His eyes were crazed.

Thompson fired two shots in quick succession. The slugs struck Harris just over the sternum, not a handspan apart. He reeled sideways in a nerveless dance, dropping the shotgun, and slammed into the bar.

A sudden pall of silence fell over the room. The crowd waited in a stilled tableau, all eyes locked on Thompson. He moved just inside the doorway, placing his back to the wall. His gaze swept the startled faces, the Colt at his side. He looked at Simms.

"Go get the sheriff," he said. "Tell him to come right along."

DEATHWALK

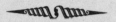

MATT BRAUN

St. Martin's Paperbacks

This is a work of fiction. All of the characters, organizations, and events portrayed in this novel are either products of the author's imagination or are used fictitiously.

DEATHWALK

Copyright © 2000 by Winchester Productions, Ltd.

All rights reserved.

For information address St. Martin's Press, 175 Fifth Avenue, New York, NY 10010.

ISBN: 978-0-312-97516-6

Printed in the United States of America

St. Martin's Paperbacks edition / September 2000

St. Martin's Paperbacks are published by St. Martin's Press, 175 Fifth Avenue, New York, NY 10010.

10 9 8 7 6 5 4 3 2

To
BOB AND JOY HEIMAN
AND
HUD
THE TOPS, ACES HIGH, THE BEST!

AUTHOR'S NOTE

Deathwalk is based on a true story.

Ben Thompson was the foremost shootist of his time. A gambler by profession, he plied his trade from the border of Old Mexico to Denver and Dodge City and countless other boomtowns. His personal code of honor allowed neither insult nor physical threat from another man. History records that those who provoked his anger were soon bound for the graveyard. He never lost a gunfight.

Bat Masterson, who was himself a noted gunfighter, stated that Thompson was without equal. In 1907, Masterson was engaged by *Human Life* to write a series of articles on famous shootists of the Old West. At the time, Masterson was a sportswriter for the *Morning Telegraph* in New York City. Yet his reputation as a frontier lawman was still the stuff of legend, and he had personally known all of the Western gunfighters. He selected for his first article none other than Ben Thompson.

Masterson wrote: "Ben Thompson was remarkable . . . it is very doubtful if in his time there was another man living who equaled him with a pistol in a life and death struggle. He was absolutely without fear and his nerves were those of the finest steel. He had during his career more deadly encounters with the pistol than any man living and won out in every single instance. The very name of Ben Thompson was enough to cause the general run of mankillers to seek safety in instant flight."

Deathwalk deals with a specific time in Ben Thompson's larger-than-life exploits. The article by Bat Masterson was, in part, responsible for the genesis of this novel. Masterson also wrote in his article: "Thompson possessed a much higher order of intelligence than the average gunfighter or mankiller of his time. He was more resourceful than any of that great army of desperate men who flourished on our frontier." These attributes, intelligence and resourcefulness, led Thompson to the most fateful decision of his life. His personal code of honor further secured his place in the mythology of the American West.

Deathwalk is the story of a man who dared against all odds . . . the story of Ben Thompson.

ONE

—======—

"Kings bet twenty."

Thompson studied the dealer's hand. On the table were an eight, a king, a ten and a king. He figured it for two pair, probably kings and eights. Homer Watts, the dealer, was a tombstone peddler who fancied himself a poker player. The other men in the game had dropped out of the hand.

Watts stared across the table with an eager smile. The game was five-card stud, and Thompson's hand revealed a jack, a three, a jack and a king. In the hole he had another jack, but it was the king that impressed him most. With three on the board, the dealer would have to hold the case king to win. The odds dictated otherwise.

"Your twenty—" Thompson shoved chips into the center of the table—"and raise fifty."

"You're bluffin', Ben."

"One way to find out."

"Call your raise," Watts cackled, "and bump it another fifty."

All afternoon the two men had butted heads. The other players were largely spectators, seldom winning a hand. Ben Thompson was the owner of the establishment, the Iron Front Gaming Parlor & Saloon. A gambler of some repute, he invariably drew players to his game. Today was no exception.

"Let's make it interesting," Thompson said casually. "How much in front of you?"

Watts quickly counted his chips. "Hundred and thirty."

"I'll tap you, then. The raise is a hundred and thirty."

"You're tryin' to buy yourself a pot. No way you've got three jacks."

"You'll have to pay to see, Homer."

The other players watched with amused looks. Watts fidgeted a moment, then pushed his chips into the pot. "You're called," he said. "What's your hole card?"

Thompson turned over the third jack. Watts glowered at the cards with an expression of dumb disbelief. "*Gawddamn* the luck!" he howled. "I would've sworn you was bluffin'."

"Another day, another time, Homer. Your luck's bound to change."

"Hold my chair!" Watts announced, jumping to his feet. "I ain't outta the game yet."

The deal passed with each hand. One of the men began collecting the cards. "We're fixin' to play poker here, Homer. You gonna be gone long?"

"Won't take a minute," Watts called, rushing toward the door. "Just gotta go to my wagon."

Thompson shook his head, chuckling to himself, and raked in the pot. He was a blocky man, not quite six feet tall, with square, broad shoulders and rugged features. His gray eyes were alert and penetrating, and even with a full mustache, he looked younger than his thirty-nine years. Over his vest, he wore a spring-clip shoulder holster, the leather molded to the frame of a Colt pistol. The lustrous blue of steel was set off by yellowed ivory grips.

The Iron Front was located just off the corner of Mulberry and Colorado. The establishment got its name from a heavy metal sign that extended the width of the building. A lifelong resident of Austin, the capital of Texas, Thompson had bought the gaming parlor two years ago. In that time, he had transformed it into one of the premier gambling clubs of the city, frequented by lawmakers and influential businessmen. The state capitol building was only two blocks away.

Homer Watts rushed back through the door. A granite tombstone, weighing at least a hundred pounds, was cradled in his arms. In the afternoon lull, there were few men at the long mahogany bar, and fewer still at the faro and twenty-one layouts along the opposite wall. Yet they paused, bemused by the sight, as he staggered toward the poker tables at the rear of the room. He lowered the tombstone to the floor with a thump.

"There you are," he said, grinning at Thompson. "Solid granite and smooth as a baby's butt. Carve anything you want on it."

Thompson nodded appreciatively. "That's a fine looking headstone, Homer. What does it have to do with poker?"

"Well, it's worth a couple of hundred, easy. You credit me with a hundred and I'm back in the game. You got yourself a bargain."

"What the devil would I do with a headstone?"

Watts gave him a crafty look. "Everybody needs one sooner or later. C'mon, Ben, be a sport. What's a hundred?"

Thompson glanced at the men seated around the table. "How about it, gents? Think it's worth a hundred?"

None of them thought Ben Thompson had any immediate need of a headstone. He was the most renowned shootist of the day, reported to have killed eight men in gunfights. The *Police Gazette*, ever in search of a sensational headline, ranked him more deadly than Doc Holliday, or the infamous John Wesley Hardin, now confined to the state penitentiary. His name on a headstone seemed as remote as the stars.

"All right, Homer," Thompson said amiably, tossing chips across the table. "Have a seat and let's get on with the game. You just made a sale."

"Five-card draw," the dealer said, shuffling the cards. "Everybody ante up."

Homer Watts found luck to be as elusive as ever. He opened with a pair of queens and failed to improve his hand on the draw. Yet he rode it to the end, confident he couldn't be beat.

A pair of aces left him poorer, if not wiser.

The game ended shortly before six o'clock. The players cashed in their chips and drifted to the bar. There, over whiskey, they commiserated with one another on the turn of the cards. Few of them had won more than the price of a drink.

Thompson walked to his office at the rear of the room. He was a family man, and unlike most gamblers, he made it a point to have supper with his wife and son. Then, around eight in the evening, he would return to the Iron Front for a night of poker. He usually played until two or three o'clock in the morning.

A dandy of sorts, Thompson was an impeccable dresser. His normal attire was a Prince Albert suit, with a somber vest and striped trousers, and a diamond stickpin in his tie. He topped it off with a silk stovepipe hat, and the result was a man who looked the very picture of sartorial fashion. As he slipped into his coat, tugging the lapel snug over his shoulder holster, the door opened. Joe Richter, who managed the club, stepped into the office.

"You're a corker, boss," he said with a toothy grin. "Everybody in town will have a good laugh over that game."

Thompson shrugged. "Homer had his mind set on playing. How could I turn him down?"

"Damn fool ought to stick to sellin' headstones. Poker's not his game."

"Joe, the same might be said about most of our customers. Sometimes it gets discouraging."

Thompson was known and respected on the Western gamblers' circuit. Over the past decade he had played poker from the Mexican border to the Dakotas. In the Kansas cowtowns, during trailing season, he'd never failed to find a high stakes game with wealthy Texas cattlemen. His name alone brought high rollers to the table.

Austin was a different kettle of fish. On occasion he would host a high stakes game with legislators from the state capitol and local ranchers. But for the most part, the Iron Front catered to a clientele who viewed gambling as a pastime. Faro and roulette, and other games of chance, made the enterprise immensely profitable, even for low stakes. Still, it was a world apart from the action he'd known on the gamblers' circuit. Some days were more boring than others.

Joe Richter saved him from the drudgery of daily operations. A slender stalk of a man, Richter was a veteran of the gaming life and a highly competent manager. His responsibility included everything from hiring and firing dealers to overseeing the bartenders. He was trustworthy and capable, and his expertise with gaming tables was reflected in the monthly balance sheet. His attention to detail relieved Thompson of the tedium associated with running a business, albeit one of a sporting nature. He was, for all practical purposes, the backbone of the Iron Front.

"Before you go," he said now. "What should I do with the tombstone? We have to get it off the floor."

"Donate it to one of the churches," Thompson replied. "Preachers are always burying somebody."

"And if they ask how we got it?"

"Tell them Homer Watts took it out in trade."

Thompson moved to the door, his stovepipe hat tilted at a rakish angle. He went through the club and emerged onto the street, struck by the cloying warmth of day's end. Austin was sometimes brutally hot in the summer, and July had proved to be a scorcher. He turned toward Congress Avenue, where the streetcar line bisected the city.

A short distance ahead, three cowhands were congregated at the corner of Mulberry and Colorado. Thompson saw that they were reasonably sober, and wondered why they had strayed into the uptown area. The cattle trade usually kept to the red light district, which was some blocks south, nearer the river. As he approached, the men inspected his fashionable attire with wiseacre grins. One of them stepped into his path.

"Well, looky here," the cowhand gibed. "We got our-selves a regular swell. Where you from, pilgrim?"

Thompson realized he'd been mistaken for an East-erner. The idea amused him, and he decided to play along. "Why, I came West for my health. I have a lung condition."

"Ain't too healthy for Yankees around these parts."

"On the contrary, I've found it quite pleasant."

"Yeah?" The cowhand reached out and swatted his top hat into the gutter. "What d'you think now?"

Thompson retrieved his hat. "I think your ma never taught you any manners. You give cattlemen a bad name."

"Listen to the sorry shit-heel talk! Maybe I'll just teach *you* some manners."

"Fun's fun and you've had yours, cowboy. Let it drop."

"Hell I will!"

The cowhand drew back a doubled fist. Thompson had survived a lifetime of random violence on sharp re-flexes and flawless instincts. The odds were three to one, and he wasn't about to engage in a street brawl. He popped the Colt out of his shoulder holster.

"Holy shit!" one of the men yelled. "He's got a gun!"

The cowhands took off running in different direc-tions. All along the street, passersby scattered and ducked for cover. Then, in an act of bravado, the cow-boy who had started the trouble skidded to a halt and pulled his pistol. He darted behind the awning post of a barbershop and winged a shot at Thompson. The slug exploded through the window of a store across the street.

Thompson extended his Colt to arm's length. The cowhand was concealed by the awning post, but the right side of his head and his wide-brimmed hat were partially visible. Drawing a fine bead, Thomson sighted carefully and feathered the trigger. The man's ear lobe vanished in a spray of blood.

A wild, gibbering screech followed upon the Colt's report. The cowhand dodged past the opposite awning post, momentarily obscured from view, and broke into a headlong sprint. Thompson kept him fixed in the sights, silently urging him not to turn and fight. He disappeared around the far corner at the end of the block.

Some thirty minutes later City Marshal Ed Creary appeared at the scene of the shooting. Thompson was waiting with a policeman who had responded to the sound of gunfire. A crowd stood watching, spilling out into the intersection, buzzing excitedly about the latest escapade of Austin's resident gunman. Creary elbowed his way through the onlookers.

"What's the trouble here?" he demanded. "Who'd you shoot now, Thompson?"

"I didn't take the time to get his name."

"Did you kill him?"

"Not likely," Thompson said in a wry tone. "Last time I saw him, he was still going hell-for-leather."

Creary was a beefy man with pugnacious features and a dark scowl that gave him a satanic look. He considered Thompson a smudge on the reputation of Austin, and the sense of dislike was mutual. For his part, Thompson thought the town's chief law enforcement officer was a politician hiding behind a badge. He'd never known Creary to take hand in a shooting involving the police. The marshal invariably appeared after the fact.

"Who started it, anyway?" Creary persisted. "Did you fire the first shot?"

"I defended myself," Thompson said. "He let loose and I returned fire. You won't have any problem recognizing him."

"How's that?"

"Look for a cowhand missing his right ear lobe."

"And you're gonna tell me you shot off his ear on purpose?"

"I generally hit just exactly what I aim at."

Creary grunted. "I'll have to charge you with the discharge of firearms. You know the law."

"Do whatever you've got to do. I'll pay the fine in the morning."

"I ought to arrest you."

"Don't even think about it, Ed." Thompson smiled at him with a level stare. "I wouldn't take kindly to being rousted for no reason."

There was a moment of leaden silence. Creary was aware of the crowd watching him, and his face flushed with anger. But he was even more aware of Thompson's stare, pinning him in place like a butterfly on a board. He knew better than to push too far.

"I'm late for supper," Thompson said when the silence held. "Send somebody around if you find that cowhand. The goofy bastard tried to murder me."

Creary ground his teeth. "You just make sure you're in court tomorrow."

"I always obey the law, Marshal. It's one of my finer virtues."

Thompson walked off toward the center of town. He thought it unlikely the cowhand would be found, and curiously unjust that he was the one who would be fined. Yet there was a bright side to any fracas.

He wasn't the one who'd lost an ear lobe.

TWO

A short walk brought Thompson to Congress Avenue. The broad thoroughfare sloped gently from the state capitol grounds to the Colorado River, which bordered the southern edge of the city. A mule-drawn streetcar clanged back and forth from the river to a residential district north of the capitol.

Thompson hopped aboard the streetcar when it stopped at the corner. He took a seat at the rear, tipping his hat to a lady with a folded parasol nestled in her lap. Directly ahead, a fiery sunset bronzed the dome of the capitol and boiled the blue out of the sky. A lamplighter walking along the avenue ignited gas vents that illuminated round globes in the quickening dusk.

The streetcar bell clanged and Thompson settled back in his seat. Outwardly calm, he was still seething from his encounter with Marshal Ed Creary. He considered himself a businessman, and many of Austin's most prominent civic leaders accorded him their respect. Yet lawmen, not to mention the press, labeled him a shootist and mankiller. He sometimes wondered if he would ever outdistance his reputation.

A native of England, Thompson's family had immigrated to the United States in 1851. He was nine years old, and along with his parents and his younger brother, the family landed at Galveston and settled in Austin shortly afterward. He was educated in a private school, but he was a hot-tempered youth, and constantly in trouble. His name first made newspaper headlines when he was fifteen, and challenged a schoolmate to a duel. They fought at forty paces, with shotguns, and both were severely wounded.

Some three years later, when he was eighteen, he became embroiled in an argument over the attentions of a girl. The affair turned deadly, and after an exchange of gunshots, Thompson was tried and acquitted on a charge of manslaughter. During the Civil War, while serving under the Confederate flag, he killed two men in gambling disputes, and was exonerated in each instance. On the gamblers' circuit, in the years that followed, he sent five more men to their graves in what were ruled justifiable homicides. By then, his reputation was known across the breadth of the West.

Two years ago, in league with Bat Masterson, Thompson took part in what was widely publicized as the Royal Gorge War. A group of gunmen were recruited in Dodge City by the Atchison, Topeka & Santa Fe Railroad. They proceeded to Colorado and fought several pitched battles with mercenaries of the Denver & Rio Grande Railroad over the right-of-way through Raton Pass. Afterward, with the five thousand dollars earned in the railroad war, Thompson returned to Austin and bought the Iron Front. Today was the first time he'd fired a gun in anger since departing Colorado.

But now, in the summer of 1881, little or nothing seemed to have changed. The *Police Gazette* still wrote articles about him, and the law jumped to the conclusion that he'd fired the first round in today's shootout. Thompson stared off into space as the streetcar trundled along, feeling oddly haunted by his own reputation. He'd killed men for what he considered sound reasons, and for the past two years he had been a model citizen and businessman. Yet he was still the most notorious figure in Austin.

The streetcar tracks circled around the state house grounds. A last ray of sunlight glinted off the capitol dome, and Thompson seemed to awaken from his ruminations. His gaze was drawn to the dome, and then downward over the immense three-story structure. He tried to recall when it was completed, and vaguely recollected the last block of limestone being laid the summer he was sixteen. A year later the Governor's Mansion had been erected catty-corner from the capitol grounds, between Colorado and Lavaca streets. He had grown to manhood watching the city double and redouble in size.

The original town site, situated along the banks of the river, had been named for Stephen Austin, the founder of Texas. The year was 1839, shortly after the war for independence with Mexico, and six years later Texas was admitted to the Union as a state. Austin spread northward from the river, and like ancient Rome, the town was built upon seven hills. The setting was pastoral, surrounded by rolling prairie and limestone mountains, and attracted immigrants by the thousands. A city began to take shape.

The decade following the Civil War brought explosive growth. In 1871, with the arrival of the Houston & Texas Central and the International & Great Northern, Austin became the railroad hub of central Texas. By 1874 gaslighting illuminated Congress Avenue, and shortly afterward waterworks and sewage systems were installed to serve the burgeoning city. The population swelled to more than ten thousand, and two of the largest banks in Texas established headquarters opposite the Capitol Square. The frontier town grown to a city led the state into an era of commerce and prosperity.

Thompson was seldom given to introspection. Yet today, reflecting inwardly, he thought his life was somehow intricately bound to the place of his boyhood. His parents had passed on some years before, and his younger brother, Billy, was a gypsy without family or roots. Over the years, that same wanderlust had taken him to cowtowns and mining camps dotting the West, always chasing the rainbow. But wherever he roamed, he was drawn, inexorably, back to the banks of the Colorado, and Austin. His inner compass seemed forever fixed on the city of his youth.

Dusk darkened the land as he stepped off the streetcar. His home was seven blocks north of the capitol, on University Avenue, with a spacious lot. The house itself was a classic Victorian, white with green trim, with a pitched roof, square towers, and arched windows. Directly across the street was College Hill, campus for the University of Texas, which now had four hundred students. The proximity to the university, in one of the city's more affluent neighborhoods, was the principal reason he'd bought the house. He wanted his son raised among decent people, well-born and educated.

Catherine was waiting in the parlor. She was a svelte woman, pleasantly attractive with lively green eyes and a mass of auburn hair piled atop her head. Five years younger than Thompson, she still had her figure, full breasts accentuated by a stemlike waist. She walked into the hallway as he entered the door.

"Home is the stranger," she said with a dimpled smile, kissing him on the cheek. "I thought maybe the streetcar had gone out of service."

"No, nothing like that," Thompson said, hooking his hat on a coatrack. "I got waylaid downtown."

"I kept your supper in the warmer oven. Tell me about it while you eat."

"Where's Bobby?"

"In his room, working on his model ship. I sometimes wonder he hasn't run off to sea."

She led the way through the parlor. The furniture was French Victorian, with slender cabriole legs and balloon-shaped cushions. Thompson took a seat in the dining room, at a glistening rosewood table with a carved rose motif bordering the edge and along the legs. She returned from the kitchen with his plate.

"Well, now," he said, studying rare cuts of roast beef surrounded by potatoes and vegetables. "I'm glad I made it home for supper."

"I just hope it's not overdone from sitting in the oven."

Catherine made several trips to the kitchen. She brought fluffy dinner rolls, fresh water, and finally a pot of coffee, all carried one at a time. Thompson had long since learned that an offer to help would be quietly refused. She insisted on doing everything herself, even though it was a chore at times with one hand. The left sleeve of her dress was folded double and pinned beneath her upper arm.

Some years ago, the summer of 1871, Thompson had

taken the family on holiday to Kansas City. He'd rented a buggy for sightseeing, and the second day there, when their horse bolted, the buggy overturned. Bobby, who was four at the time, was thrown clear, and Thompson's leg was broken. Catherine was pinned underneath the frame of the buggy, her left arm crushed beyond repair. A surgeon at the city hospital performed an amputation just above the elbow. Undaunted, never once expecting pity, she emerged from the ordeal with her spirit intact.

Thompson had long ago grown accustomed to her shortened arm. Over the years, in some way he couldn't define, he'd come to admire her even more than before. Her indomitable will, her refusal to withdraw in the face of adversity, was to him the measure of the woman. They had been married in 1863, while he was on furlough during the Civil War, and eighteen years had done nothing to diminish what he felt for her. Nor had the loss of her arm affected the physical bond between them. Her appetite matched his own, and she was still the most sensual woman he'd ever known. He never got enough of her.

"Well—" She paused, pouring him another cup of coffee. "I'm dying of curiosity. Aren't you going to tell me how you got—what was it—waylaid?"

Thompson rarely kept any secrets from her. All the more so when he knew she would read about it in the morning paper. He speared a chunk of beef with his fork, waved it with an idle motion. His expression was one of feigned innocence.

"Some fool cowboy braced me," he said, popping the beef into his mouth. "Knocked my hat off, and tried to take a swing at me. So, naturally, I had to defend myself."

"Oh, no!" she exclaimed, her eyes wide. "You drew your gun?"

"Now keep in mind, he fired first. Not that there's a cowboy alive any good with a gun. I just winged him a little bit. Nothing serious."

"How serious is 'nothing serious'?"

"Took a little piece of his ear."

"You intentionally shot him in the ear?"

"Katie, I don't mind saying I'm surprised at you. Have you ever known me to miss?"

Catherine had no trouble at all imagining the scene. Her husband lived by a code that was immutable as day and night. He would not be insulted, and he would not tolerate being manhandled, or struck a blow. Any man who violated the code was at risk.

"I'm so sorry, Ben," she said in a soft voice. "I know you've tried your best to avoid problems. It's been what—two years?"

"Two years, three months," Thompson observed, chewing thoughtfully. "Guess it was too good to last."

"Were the police involved?"

"Ed Creary tried to play the big lawdog. I'll have to pay a fine in city court."

"But that's not fair!" she said in a sudden temper. "Why should you be fined when the cowboy fired first?"

"I haven't got the least notion," Thompson said. "Especially when he's the one that started it. Anybody that dumb deserves to get shot."

"You shot somebody, Pa?"

The voice brought them around. Bobby, addressed as Robert only when being scolded, was standing in the parlor doorway. He was tall for his age, barely fourteen, with the promise of his father's sturdy build. His eyes bright with excitement, he advanced into the dining room.

"You've turned Injun on me, son," Thompson said. "How'd you sneak downstairs so quiet?"

"I dunno," Bobby said, refusing to be sidetracked. "Who'd you shoot, Pa?"

Catherine motioned him to a chair. "Have a seat and let your father eat in peace. No more questions."

"Cripe's sake, Ma, all I asked was who he shot. What's wrong with that?"

"Listen to your mother," Thompson admonished him. "Let's not have any back talk, buddy boy. Understand?"

Bobby pulled a face. "I never get to hear anything. It's not fair."

Thompson playfully tousled his hair. "Some things are better left to grown-ups. Maybe we'll talk about it when you're older."

"All the guys will be talkin' about how you shot somebody. What am I gonna say when they ask me, Pa? I'll look like a stupe."

"You heard your father," Catherine said sternly. "We'll not have any more discussion on this subject. That's final!"

Thompson nodded agreement. The boy was overly fascinated with his father's reputation as a gunman, often badgering him for details. He remembered that he was hardly older than Bobby when he'd engaged in his first shootout, and it was an unsettling thought. There was nothing particularly heroic about the life he'd led; he didn't want the boy following in his footsteps. He intended an altogether different life for his son, something respectable and proper. A doctor, or perhaps a lawyer. Anything but a gambler.

"How's the model ship?" he asked, diverting the boy onto safer ground. "Have you about got it finished?"

"Well, just about," Bobby said in a sulky voice. "I've got the masts and everything pretty much finished. Still needs sails."

"What was it you called it—a brigantine?"

"No, Pa, that's a pirate ship. This's gonna be a schooner, a big one. Like for the China trade."

"Your mother worries you're liable to run off to sea someday. Think you'd like to be a sailor?"

"Maybe," Bobby allowed. "I dunno yet."

"You've got plenty of time to decide. No rush."

Thompson took a last swig of coffee. He fished a thin cheroot from his inside coat pocket and struck a match, puffing wads of blue smoke. There was no real concern that Bobby would run off to sea and follow the China trade. The boy was bright, one of the better students at school, and got top marks. One day, he would attend the university, and from there . . . anything was possible.

A little later, Thompson allowed himself to be led upstairs for a look at the model ship. Catherine began clearing dishes from the table, carrying them to the kitchen sink. Yet her mind was on the men in her family, and how impressionable young boys were at fourteen. She saw so much of her husband in her son.

Not that there was anything wrong with that. Her husband was faithful and loving, generally even-tempered, and a good father. All a wife could ask for in a man.

She just wished he weren't so quick with a gun.

THREE

Thompson was seated at the desk in his office. His eyes glazed as he stared at rows of figures in an accounting ledger. The numbers seemed to blur.

Twice a month, on the first and the fifteenth, he went over the books. Today was July 15, and he'd been dreading the chore since awakening that morning. He was not a bookkeeper, and reconciling daily operating expenditures with gross revenues seemed to him an exercise in boredom. The task invariably put him in a foul mood.

Joe Richter was meticulous with the books. His penmanship was flawless, and he accounted for every dime as though he owned a part of the Iron Front. Still, Thompson thought it only appropriate that he fulfill his duties as proprietor, and however tedious, perform the role of a businessman. The one saving grace was the impressive financial balance shown in the ledger. Every month added to his already sizeable net worth.

The door rattled under a hammering fist. He turned from the desk, a scowl on his face, and started out of his chair. Halfway to his feet, the door flew open and his expression abruptly turned to one of amazement. His brother Billy strode into the office.

"Goddamn, I knew it!" Billy howled. "Got you chained to a desk!"

"Where the hell'd you drop from?"

"Here, there, and yon. Never let the dust settle under your feet. That's my motto."

"You no-account rascal!"

Thompson smothered him in an affectionate bear hug. Billy was three years younger, lithe and muscular, with a sweeping mustache. The family resemblance was striking; even in a crowd, they would have stood out as brothers. Their features were all but a mirror image.

"Never thought I'd live to see it," Billy chided. "You slaving over the books like some blue-nosed banker. I'll bet you're rich as Midas."

"I eat regular," Thompson said expansively. "How about you?"

"Livin' high on the hog, big brother. Things couldn't get no better."

Their closeness was born not just of blood. They genuinely liked one another, and each considered the other his staunchest friend. Hardly more than boys, they had joined the Second Texas Cavalry Regiment and fought under the Confederate flag for four long, bloody years. Their wartime service included engagements in Texas, New Mexico, Louisiana, and finally, skirmishes along the Mexican border. They emerged from the conflict as veterans of the killing ground, having killed their share. Neither of them ever flinched in the heat of battle.

Following the Civil War, thousands of Rebels could

not come to terms with the Yankee occupation of their homeland. The Thompson brothers, like many Confederates, crossed the border and joined the army of Emperor Maximilian. Under the patronage of France's Louis Napoleon, Maximilian was then waging war on the forces of Benito Juarez, a Mexican revolutionary. In 1867, when Maximilian was captured and executed, the imperial army scattered to the winds. Thompson, by then the captain of a cavalry troop, escaped with Billy and returned to Austin.

A year later, Billy killed a Union army sergeant during a drunken argument in a brothel. Thompson, working quietly and quickly, engineered his brother's escape to the sanctuary of Indian Territory. But the incident pushed Billy into the wild life, and he began a wayward pilgrimage that had yet to end. He never married, and like so many drifters in the West, he was forever in search of the next El Dorado. He became a vagabond gambler, occasionally joining Thompson in a cowtown or mining camp, only to disappear with news of the latest bonanza. Over a year had passed since his last visit to Austin.

"Where have you been?" Thompson asked. "Wouldn't hurt you to write a letter now and then."

Billy waved it off. "I never was one for letters. By the time you answered, I would've been somewheres else, anyhow."

"So where's somewheres else?"

"Tombstone."

"Arizona?"

"Last time I checked," Billy said with a crooked smile. "Lots of the old Dodge City crowd out there, too. Damnedest silver strike this side of kingdom come."

Thompson nodded. "I heard Wyatt Earp and his brothers were there. Who else?"

"Doc Holliday showed up right after Wyatt. Those two always were thicker'n fleas on a dog."

"How's Doc's health these days?"

"Still coughin' his lungs up a piece at a time. Most days, he looks like death warmed over."

"Billy, he'll probably outlive us both."

"Speak for yourself," Billy said, rolling his eyes. "I aim to live till hell freezes over."

"Sure you do," Thompson said dryly. "The Devil himself will be there to crack the ice."

"You interested in hearin' about Tombstone or not?"

"What's there to tell besides Wyatt and Doc?"

"Bat Masterson."

"Now that I hadn't heard."

"And Luke Short."

"I'll be damned."

"Told you it was the whole crowd."

Thompson counted all of the men as longtime friends. He'd first met Earp and Masterson in Wichita, and later renewed the acquaintance when the cattle trade moved to Dodge City. Through them, he had been introduced to Holliday and Short, two of the more widely known names on the gamblers' circuit. But he was particularly close to Masterson, whom he admired as both a man and a lawman. He considered Masterson a cut above the others.

"What's Bat doing in Tombstone?"

"Dealin' faro," Billy said, wagging his head. "Him and Luke Short are workin' for Wyatt. Don't that take the cake!"

"Sure as hell does," Thompson agreed. "Are you saying Wyatt owns a gaming club?"

"Well, he's partners in a place called the Oriental Saloon. Fanciest dive in Tombstone."

"And Bat's just a dealer—that's all?"

"Yeah, that's it," Billy said. "'Course, I guess he wore a badge too long. He still tries to play the peacekeeper."

"Peacekeeper?" Thompson repeated. "How so?"

"That dust-up between Short and Charlie Storms. Bat tried to talk 'em out of it."

"Who's Charlie Storms?"

"Don't they print the news in Austin anymore? I thought everybody knew about that."

"I haven't read anything."

"Then you missed a humdinger. I was there that night, playin' poker. Saw the whole thing."

Billy quickly related the details. Charlie Storms, who was playing faro at Short's table, questioned the deal. An argument ensued, and the two men were on the verge of drawing guns. Masterson intervened, talking fast, and persuaded them to call a truce. Storms stalked out the door, only to return later in the day, with gun in hand. Short rose from behind his faro layout and calmly fired three shots. The first broke Storms's neck and the other two slugs struck him in the heart. He fell dead with the cocked gun still in hand.

"Never got off a shot," Billy concluded. "Damnedest thing you ever saw."

"Sounds like Luke hasn't lost his touch."

"Went back to dealin' faro—cool as you please."

Thompson, unwittingly, was reminded of another shooting, long ago. The summer of 1873, he and Billy were running faro games in Ellsworth, a Kansas cowtown. They got into an altercation with a couple of gamblers, one of whom owed Thompson money. The local sheriff attempted to defuse the situation, only to be caught in the middle. Billy, who was drunk at the time, accidentally discharged a shotgun, and the sheriff was killed. In the confusion, Thompson spirited his brother out of town and put him on a horse for Texas. Murder charges were promptly brought against Billy.

Four years passed, with Billy on the dodge and Thompson working to have the charges dismissed. Then, in 1877, Texas Rangers finally captured Billy, and he was extradited to Kansas. Thompson hired a battery of lawyers, who mounted an aggressive defense when Billy was brought to trial. The lawyers managed to obfuscate the facts, and witnesses to the shooting, fearful of offending Thompson, suffered a lapse of memory. The jury rendered an acquittal verdict, and Billy was once again a free man. The legal bills, and four years in hiding, came at a stiff price. Thompson ultimately shelled out more than ten thousand dollars.

"So anyway," Billy went on, "Virgil Earp practically walked Luke through the coroner's inquest. Took about ten minutes to get a ruling of self-defense."

Thompson appeared surprised. "Virgil's a lawyer now?"

"That'll be the day! Virgil's the city marshal of Tombstone. Still wearin' a badge."

"What about Wyatt?"

"Wyatt's got his hand in lots of things," Billy said. "I told you about the gaming dive, and he's bought some mining claims. 'Course, everybody knows he's got his eye on the sheriff's job."

Thompson chuckled. "Wyatt always was the ambitious one in the family."

"Hell, you don't know the half of it. Him and Virgil mean to take over the law and run the whole show. They'll wind up ownin' Tombstone."

"That's a little too ambitious—even for Wyatt."

"Ben, I'm tellin' you, he's got brass balls."

Billy recounted the story with some gusto. Wyatt Earp intended to make his fortune in Tombstone, where the silver mines were turning out millions in ore. His brothers, Virgil and Morgan, were part of the grand design, one the city marshal and the other a deputy. Wyatt, meanwhile, was campaigning to discredit the sheriff, a man named Behan. The campaign was directed at the Clanton gang, a band of robbers operating under Behan's protection, and a connection that could bring about his downfall. The accusations by Wyatt were the talk of Tombstone.

"These Clantons are a hard bunch," Billy finally said. "Wyatt's liable to get more than he bargained for."

"But if he gets in as sheriff," Thompson remarked, "he'll control the county. He can write his own ticket."

"Yeah, he could wind up a goddamn millionaire. Or get himself bushwhacked some dark night."

"Is Bat in with the Earps on the deal?"

"Funny thing about Bat," Billy said in a musing voice. "Way he talks, he's plumb done wearin' a badge. Guess he got a bellyful back in Dodge City."

"Politics is a rough game," Thompson noted. "Even so, I'm still surprised to hear that Bat's turned faro dealer. He was a damn fine peace officer."

"Not everybody's like you and Wyatt," Billy joshed. "Some men weren't cut out to be business tycoons. There's more to life than money."

"Spoken like a man who sleeps wherever he hangs his hat. I offered to go partners with you years ago. What would you say if I asked you now?"

"Well, you know me, Ben. A rolling stone gathers no moss. I like to keep movin'."

Thompson couldn't argue the point. All their lives, he'd been the one determined to make his mark in the world. Perhaps being the older brother was the driving force, but his reach had always exceeded his grasp. Billy, on the other hand, was happy-go-lucky and irresponsible, and not the least bit ashamed of his shiftless attitude. He was a nomad who wandered wherever the impulse took him. Tomorrow was his vision of the future.

"You're a case, little brother," Thompson said ruefully. "I suppose you're just passing through to somewhere else. Am I right?"

Billy laughed. "I need a change of scenery every now and then. Never was one to get stuck in a rut."

"So how long can you stay?"

"I reckon I could spend the night. Wouldn't want to wear out my welcome."

"One night!" Thompson barked. "Haven't seen you in a year and all you can spare is one night? What's your rush?"

"No rush a-tall," Billy said, spreading his hands. "We'll be talked out long before mornin' anyhow. One night ought to do it."

"Katie's gonna raise the roof. You're her only brother-in-law, and believe it or not, she likes you. She'll be damned upset."

"I'll sweet-talk her out of it, don't you worry. How's she been?"

"She's been just fine, thank you. Too bad you never found somebody like her."

"No weddin' bells for me," Billy said, amused by the thought. "I never was much for strings and things. How's little Bobby?"

"Not so little anymore," Thompson said. "You might recollect, he's going on fifteen."

"Fifteen."

Billy spoke the word in a subdued voice. He stared off into the middle distance, as though looking backward through a cobweb of years. He was silent for a long moment, then he blinked, the reverie broken. His mouth curled in the old devil-may-care grin.

"Time flies when you're havin' fun, don't it, Ben?"

Thompson felt a lump in his throat. He thought he'd never seen a lonelier man than the one across from him, his brother. The insouciant manner and the easygoing charm were all pretense, a veneer to mask what was inside. He debated whether to insist—demand—that a single night in a year was not nearly enough. But then, knowing his brother all too well, he discarded the notion. Some men were not meant for strings and things.

"So tell me, Mr. Fiddlefoot," he said, forcing a jocular tone. "Where're you headed like your pants are on fire?"

"Brownsville," Billy said with his loopy grin. "Figured I'd sashay on down to the border."

"What the hell's in Brownsville?"

"I hear the Rio Grande's the last holdout for riverboats. I always fancied myself a riverboat gambler."

"You know something—" Thompson studied him a moment, "I think you might have found your calling. By God, a riverboat gambler!"

Billy looked pleased. "Got a good ring to it, don't it?"

Thompson nodded, smiling, as though he agreed. But in the back of his mind, he was wondering how long it would last. The answer came to him almost immediately.

Not long.

FOUR

The men began arriving at the Iron Front shortly before eight o'clock. The evening of July 20 was sultry, with roiling clouds and the smell of rain in the air. Off to the west, beyond the mountains, jagged streaks of lightning split the sky.

Thompson hosted a private game every Tuesday night. The players were drawn from a list of businessmen and politicians, and the game was by invitation only. Those attending tonight's session were shown to a back room, opposite Thompson's office. The walls were paneled in dark hardwood, with plush maroon carpeting on the floor, and a walnut sideboard stocked with liquor. The baize top of the poker table was bathed in the cider glow of an overhead lamp.

The men represented a cross-section of Austin's civic leaders. Among those present tonight were Mayor Tom

Wheeler; James Shipe, president of the Mercantile National Bank; and Will Cullen, the largest liquor wholesaler in Central Texas. Luther Edwards and Jack Walton, partners in a law firm, were noted litigators and Thompson's personal attorneys. They all enjoyed a friendly game of poker, even though they played by cutthroat rules. The stakes were ten-dollar limit, with three raises, check and raise permitted. No one thought to make his fortune at the Iron Front.

The mood of the game was genial, a once-a-week rivalry with cards. Thompson was by far the most seasoned player, and he often folded decent hands rather than win too heavily. Yet the men relished testing themselves against a professional, particularly one whose name commanded respect within the gambling fraternity. There was, as well, the fact that he was considered the most deadly shootist of the day. Only a week ago, according to the newspapers, he'd shot off a cowboy's ear! A sense of danger added spice to the game.

The mayor won the first hand for a modest pot. The deal passed from man to man, with agreement that only standard draw and stud were allowed. Jim Shipe, the banker, dealt five-card draw, and raised the opener upon discovering he'd dealt himself three fours. Thompson, who was nursing a pair of kings and easily read Shipe's gloating expression, folded after the draw. Everyone else stayed in, contributing to the pot, as Shipe and Cullen, the liquor wholesaler, took it to three raises. Shipe, certain he'd won, proudly spread his three fours on the table. Cullen turned over three sixes.

"Well now," he said, raking in the pot. "You boys better be on your toes. Tonight looks to be my night."

"Talk about luck of the draw," Shipe countered. "I

deal myself three of a kind and you stumble onto another six. What, may I ask, are the odds on that? Any idea, Ben?"

Thompson chuckled. "I'd take your hand anytime. Like you said, Jim—luck of the draw."

The deal passed to Walton. As he shuffled, his law partner, Luther Edwards, glanced at the mayor. "Did you read the editorial in the *Statesman* this morning? John Cardwell certainly minced no words about the sporting district."

"John likes to play the moralist," Wheeler said indignantly. "Guy Town is one of our city's oldest institutions. Not that I'm defending prostitution, you understand."

"If you don't I will," Cullen said with ribald humor. "Where would City Hall be without the fines on whores? Our property taxes would go sky high."

"Excellent point," Edwards added with a sly smile. "Not to mention that some of our best friends expend all their carnal lust downtown. Who knows how many marriages the floozies have saved?"

Walton, in the midst of dealing the cards, snorted laughter. "Now *that* would make an editorial!"

The newspapers adopted a moral tone when lambasting the world's oldest profession. Yet, along with righteous indignation, there was frequently a tongue-in-cheek twist that lent a note of levity. The *Statesman* editorial that morning had hinted at the name of a prominent legislator seen in the company of a *"fille de joie,"* and demanded that the prostitutes be subjected to higher fines. No one objected to stiffer fines; but apart from clergymen, few people favored reform. Somewhat like their mayor, the citizens of Austin looked upon the sporting district as a landmark. A holdover from the frontier days.

The immediate area north of the railroad depot was known locally as Guy Town. Located between the river and Cedar Street, it was the heart of the sporting district, occupying several square blocks. The streets were lined with saloons, gaming dives, dance halls, and whorehouses, devoted solely to vice and separating working men from their wages. Over the years, as Austin doubled and doubled again in size, the district had grown to encompass the entire southwestern part of the city. People called it Guy Town because it was the haunt of men out for a night's fun. The bordellos, with sin for sale, catered to their most exotic tastes.

Austin itself had been transformed from a riverside outpost into a thriving center of commerce. With the advent of the railroads, business and industry had replaced cattle and ranching as the mainstay of the economy. Yet there was an odd mix of the old and the new, with spurred cowhands still jostling among the sidewalks among laborers, railroad men, and factory workers. The town itself might have changed, but some aspects of life were seemingly immutable to the upheaval of the modern era. A generation of men had frolicked to the pulse of the sporting district, and they remarked on only one change. Guy Town had simply grown larger.

Austin, like many cities in the West, was still reasonably broad-minded about vice. Though it was the county seat of Travis County, and the state capital, the community itself was largely controlled by local politicians. The city government imposed so-called occupation taxes on saloons, gaming dives, and bordellos. Further revenues were generated through periodic raids on the brothels, with court fines levied against madams and prostitutes. The city treasury was kept afloat, and a truce was maintained with the sporting crowd. So long as immorality was confined to Guy Town, the law was tolerant.

Uptown, where the better class of people conducted their business, nothing unseemly was tolerated. There were gambling clubs, saloons, and variety theaters, but none of the depravity to be found in the sporting district. As though the town fathers had drawn a line of demarcation, everything north of Guy Town was held to a different standard. There the streets were free of violence and whores, and clubs such as the Iron Front operated under the benevolence of City Hall. Everyone, saint and sinner alike, benefited by the arrangement.

"Speaking of whores," Cullen said, as another hand was dealt, "I was in Guy Town yesterday afternoon. Even on a Monday, business was really quite brisk. Amazing."

Edwards looked at him with a satiric smile. "Getting your ashes hauled, were you, Will? What would the little woman say?"

"Nothing of the sort!" Cullen protested. "We move carloads of liquor in Guy Town, and I sometimes go out on calls with my salesmen. A man has to keep his eye on business."

"And maybe a little monkey business on the side? Sounds very suspicious to me, Will."

"Leave it to a lawyer to think the worst. Although, I have to admit I did something damned foolish."

"Uh-*huh*!" Edwards crowed. "Now the story comes out."

Cullen glanced at Thompson. "Do you know Al Loraine? He has the faro concession at the Tivoli Saloon."

"I know the name," Thompson said. "I've never had any dealing with him. Why do you ask?"

"We had some time to kill before our next call. I thought I'd amuse myself with a few hands of faro . . ."

"And he took you to the cleaners."

Cullen nodded soberly. "I've never seen such a run of cards. Do you think he's honest?"

"I'll ask around," Thompson replied. "What if he's a sharper? Do you want to press charges?"

"No, no," Cullen said hastily. "I wouldn't want it made public I'd been duped. My wife would never let me hear the end of it."

"Well, I'll check it out, anyway. Never hurts to know who's straight and who isn't."

"Don't put yourself to any trouble. I was really just curious."

"No trouble at all, Will."

Their attention was drawn to their cards as the mayor opened for ten dollars. The conversation about Al Loraine seemed casual enough, but Thompson considered it a serious matter. Gambling, more so than most professions, was susceptible to adverse public opinion. A cardsharp, even in Guy Town, was bad for business.

His mind elsewhere, he idly called the mayor's bet.

The Tivoli Saloon was located on the corner of Cypress and Congress Avenue. A knot of revelers burst from one of the nearby dance halls, lurching drunkenly along the sidewalk. Their raucous laughter mingled with the strains of a rinky-dink piano.

Thompson stepped off the streetcar at the corner. The game had ended shortly after midnight, and nothing more had been said about the faro dealer at the Tivoli. After the mayor and the others were gone, he'd caught the streetcar down to Guy Town. He decided to check it out for himself.

The inside of the saloon was thick with smoke. The bar was lined with men, mostly railyard workers fresh off the late shift. Thompson was known here, as he was anywhere in Austin, and the bartender greeted him with a nod. He seldom ventured into Guy Town, and his frock coat and top hat gave the impression that he was slumming. He ordered a whiskey.

Al Loraine was operating a faro game directly opposite the bar. Thompson knew him on sight, though he couldn't recall ever having spoken to the man. He was hesitant to take a seat at the faro layout, for no one would risk offending him by dealing crooked cards. Instead, as though he'd just stopped by for a nightcap, he watched the game with mild interest. He noted that Loraine was slick, a man with nimble hands.

Faro, even more than poker, was governed by the luck of the draw. An old and highly structured game, it had originated a century before in France. The name was derived from the king of hearts, which bore the image of an Egyptian pharaoh on the back of the card. All betting was against the house, with the odds weighted in favor of the dealer. In Western parlance, it was known as "bucking the tiger."

A cloth layout on the table depicted every card from deuce through ace. After being shuffled, the cards were placed in a dealing box, and then drawn in pairs, displayed face-up. Before the turn of each pair, players placed bets on one or more cards of their choice. The first card out of the box was a losing bet, and the second was a winner. All bets were canceled if there were no wagers on either card.

To one side of the table was an abacuslike device known as the casekeeper. The casekeeper indicated the cards already dealt and allowed a player to figure percentages on cards remaining in the deck. Players could bet win or lose on the layout, and a losing wager was "coppered" by placing a copper token on the chips. A daring player would often bet win and lose on the same turn of the cards.

Thompson caught the gaff within a few minutes. A crooked dealer rigged a faro game in advance with a small rectangular device known as a card trimmer. The metal device was flat on top, with a gauge to position and measure cards, and what resembled a hinged cleaver on one side. By turning a knob on the left side, a thin plate moved the card a millimeter to the right, the edge held firmly in place. The cleaver was then snapped downward in a slicing motion.

The razor-sharp blade cleanly trimmed a millimeter off the side of the card. The trim was discernible only to an educated finger, and left the edge smooth and undetectable to anything but a magnifying glass. A deck of cards put through a trimmer allowed a skilled dealer to "read" individual cards simply by touch. By watching the wagers on the layout, a dealer could hold back certain cards and deal "seconds" to put losing cards into play. The result was akin to shooting fish in a barrel.

Halfway through the deck, Thompson walked to the table. Loraine paused, about to deal a card, and looked at him with a strange expression. The players turned, confused by the halt in the game, uncertain as to what Thompson was about. He nodded to Loraine.

"You're slick," he said with a hard smile. "But I never could abide a goddamned tinhorn. You're running a crooked game."

Loraine blanched. "I've got no quarrel with you, Mr. Thompson. What's going on here?"

"Yesterday you clipped a friend of mine. Trash like you give gamblers a bad name."

"I've never dealt crooked in my life. Your friend is mistaken."

"Save your breath," Thompson told him. "Those cards are trimmed and you're dealing seconds. I know it when I see it."

"That's one man's opinion," Loraine said reasonably. "You'll never prove it."

"Here's your proof."

Thompson snapped the Colt out of his shoulder holster. He thumbed the hammer and brought the pistol to bear as the players dove for cover. Hardly a heartbeat apart, he fired two shots and the dealer's box exploded in splinters of wood and cards shredded into pasteboard. He leveled the Colt on Loraine.

"You care to argue the point?"

Loraine sat frozen in his chair. "No . . . no argument."

"Thompson!"

Sol Simon, owner of the Tivoli, pushed through the crowd. Thompson lowered the hammer on his Colt, shoved it into the holster, and turned away from the table. Simon skidded to a halt.

"What the hell you mean shootin' up my place?"

"You ought to be more careful, Sol. You've got a cardsharp running your faro concession."

Simon went beet red. "You accusing me of operating fixed games?"

"What size shoe do you wear?" Thompson glanced down at the dive owner's feet. "Well, what d'you know about that, Sol? Looks like it fits."

"I'm gonna call Creary and his whole damn police force. I'll put you in jail!"

"Don't lay odds on it."

Thompson walked to the door. As he went out, the northbound streetcar stopped at the corner. He stepped aboard, handing the driver the nickel fare. His mouth creased in a slow smile.

He thought he'd done a good night's work.

FIVE

Thompson awoke around nine the next morning. The thunderstorm had passed overnight, and brilliant shafts of sunlight flooded through the bedroom windows. He rarely lingered in bed, for when he awoke he was instantly and fully awake. A wide, jaw-cracking yawn usually got him off to a quick start.

In his nightshirt, he padded barefoot into the bathroom. He first relieved himself in the commode, an invention he still considered the marvel of the age. Then he set about his morning ritual, scrubbing his teeth, bathing and shaving, and trimming his mustache. Upon emerging from the bathroom, his checks glowed from a splash of bay rum.

A tall armoire occupied one wall of the bedroom. His array of suits were somber in color, each one hand-tailored, cut from the finest fabrics. His shirts, imported from New Orleans, and his underclothing were neatly arranged in separate drawers. For casual wear, his garments were store-bought and somewhat less sedate in tone. He selected twill trousers and a cotton shirt, and shrugged into his shoulder holster. A lightweight corduroy jacket completed his outfit.

Downstairs, he found Catherine in the kitchen. Her hair was upswept and she was wearing a brightly patterned calico dress. Today was the day she baked bread, and her forehead was dotted with beads of perspiration from the heat of the stove. She removed a golden loaf from the oven, gingerly holding the pan with a folded towel, and set it on a rack to cool. He wrapped his arms around her from behind, and placed his hands over her breasts. She laughed a low, throaty laugh.

"Your timing is terrible," she murmured, blowing a damp wisp of hair off her forehead. "Why didn't you think of that last night?"

"I got in late," Thompson said, teasing her nipples with his fingertips. "And besides, you were asleep."

"That has never stopped you before."

"Maybe I'll surprise you tonight."

"Promises, promises."

"Where's Bobby?"

"Off playing somewhere. And don't let that give you any bright ideas."

She slipped out of his embrace. Turning, she gave him a quick kiss, tugging playfully at his mustache, and moved away. He took a chair at the kitchen table, watching as she arranged strips of bacon in an iron skillet and collected a bowl of eggs. His eye fell on the morning *Statesman* which was positioned by his silverware. A headline leaped off the front page.

THOMPSON TERRORIZES GUY TOWN

"I'll be damned," he said blankly. "How'd they get it in the morning edition?"

"Sweetheart, I just imagine they stopped the presses. After all, you are the hottest news in town."

Catherine placed a steaming mug of coffee on the table. She walked back to the stove while he read the account of his raid on the Tivoli Saloon. When he looked up, he found her watching him with a curious expression. He smiled sheepishly and took a swig of coffee. She waited him out.

"Anything for a headline," he said, rapping the newspaper with his finger. "They make too much of it, way too much. I shot the dealer's box, not the dealer."

"Oh, that makes all the difference." She removed bacon from the frying pan and cracked an egg. "The paper says you accused the dealer of being a cheat. Why would you care?"

"Will Cullen was in the game last night. He told me he'd been taken by this dealer at the Tivoli. I promised I'd look into it."

"So you did it for a friend?"

"Well, partly," Thompson allowed. "Guess I did it for myself, too. Tinhorns give all gamblers a bad name."

"Why not let the police handle it?"

She brought his plate to the table. He tore off a chunk of warm fresh bread and dipped it in egg yolk. As he chewed, he smeared butter and jam on the slice of bread, and then took a bite of bacon. She waited for him to answer her question.

"The police would have botched it," Thompson finally said. "First off, they would've never spotted the gaff. Takes a good eye to catch a man dealing seconds."

"And?" she pressed. "There's something else, isn't there?"

"Word's around that Ed Creary is on the take. The dives in Guy Town pay him off to look the other way. Not much chance of a crooked dealer getting arrested."

"Have you told Mayor Wheeler?"

"Didn't have to," Thompson said, loading his fork with hunks of egg. "So I hear on the grapevine, the mayor wants Creary off the ticket in the next election. Trouble is, there's nobody who could beat him at the polls."

She was thoughtful a moment. "Is that the reason you've never liked Creary? Because he takes payoffs?"

"I suppose that's part of it. But mainly it's because he's a pitiful excuse for a lawman. He's just another jackleg politician."

A knock sounded at the front door. Catherine left him to finish breakfast and hurried through the parlor. As he drained his coffee mug, she returned to the kitchen. She looked upset.

"There's a policeman at the door. Are they going to arrest you?"

"Don't get yourself worried."

Thompson walked through the parlor into the hallway. Lon Dennville, a sergeant on the police force, stood on the porch. He was a tough, no-nonsense officer and one of the few men on the force that Thompson respected. He nodded with an apologetic smile.

"Ben, I'm sorry to bother you at home. So far as I'm concerned, it could have waited till you got to the Iron Front. Marshal Creary ordered me to come here."

"Orders are orders," Thompson said evenly. "What can I do for you, Lon?"

"That incident last night—" Dennville offered him

a lame shrug. "You'll have to pay the fine for discharge of firearms, and Creary wants you in court at one o'clock. Otherwise, he'll swear out a warrant for your arrest."

"And he'd probably make you serve it. I doubt he's got the brass to try it himself."

Dennville tactfully held his silence. After a moment, Thompson gestured aimlessly. "Tell Creary he's lucky to have a man of your caliber on the force. I'll be there and pay the fine."

"You've taken a big load off my mind, Ben. I'd hate to be the one to serve that warrant."

"Let's consider it water under the bridge. I'll see you in court."

Dennville looked relieved. Thompson watched as he went down the porch stairs and turned toward the street-car stop at the corner. He felt no animosity for the sergeant, but he was boiling mad at being confronted in his home. Ed Creary was, plain and simple, a son-of-a-bitch.

He told himself there were ways to settle the score.

Bobby always accompanied his father to Waller Creek. For a gambler, a gun was a tool of the trade, and Thompson considered routine practice all part of the profession. He spent every Wednesday morning in pistol drills.

The creek was a mile east of the house. Bobby was awed by his father's skill, and these outings were his favorite time of the week. Thompson was nonetheless ambivalent, and Catherine shared his mixed feelings. He believed that every boy should be taught the proper use of a gun, and respect for a deadly weapon. Yet he was wary of his son following in his footsteps, either as a gambler or a gunman. On their trips to the creek, he generally spoke more of college than of firearms. The message he instilled was clear, and simply stated.

A man with an education was the odds-on favorite in life. A gun, on the other hand, was merely a tool. One should never be confused with the other.

Whatever his plans for his son, Thompson was pragmatic about himself and the life he led. Over the years, he had been involved in far more gunfights then he cared to remember, and witnessed countless others. Experience, and personal reflection in the aftermath of shootings, led to the conclusion that the victor was not necessarily the faster man. Speed was fine, but in his view, accuracy was final.

Thompson operated by a cardinal rule. The shot that killed an opponent, rather than the first shot, was what counted. More often than not, the man who hurried his first shot, the victim of his own nerves, was soon bound for the graveyard. So in his weekly drills, he practiced on a speedy draw, yet his focus was on placing every shot dead center. He was quick, but deliberate.

Bobby positioned himself upstream. He carried a gunnysack filled with empty whiskey bottles collected from the Iron Front. The bottles were corked and airtight, guaranteed to float, and made targets that required deadly accuracy. The boy tossed a bottle into the creek, and then lobbed four more in rapid succession. The bottles bobbed to the surface and floated downstream.

Thompson's hand snaked beneath his jacket. His arm leveled, time fragmented into split seconds, and the pistol roared. The first bottle erupted in a geyser of water and glass, and he locked onto the second. His eyes sighted along the barrel, bottles exploding in quick order, until the last one burst as the current swept it past his position. Less than five seconds had elapsed from the moment he pulled the gun.

Timing himself, Thompson shucked the empty shells and reloaded. On the count of ten, he holstered the Colt, looked upstream at Bobby, and nodded. The drill was repeated, five shots at a time, until thirty bottles had gone to the bottom. Finally, he reloaded, lowering the hammer on an empty chamber, and wedged the Colt into his shoulder holster. He was satisfied that his reflexes were still sharp.

"Goldurn!" Bobby shouted, scampering along the creekbank. "You never miss, Pa!"

"That's the whole idea," Thompson said genially. "I'd hate to lose my touch."

"When you gonna teach me to shoot, Pa? I just bet I'd be good, too."

"We'll get around to it, son. You're a little young yet."

"You always say that," Bobby sulked. "How old do I hav'ta be?"

Thompson tousled his hair. "I'd judge sixteen's a good age. No need to rush things."

"Holy Hannah, that's almost two years off! C'mon, Pa, have a heart—*pleeeze.*"

"Keep your grades up and maybe we'll work something out. Your schooling's more important than popping away at bottles."

"School don't start till September. What about between now and then?"

"We'll wait to see your first report card."

Bobby groaned and pulled a face. Thompson understood his disappointment, for a boy's first gun was thought to be a rite of passage into manhood. But he wanted something more for his son, something better. A life where knowledge, not force of arms, made the difference.

His legacy to the youngster would never be a gun.

City Hall was located at the corner of Mesquite and San Jacinto. The offices of city officials were on the ground floor of the two-story structure, and the jail was in the basement. The city court was on the second floor.

Judge Horace Warren presided over the court. His authority extended to misdemeanor offenses committed within the city limits. For the most part, he dealt with drunk and disorderly, breach of peace, and family disputes. Graver crimes, such as robbery and murder, were tried at the county courthouse.

Thompson walked into the courtroom on the stroke of one o'clock. Marshal Creary, who was standing near the bench, gave him a sour look. The marshal's job, since there was no prosecutor for misdemeanors, was to present the case to the judge. His expression upon spotting Thompson was somehow disgruntled. He clearly would have preferred to request an arrest warrant.

Judge Warren was on the sundown side of fifty. He was squat and pudgy, with rheumy eyes, and noted for dispensing evenhanded justice. He motioned Thompson forward, and waited until he stopped before the bench. Then he nodded to Creary.

"All right, Marshal, let's hear the particulars."

Creary laboriously outlined the case. He dwelled on the fact that Thompson had discharged a firearm in a public establishment, at great risk of bodily injury, perhaps even death, to the patrons. The incident was unprovoked and a clear violation of the city ordinance.

"Your Honor, it's just not tolerable," he concluded. "This is the second time in less than two weeks he's appeared in court for the same offense. I'd hope you'd see fit to give him some jail time."

"Well, Mr. Thompson?" Judge Warren peered down from the bench. "Two times in two weeks is twice too often. What do you have to say for yourself?"

Thompson looked unrepentant. "Judge, for openers, nobody was in any danger. You know yourself, I've never missed in my life." He paused, shook his head. "I hit the mark dead center."

"I grant you are a marksman of the first order. But that doesn't make it any less a violation of the municipal code."

"Maybe not, but I had good cause. That dealer, Al Loraine, he's crooked as they come. I caught him dealing seconds."

"Did you now?" Judge Warren sounded personally offended. "Dealing seconds violates the code to hell and gone. There's no place for a cardsharp in Austin."

"Those are my sentiments exactly, Judge. A man has a right to expect a square deal."

"Your Honor!" Creary interjected loudly. "This isn't about a crooked dealer. It's about firing a gun in public."

The judge squinted at him. "Perhaps you ought to devote more time to cleaning up Guy Town, Marshal Creary. Tinhorn card cheats are a blight on our city's fair name."

"But that's not the point here! We're faced with—"

"Hundred dollar fine," Judge Warren interrupted, banging his gavel. "Pay the bailiff, Mr. Thompson. Case dismissed."

Thompson peeled a hundred off his roll. He grinned

at Creary and let the bill flutter onto the bailiff's desk. Judge Horace Warren rose from the bench, quickly smothering a laugh, and walked toward his chambers. He called back over his shoulder in what he hoped was a stern voice.

"Let's not see you in my courtroom again, Mr. Thompson."

SIX

On the first Friday in August, business was brisk. There was a cattlemen's convention in town, and many of the larger ranchers were inveterate high rollers. By late evening, several of them would gravitate to the tables at the Iron Front.

Thompson nonetheless went home for supper. A table stakes poker game, which attracted the high rollers, wouldn't get under way before eight or so. Until then, he was content to leave the club in the capable hands of Joe Richter. The house odds virtually guaranteed a profit no matter who was on the floor.

Around seven, Thompson hopped aboard the streetcar across from College Hill. He was stuffed with Catherine's meatloaf, savoring the aroma of a half-smoked cheroot. The sky blazed with stars, and a pale sickle moon hung lopsided on the horizon. As the streetcar pulled away, he took a long draw on the cheroot, his gaze fixed on distant, blinking stars. He felt all was right in his world.

For no particular reason, he was in a jolly good mood. Perhaps it was Catherine's meatloaf, or perhaps it was the promise of a high-stakes poker game. Or perhaps, as he reflected on it further, it was the pleasant memory of having bested Ed Creary in court. Some two weeks had passed, but rarely a day went by that it didn't pop into his mind, and he still relished the moment. He'd left Creary with egg on his face!

Not that he had done it without friends. Judge Horace Warren, along with the mayor, shared his distaste for Ed Creary. Granted, the customary fine for discharge of firearms was fifty dollars, and the judge had doubled it to a hundred. But Creary had pressed for jail time, doubtless reveling in the thought of Thompson confined to the dungeon beneath City Hall. The fine, however stiff, had amounted to little more than a slap on the wrist.

Yet the crowning moment was Judge Warren's sharp rebuke of Creary. In blunt terms the judge had admonished him to police Guy Town, and put an end to card cheats. Though unstated, there was the implicit charge that Creary was taking payoffs from the gaming dives. The look on Creary's face still gave Thompson a chuckle, and even greater appreciation of Judge Warren. Good friends, particularly in a courtroom, were a blessing.

Downtown, Thompson walked from Congress Avenue to the Iron Front. With the supper hour over, the bar was already crowded, and men were starting to congregate around the gaming tables. He moved to the end of the bar, where Richter stood watching the action. One of the barkeeps brought him a brandy, which was the only drink he would have until the place closed for the night. He lit a fresh cheroot, nodding to Richter.

"Looks to be a good night," he said, exhaling smoke. "I expect some of the cowmen to drift in later."

"They throw quite a shindig," Richter said. "Word's out they rented the ballroom at the Austin Hotel for their final banquet."

"Joe, money's no object when they hold a convention. They're all trying to impress one another with how rich they are."

"Somebody told me Shanghai Pierce is in town. Think he'll join your game?"

"I sincerely hope so. He's my kind of poker player—a happy loser."

Abel Pierce was one of the largest ranchers in Texas. His Rancho Grande cattle spread in Wharton County covered a quarter-million acres, and ran a herd of thirty thousand longhorns. A sailor in his youth, he'd been dubbed "Shanghai" for bragging about his seafaring adventures. His vast holdings made him one of the wealthiest men in the state.

Thompson knew him from Dodge City. A heavy drinker, Pierce was six-foot-four, loud and boisterous, and overly impressed with himself as a poker player. Some years ago, after he'd trailed a herd to railhead in Kansas, Thompson had relieved him of several thousand dollars in a marathon poker game. Despite his size, and a rowdy manner fueled by alcohol, he had proved to be a congenial loser. He was, in many respects, still something of a drunk sailor.

"Maybe he'll drop by," Richter said. "Everybody says he's got more money than God."

Thompson smiled. "God doesn't play poker. I'll take Shanghai Pierce any day."

Luther Edwards slammed through the door. His features were the color of oxblood, and his eyes were dark with anger. Thompson thought he'd never seen the lawyer in such an agitated state, and wondered what might have happened. He motioned Edwards to the rear of the bar.

"Luther, you're a sight," he said. "Somebody light your fuse?"

"Whiskey!" Edwards pounded on the bar. "I've never been so insulted in my life. Dirty bastards!"

"Who?"

"The goddamn cattlemen. They threw me out!"

"Threw you out of what?"

The bartender placed a shot glass on the counter. Edwards downed the whiskey neat, shuddering as it struck bottom. He waved a hand in wild outrage. "Threw me out of their banquet. That's what! Goddamn them."

Thompson appeared confused. "Why would you go to their banquet? You're not in the cow business."

"Captain Lee Hall is their keynote speaker. I wanted to hear his speech."

"I didn't know you were an admirer of Captain Hall's."

"Christ, Ben, who wouldn't want to hear him? He's only the greatest Ranger of our time."

There was no arguing the point. Captain Lee Hall, though scarcely in his thirties, was already a legend among Texas Rangers. Under his command, a troop of Rangers had all but ended the infamous Sutton-Taylor feud, arresting over four hundred men in the process. Some three years ago, he was with the Rangers in

Round Rock, the day they killed Sam Bass, a daring young robber who was now the subject of ballads. No one doubted that ballads would one day be sung about Lee Hall.

"So what happened?" Thompson asked. "How'd you come to be thrown out?"

Edwards quaffed another shot of whiskey. "I walked in, polite as you please, and took a seat at the rear of the room. One of the ranchers, the tallest son-of-a-bitch you've ever seen—"

"Sounds like Shanghai Pierce."

"Yes, that's what the others called him, Shanghai. They told him, and I quote, 'boot his ass out the door.'"

"Because you're not a cattleman?"

"Well, I tried to explain. But I hardly got a word out of my mouth when he grabbed me by the neck and waltzed me to the door. Ben, he picked me up and actually *threw* me out."

"Got yourself manhandled," Thompson said thoughtfully. "Not a hospitable bunch, are they?"

"Hospitable?" Edwards hooted. "The bastards aren't even civil! They laughed to beat the band."

"All a big joke . . . at your expense."

"I was ridiculed, Ben. Ridiculed!"

Thompson was silent a moment. Over the years, Edwards had proved to be a good and loyal friend, and indispensable in legal matters. But he was a thinker, not a physical man, and incapable of defending himself. A valued friend, Thompson told himself, deserved loyalty in return. He started toward the door.

"Let's go."

"Go?" Edwards said. "Go where?"

"To the hotel."

*　*　*

The Texas Livestock Association held a convention every year. The membership roll included the largest and most influential cattlemen in the state. Their combined herds numbered in the hundreds of thousands.

Shanghai Pierce sat at the head table. Seated beside him was Captain Lee Hall, and ranged along the table were such notable cowmen as Richard King, Alonzo Millett, and Seth Mabrey. They listened as the president of the association, Ellsbery Lane, droned on about issues vital to their industry. Issues that would determine the future of the cow business in Texas.

Lane was anything but a fiery speaker. Yet the message he delivered was a summation of two days of intense, and often rancorous, debate. There was now a consensus among the members that a policy of open range led to increased cattle rustling and sometimes violent disputes about land boundaries. A resolution would be presented to the state legislature requesting laws that would require the fencing of all rangeland, from the smallest spread to the largest. Open range, a tradition in Texas for generations, was about to become a thing of the past.

Richard King, the largest landholder in the state, was a staunch advocate of the proposal. His Santa Gertrudis Ranch was located near the lower Rio Grande, a sprawling empire founded in 1853 with the purchase of an old Spanish land grant. The original grant was for fifteen thousand acres, and over the years, King had transformed it into a virtual fiefdom encompassing one-and-a-quarter million acres. He saw barbed-wire as a means to protect his range.

Another rancher, conspicuous by his absence, was the second largest landholder in Texas. Charlie Goodnight, fabled for having blazed the Goodnight Trail to

Colorado, ruled his own fiefdom in the Texas Panhandle. His JA spread was located along Palo Duro Canyon, encompassing a million acres and a hundred thousand head of cattle. A year ago, he had formed the Panhandle Stockgrowers Association, and he remained an advocate of open range. He dissuaded rustlers by the simple expedience of hanging them.

Pierce and King swapped a glance as Ellsbery Lane plodded on with his speech. There were twenty ranchers seated at the banquet tables, and all of them were bored with Lane's recital of the agreement hammered out over the past two days. They were eager to hear a rousing oration from their keynote speaker, Captain Lee Hall. They fully expected to be regaled with tales of the Sutton-Taylor feud, and who actually fired the shot that killed Sam Bass. To a man, they wanted the business to end and the fun to begin. Their eyes glazed as Lane went on and on . . . and on.

The ballroom was stuffy from the lingering warmth of an August evening. To stir the air, the windows directly behind the head table had been opened earlier. Pierce was momentarily distracted by sounds from the street, and heaved a heavy sigh, wondering if Lane would ever finish. He leaned sideways in his chair, looking around at Richard King. He spoke in a low, disgruntled rumble.

"You reckon Ellsbery's ever gonna quit?"

"The man's a talker," King murmured softly. "You'd think he was running for political office."

"Hell's bells, we already elected him president."

"Maybe that was our first mistake."

"Shanghai Pierce!"

The booming shout froze everyone in the room. They turned and saw Thompson standing in the doorway, Luther Edwards at his side. Thompson moved forward, the Colt Peacemaker in his hand, covering the men seated at the tables. His gaze drilled into Abel Pierce.

"You recognize this man?" he demanded, jerking a thumb over his shoulder at Edwards. "You tossed him out of here on his butt. Time to pay the piper, Shanghai!"

Thompson started toward, the speakers' table. Ellsbery Lane ducked beneath the podium, and the other cattlemen dropped to the floor. Shanghai Pierce bolted, his nerves deserting him, overturning his chair as he spun around. He dove headlong through an open window and landed in the alleyway beside the hotel. He sprinted off into the night.

Captain Lee Hall hadn't moved until now. He knew Thompson on sight, though they had never met. Careful of sudden moves, he rose from his chair and walked around the end of the table. He kept his hands at his sides.

A tomblike silence settled over the room. The cattlemen eased from beneath the tables, and watched bug-eyed as Hall moved forward at a measured pace. He was a man of square features, with steely blue eyes and a thatch of red hair. His expression was composed, almost phlegmatic, betraying nothing. He halted in front of Thompson.

"I'm Lee Hall," he said levelly. "I don't believe we've met, Mr. Thompson."

"No, we haven't," Thompson acknowledged. "The pleasure's all mine, Captain."

"Sorry I can't say the same. I'll thank you to hand over that gun."

Thompson smoothly snapped the Colt into his

shoulder holster. "I've never surrendered my gun to any man, Captain. Tonight's no different."

"Don't push me," Hall said in a flat voice. "I mean to disarm you."

"Well, I suppose you could try, if you've got your mind set. I wouldn't recommend it."

Their eyes locked in a staring contest. After a prolonged moment, the tense look went out of Hall's features. He cocked his head with an inquisitive frown. "You've scared the living hell out of these men, Mr. Thompson. What's your purpose here?"

"I'd like you to meet a friend," Thompson said. "This is Luther Edwards, one of Austin's finest attorneys."

Edwards stuck out his hand. "Captain Hall, I consider it a personal honor. I've admired you for many years."

"I'm obliged," Hall said, accepting his handshake. "I apologize for the rough treatment you got earlier. Pierce had you out the door before I could stop him."

"That's why I'm here," Thompson injected. "Luther just wanted to hear your speech, and he meant no harm. Shanghai had no right to manhandle him."

Hall allowed himself a tight smile. "I just imagine we've seen the last of Shanghai Pierce. He's probably halfway back to Wharton County."

"Good riddance," Thompson' said. "Maybe he's learned his lesson."

"Did you intend to use that gun?"

"Captain, I thought to teach the rascal some manners. I won't tolerate an insult to a friend."

"I'll take you at your word, Mr. Thompson." Hall motioned them toward the tables. "Why don't you gents have a seat and make yourselves comfortable? I was just about to give a speech."

Luther Edwards grinned like a frog. As Hall turned toward the speakers' dais, Thompson led his friend to the nearest table and got him seated. The cattlemen slowly filed into their chairs, not quite sure what they'd witnessed. Their attention was drawn to the square-jawed Ranger at the podium.

Captain Lee Hall told them who really shot Sam Bass.

SEVEN

Macbeth was playing a limited engagement. Everyone who was anyone in Austin was attending the opening performance, and a line of carriages blocked the street outside the opera house. Opening night was sold out.

Drivers hopped down to assist their passengers from the carriages. For the gala occasion, the men were dressed in white tie and tails and tall top hats. The women wore fashionable gowns and were adorned with their finest jewelry. One carriage after another disgorged a gathering of the town's elite. They slowly made their way into the opera house.

Thompson stepped from the coach of a brougham. The elegant carriage was drawn by a team of blood-red bays, rented for the evening from Purdy's Livery. As he assisted Catherine from the coach, her features bathed in the lights from the marquee, he thought she had never looked lovelier. She wore a pale rose gown of gossamer silk and a matching cape, her hair arranged in the latest chignon style, with an exquisite pearl choker at her throat. She was a vision, somehow regal.

A breeze off the river cooled the late August evening. As carriages pulled away, the crowd filed into the opera house with a buzz of excitement. Opening night was a major social event, and the lobby was packed with people who paused to exchange greetings. Thompson checked his hat at the cloak room, and turned back to Catherine, wending a path through the throng. Up ahead, near the theater entrance, he saw James Shipe, whose wife dripped with diamonds. The banker was talking with Mayor Tom Wheeler, also accompanied by his wife.

"Good evening," Thompson said cordially. "A pleasure to see you all again. Looks to be quite an affair."

"Indeed it does," Wheeler agreed. "Nothing like a little culture to bring out the best in folks."

After a round of handshakes, the ladies quickly engaged in animated conversation. Thompson counted it a source of pride that he and Catherine were accepted in the better circles of Austin. A gambler, particularly one with his reputation for gunplay, was more often than not excluded from polite company. He was especially gratified that the women were fond of Catherine. She enjoyed mixing with cultivated people.

"Just think of it," Shipe marveled, as the women chattered away. "Edwin Booth on the stage in Austin. We have reason to celebrate."

"We are the envy of Texas," Wheeler added. "Imagine that he bypassed Dallas in favor of Austin! I'm drunk with the thought of it."

Edwin Booth was the foremost Shakespearean actor of the day. His renown as a tragedian was unsurpassed, and even in England, the home of Shakespeare, he was considered a master of the art. In 1865, his younger brother, John Wilkes Booth, an actor of lesser fame, had assassinated Abraham Lincoln at the Ford Theater in Washington. Yet the public adoration of Edwin Booth went undiminished, and he remained an icon of the stage. His current tour would take him to twenty cities throughout America.

"There's the governor," Shipe said, pointing off into the crowd. "I understand he held a reception for Booth at the state house this afternoon. He must be quite an admirer."

The men watched as Governor Oran Roberts and his entourage moved through the theater doors. Wheeler shook his head with a rueful smile. "One of his aides called on me last week," he said, glancing at Thompson. "The governor's no admirer of yours, Ben."

"What's he got against me?" Thompson asked, somewhat taken aback. "I've never even met the man."

"Apparently he got a sizzler of a letter from the cattlemen's association. They filed a protest about your disrupting their banquet."

"I'd lay odds the protest came from Shanghai Pierce. Last time I saw him, he was still running."

Shipe chuckled with some humor. "Is it true that Pierce jumped out a window? That's what I read in the paper."

Articles had appeared in both the *Statesman* and the *Republican*. For several days following the incident, Thompson's encounter with Captain Lee Hall had been the talk of the town. The papers had treated the affair with satirical wit, chastising the cattlemen more than Thompson. The public, in turn, thought the matter somewhat laughable.

"So what's the governor's problem?" Thompson said. "All I did was take up for Luther Edwards."

"Oh, it's politics as usual," Wheeler said dismissively. "The cattlemen's association contributed to the governor's war chest in the last election. He felt obligated to complain that you hadn't been arrested."

"Well, it wasn't exactly a matter for the Rangers. Captain Hall was there, and he didn't arrest me."

"Didn't or couldn't?" Shipe joked. "The papers say he tried to disarm you. What happened?"

Thompson smiled. "Captain Hall's a reasonable man. We came to an understanding."

"Yes, I'm sure you did, Ben. I'm sure you did."

Wheeler snorted laughter. "I'd like to have been a fly on the wall."

Their conversation was cut short when curtain time was announced. Thompson nodded genially to the men, collected Catherine, and moved toward the doors. An usher escorted them to the best seats in the house, fifth row center in the orchestra. A vaulted ceiling rose majestically in the theater, with intricately carved woodwork bordering a spacious mural of robed figures and fleeting nymphs. The proscenium stage was crowned by an elaborate arch, bounded on the front by an orchestra pit, empty of musicians for tonight's performance. A few moments after they were seated, the house lights dimmed. The audience quieted.

Edwin Booth entered from stage left in Act One, Scene One. He was playing the lead role, Macbeth, a Scottish general of the King's army in ancient times. His costume revealed a fine figure of a man, lithe and tall, strikingly handsome, with a stage presence that dominated the play. His voice was a rich baritone, commanding and resonant, ringing out over the footlights into the farthest corner of the theater. His opening scene was with a fellow general, Banquo, and three haggish creatures revealed to be witches. From his first line, he held the audience enthralled.

Thompson was no stranger to Shakespeare. His schooling as a boy had given him a taste for the Bard, and he'd carried it with him into manhood. On occasion, in idle moments, he still perused favored passages in a well-thumbed volume of the poet's complete works. Tonight, watching Edwin Booth move about the stage, he soon found himself caught up in the lyrical rhythm of the verse. He was not as familiar with *Macbeth* as he was *Hamlet* and *Julius Caesar*, and he strained to follow every nuance of the story. He was quickly engrossed in Booth's performance.

The play opened when Duncan the Meek reigned as King of Scotland. Macbeth and Banquo, victorious generals returning from a great battle, were stopped in a desolate place by three unearthly creatures. The witches prophesied that Macbeth would become king of Scotland, a prophecy that amazed him since Duncan had legitimate heirs, two sons. Then, no less astounding, the witches foretold that though Banquo would never wear the crown, his sons would rule Scotland. Macbeth and Banquo were left to ponder the meaning of their strange encounter.

By the end of Act One, it became apparent to Thompson that something foul was afoot in Scotland. Upon returning to his castle, Macbeth related the incident with the witches to his wife. Lady Macbeth, a woman of cunning and evil, saw opportunity in the prophecy. By playing on his ambition, she convinced Macbeth that murder was an acceptable means to the crown. A visit to their castle by King Duncan and his sons, Malcolm and Donalbain, set the plan in motion. The sovereign would be killed in his sleep.

Catherine gripped Thompson's arm as the death scene unfolded. Edwin Booth masterfully portrayed a Macbeth who turned squeamish at the last moment. But Lady Macbeth was resolute, far more ruthless than her husband, and she goaded him to murder. Macbeth, armed with a dagger, entered the king's bedchamber and killed him in a bloody attack. The following morning, with discovery of the murder, the king's sons, and the rightful heirs to the throne, feared for their own lives. Malcolm, the eldest, fled to England, and Donalbain escaped to Ireland.

Macbeth, with no one to dispute his claim, was crowned King of Scotland. Yet Lady Macbeth could not forget the witches' prophecy that Banquo's children would one day claim the throne. She and Macbeth again plotted murder, and their henchmen, in the dark of the night, waylaid and killed Banquo. Scottish noblemen were repulsed by still another murder, and they joined Malcolm, the late king's heir, in England. An army was raised, with the purpose of restoring Malcolm to the throne, and marched on Scotland. Lady Macbeth, suddenly overcome by guilt and perhaps fearful of reprisals, was unable to face the consequences. She took her life by her own hand.

Edwin Booth, thoroughly immersed in the role of Macbeth, appeared devastated when informed of the queen's death. He moved downstage, his anguished features almost ghastly in the footlights, and stared out over the audience. His voice resonated with sorrow.

Tomorrow, and tomorrow, and tomorrow,
Creeps in this petty pace from day to day,

To the last syllable of recorded time;
And all our yesterdays have lighted fools
The way to dusty death. Out, out, brief candle!
Life's but a walking shadow; a poor player,
That struts and frets his hour upon the stage,
And then is heard no more: it is a tale
Told by an idiot, full of sound and fury
Signifying nothing.

Thompson was electrified by the words. His eyes were riveted on the stage, but the words resounded in his head. He was struck by the eerie sensation that something within him was no longer the same. Still, even as his mouth went dry and his scalp tingled, he was unable to formulate the change into thought. He stared, uncomprehending, at the actors.

The play moved to swift conclusion. Macbeth and his forces engaged the army besieging his castle. In the ensuing battle, he clashed in mortal combat with Macduff, one of the Scottish noblemen aligned with Malcolm. The fight ended with Macbeth defeated, his head chopped off (gruesomely depicted through stage magic), and the grisly trophy displayed on the tip of a sword. Malcolm, the rightful heir, then ascended the throne, at last victorious. The noblemen, one and all acclaimed their new monarch. *Hail, King of Scotland!*

The audience broke out in cheers as the curtain fell. Then, as the applause swelled to a crescendo, the curtain parted and the actors stepped forward to take their bows. Edwin Booth, the star of the show, was the last to appear onstage, his head magically restored. The theater reverberated with applause, and the crowd rose to give him a standing ovation. He took four curtain calls, bathed in a spotlight, glorying in the adulation. Finally, his arms raised in triumph, he backed away as the curtains swished closed for the last time. The house lights came up full.

"Oh, Ben," Catherine said, her eyes misty. "Wasn't he just magnificent!"

Thompson nodded. "Nobody will top that."

"I've never seen anything so tragic in my life. I simply loathed Macbeth—but then, somehow . . . I felt sorry for him."

"Shakespeare knew how to pull all the strings."

Thompson eased into the aisle, taking her arm. They joined the crush, moving toward the doors, aware of excited exclamations all around them. Everyone in the theater was talking about the remarkable performance delivered by Edwin Booth. A common thread, expressed in one fashion or another, ran through their comments. None of them would ever forget tonight.

Outside the opera house, Thompson waited with Catherine for their carriage to be brought around. Mayor Wheeler and James Shipe appeared with their wives, and the conversation centered as much on Edwin Booth as on the power of the play. The women were taken with the actor, and the men were perhaps more impressed with the story of a good man gone wrong. All of them agreed that it was tragedy at its best.

On the way home, Thompson lapsed into a brooding silence. As the carriage turned north, he stared out into the night, remembering the moment that had so electrified him during the play. The sensation washed over him again, and he heard the words, not altogether in order, but with ringing clarity. *Life is a tale told by an idiot, full of sound and fury—signifying nothing.*

The words seemed to hammer at him. A realist, seldom at odds with himself or his world, he was not given to moments of philosophical deliberation. But now his thoughts turned inward, sparked by some greater wisdom penned to paper by Shakespeare. He weighed in the balance all he'd done with his life, from the vast sums of money he had won at gaming tables to the men he had killed in the name of honor. Oddly, in a way he didn't quite understand, he suddenly found it wanting.

A tale signifying nothing.

"You're awfully quiet." Catherine snuggled against his shoulder. "Thinking about the play?"

"After a fashion," Thompson said, mentally switching gears. "I was wondering what the moral was. What Shakespeare meant."

"Does there have to be a moral?"

"I just suspect that's what he intended."

She looked at him. "And what was the moral you got from the play?"

"I'm not sure," Thompson said absently. "Maybe a man ought not to listen to witches. Macbeth damn sure got steered the wrong way."

"Honestly, aren't you the big tease! I thought you were serious."

"Nope, just having a little fun. I'll leave the serious stuff to Shakespeare."

Thompson knew he'd fobbed her off with nonsense. For again, as his gaze was drawn to the starlit sky, he heard the words, a different stanza. Words that stuck like a spear in his mind.

Life is but a walking shadow. A player struts his hour upon the stage, and then is heard no more.

He wondered what he'd done with his life, all those years. His hour upon the stage . . .

EIGHT

‹‹‹‹‹‹‹‹‹‹‹ ◊ ›››››››››››

"Deuces bet twenty."

"Too rich for my blood."

"I'll fold."

"I'm right behind you."

The man with the deuces was Roger Tucker. A stock-broker, and by his very nature a gambler, his passion was poker. He generally wandered into the Iron Front every Friday afternoon in search of a game. Today, the first Friday in September, was no exception.

There were five men at the table. Tucker, a notions drummer, a railroad superintendent, an insurance sales-man, and Thompson. The game was five-card stud, and Thompson was the last man in the hand. He was hold-ing two pair, but something told him that Tucker had a third deuce in the hole. He felt obliged to find out.

"I'll just call," he said, tossing chips into the pot. "Have to keep you honest, Roger."

Tucker turned over the third deuce. "Read 'em and weep," he said with a wide grin. "Got you that time, Ben."

"No question about it, Roger. You won yourself a pot."

Thompson folded his hand. Tucker and the other men were mediocre players, several notches below the competition he'd faced on the gamblers' circuit. They lacked insight into percentages and odds, often betting on the come, hoping to improve a poor hand. Even on a good hand, they seldom played it with finesse.

The proper play for Tucker would have been to check his deuces. The drummer, with queens on the board, would likely have bet the limit. One or more of the other players might have called, and Thompson would have probably tested the waters with a raise. If Tucker was able to read players as well as he read cards, he would then have raised the limit. A little finesse would have allowed him to drag down a large pot.

Over the years, Thompson had developed his own technique for winning at cutthroat poker. There was no pattern to his betting and raising; his erratic play made him unpredictable, and he won on what appeared to be weak hands. He would bluff on a bad hand as often as he folded, and he seldom folded. More often than not his bluff went undetected. The secret was to keep them guessing.

On good hands, he would sometimes raise the limit, allowing the money to speak for itself. At other times, when he held good cards, he would lay back and sucker his opponents into heedless raises. On occasion, merely calling all bets and raises, he let the other players build the pot only to turn up the winning hand. No one was ever sure of what he held.

Tucker, still grinning, raked in the pot. The deal passed to Thompson and he called five-card draw. In some Eastern casinos the traditional rules of poker had been revised to include straights, flushes, and the most elusive of all combinations, the straight flush. The highest hand back East was now a royal flush, ten through ace in the same suit. By all accounts, the revised rules lent the game a whole new element.

Poker in the West was still played by the original rules observed in earlier times on riverboats. There were no straights, no flushes, and no straight flushes, royal or otherwise. There were two unbeatable hands west of the Mississippi. The first was four aces, drawn by most players only once or twice in a lifetime. The other cinch hand was four kings with an ace kicker.

Four kings, in combination with one of the aces, surmounted almost incalculable odds. The ace kicker precluded anyone from holding what amounted to the granddaddy of all hands, four aces. Seasoned players looked upon it as a minor miracle, or the work of a skilled cardsharp. Men spoke of it in mystical terms.

A waning afternoon sun filtered through the front windows. Thompson was bored with the game, even though he was ahead almost two hundred dollars. Sometimes he felt mired in quicksand, slowly being dragged under, and all the more so since the performance of *Macbeth*. A fortnight had passed, but he was still troubled by thoughts that his life was a circle within a circle, slogging ever deeper into the mire. One day was like any other.

The man on his right cut the cards after he'd shuffled. He dealt around the table, than placed the deck beside his chips. A cheroot jutted from the corner of his mouth, and he puffed a cloud of smoke as he spread his cards. He managed a deadpan expression, though he was suddenly no longer bored with the game. He had three sevens.

Tucker, who was on his left, checked. The drummer, a pudgy man named Willis Orcutt, bet twenty. The next two players folded, and Thompson, exhaling a streamer of smoke, airily raised twenty. Tucker reluctantly folded, and Orcutt bumped it another twenty. Thompson took the last raise.

On the draw, Orcutt held four and drew one. Thompson kept the three sevens and dealt himself two. When Orcutt squeezed his cards apart, the corners of his mouth lifted in a fleeting telltale smile. He checked.

Thompson caught the smile. He figured Orcutt had filled on two pair and was trying to sandbag him. He fanned his cards, inwardly amazed that he'd drawn the case seven. He hesitated, as though weighing his options, and bet twenty. Orcutt beamed.

"Your twenty," he said smugly—"and twenty more."

Thompson feigned surprise, pausing a moment, and raised. Orcutt took the last raise, waiting for Thompson to call, and barked a short laugh. He spread his cards.

"Full house! Jacks over nines."

"Very pretty," Thompson said, turning his cards. "Unfortunately, I filled out too, Mr. Orcutt. Four sevens."

Orcutt stared at the cards. "You dealt yourself the case seven."

"Appears to be my lucky day."

"Anybody else, I'd raise the roof. Good thing you run a straight game."

"I'll take that as a compliment, Mr. Orcutt."

"Tried to sandbag you and sandbagged myself. Helluva note!"

"Well, like they say, that's poker."

The game ended shortly before five o'clock. Thompson treated everyone to a drink on the house, then walked to his office. As he shrugged into his suit coat, there was a knock on the door and he turned to find Jim Burditt. A fellow gambler and an old friend, Burditt generally plied his trade in clubs other than the Iron Front. There was common agreement among professionals that friendship and cards were a poor mix.

"Hello there, Jim," Thompson said, pleased to see him. "How's tricks these days?"

Burditt closed the door. "Not worth a damn, and that's a fact. Guess you heard about last night?"

Everyone in the sporting crowd had heard the story. Last night, celebrating a big win at the faro tables, Burditt had gotten drunk and attended a show at the Capital Variety Theater. Overly rambunctious, he'd disrupted the performance and then turned belligerent when confronted by the owner, Mark Wilson. A tough Irishman, with a hair-trigger temper, Wilson had bodily thrown him out of the theater. The word was out that Wilson had threatened harsher treatment if he ever came back.

"I've come to ask your help," Burditt said solemnly. "I think Wilson will try gunplay the next time I walk in there."

"That's simple enough," Thompson said. "Stay out of the place."

"Would you let him scare you off?"

"We're not talking about me."

"I won't have people say I'm yellow. I'm going back in there tonight and I'm asking your help. How about it, Ben?"

Thompson frowned. "I've been in two shooting scrapes the last month or so. Another one and Judge Warren will nail my hide to the wall."

"Nobody's gonna get shot," Burditt protested. "I just need you to watch my back. Wilson likes the odds stacked in his favor."

"What if things go haywire? What if I have to plug somebody to keep them off your back?"

"Things won't come to that. This here's strictly between me and Wilson. You being there will make him think twice about loading the dice. He wouldn't mess with you."

"And if somebody goes stupid and still deals me a hand? What then?"

"For chrissakes, Ben!" Burditt flung out his arms. "You took on Lee Hall and the cattlemen's association for your lawyer friend. Are you telling me I don't rate that high anymore?"

Thompson looked offended. Yet he was unable to muster a reasonable argument. Some years ago, when the Rangers were chasing his brother, Burditt had volunteered to assist in Billy's escape. On any number of occasions, particularly in the Kansas cowtowns, Burditt had proved to be a steadfast friend. A friend in need, Thompson told himself, should never go begging. A debt was a debt.

"All right," he said at length. "What's your play?"

Burditt explained what he had in mind.

The Capital Variety Theater was located on Brazos Street, a block east of Congress Avenue. A number of vaudeville acts were presented every night, with the usual array of chorus girls, jugglers, and magicians. The clientele was largely composed of workingmen and their women, and the sporting crowd. Few of the so-called respectable element ever set foot in a variety theater.

A large barroom occupied the front of the building. The bar extended the length of the room, with tables and chairs along the opposite wall. At the rear of the bar, there was a spacious theater, with seating for a hundred patrons, and a raised stage. There were three shows a night and people were already filing in for the early performance. Friday nights always drew a sellout crowd.

Thompson and Burditt arrived a few minutes before eight. As they walked through the barroom, they saw Mark Wilson, the proprietor, stationed at the entrance to the theater. He was a beefy man, thick through the shoulders, with florid features and quick eyes. He looked around, surveying the crowd, and his gaze suddenly stopped when he spotted them. His expression went flat and cold.

A moment elapsed, then Wilson darted a glance at the bar. Thompson followed his gaze and saw Charlie Mathews, one of the bartenders, slowly nod his head. Mathews was a local toughnut, handy with his fists and a gun, and also served as the house bouncer. The look that passed between Wilson and Mathews was clearly a signal, and Thompson sensed there was some sort of prearranged plan of action. Mathews would cover his boss in the event of trouble.

Burditt strolled past Wilson as though he hadn't a care in the world. He took a seat at the rear of the theater, turning slightly in his chair, so that he could keep one eye on the barroom. As they had agreed beforehand, Thompson casually moved to the end of the bar and placed his back to the wall. From there, he could watch Burditt and Wilson, and ensure, no matter what happened, that his friend got a fair shake. One of the bartenders drifted over and he ordered a whiskey, which he left untouched. He noted that Mathews was positioned farther along the bar.

Halfway through the show, a magician produced a dove from beneath a silk scarf. A group of rowdies seated in the front row were obviously waiting for the moment. One of them, the practical joker in the bunch, tossed a lighted string of firecrackers onto the stage. The dove took wing at the first explosion, and the magician backpedated furiously as the firecrackers popped and danced at his feet. The crowd roared with laughter, hurling jeers and catcalls at the magician. They thought it was the best part of his act.

A city policeman rushed through the street door. Thompson recognized him as Carl Allen, and wondered that an officer was so conveniently handy when the commotion started. Then, all in an instant, he realized that it was a setup, the rowdies and the firecrackers orchestrated by Wilson. Jim Burditt was about to be blamed, at the very least arrested, perhaps killed if he tried to resist arrest. His appearance at the theater had set the plan in motion.

Thompson moved away from the wall. Wilson, just as he'd suspected, was blaming the incident on Burditt, and demanding his arrest. Carl Allen, gesturing wildly with his nightstick, grabbed Burditt by the collar and hustled him toward the door. Thompson got ahead of them, by now convinced that Burditt would never make it to the street alive. Wilson and Mathews were too alert, swapping hurried glances, as though awaiting some sign of resistance. Thompson stepped in to Allen's path.

"Let him go," he said sternly. "Jim didn't set off those firecrackers. I saw the whole thing."

Allen waved his nightstick. "Stand aside and don't interfere. I'm taking him to jail."

"Why put yourself to the trouble? Let me be responsible for him and I'll have him in court first thing in the morning. We'll get to the bottom of things then."

Wilson pushed forward. "You're out of line, Thompson. I want him arrested."

"Nobody's arresting him," Thompson said roughly. "You know damn well he wasn't involved. You rigged the whole game yourself."

"You're a lying son-of-a-bitch—"

Thompson backhanded him in the mouth. Wilson lurched sideways, blood spurting from a split lip. Allen moved to separate them, and Thompson pulled Burditt to his side. He looked directly into the policeman's eyes.

"I'm taking Jim out of here. Any objections?"

"No, go on," Allen said lamely. "Maybe it's for the best."

Thompson backed away a few steps. Then he turned, Burditt still at his side, and started toward the door. Wilson, his features twisted with rage, motioned frantically to his bouncer, Charlie Mathews. Ducking down, Mathews brought a sawed-off shotgun from beneath the counter and handed it across the bar. Wilson eared back the hammers.

"Watch out!" someone screamed. "He's got a gun!"

Officer Allen whirled around, losing his balance. His shoulder collided with the shotgun, which was centered on Thompson's back, jostling the barrels upward. Wilson tripped the trigger and the crowd scattered as a load of buckshot punched a hole in the ceiling. Thompson spun, drawing his Colt, and fired three shots in a staccato roar. The slugs stitched bright red dots up Wilson's shirtfront.

Arms flailing, the shotgun spinning away, Wilson went down like a felled tree. As he struck the floor,

Mathews came up with a pistol from beneath the bar. He fired a hurried snap-shot that plucked at the sleeve of Thompson's coat and ripped through the flesh of his left arm. Thompson staggered, quickly righting himself, and leveled the Colt, caught the sights. He feathered the trigger.

The slug drilled into Mathews's throat. His head arched upward and the back of his neck blew out in a gout of blood and bone matter. He stood there an instant, dead on his feet, then his legs buckled and he collapsed behind the bar. A pall of gunsmoke hung over the barroom, and for a long moment, no one moved. Finally, levering himself off the floor, Officer Allen got to his feet. He took a tentative step toward Thompson.

"Jesus Christ A'mighty," he said in a piping voice. "Just put your gun away and don't kill nobody else. I'll let you surrender to Marshal Creary."

"Not tonight," Thompson said, his features hard as stone. "I'll turn myself in to the sheriff. Anybody wants me, that's where I'll be."

"The marshal's not gonna like that."

"Tell him I said to stuff it."

Thompson backed out of the barroom. Droplets of blood leaked from his sleeve, but he kept the Colt trained on Allen. Burditt fell in beside him and they went through the door onto the street. Thompson turned in the direction of Congress Avenue.

Burditt looked ashen. "Goddamn, I'm sorry as hell, Ben. I never meant for it to come to that."

"Then you shouldn't have asked," Thompson said gruffly. "Next time, do your own killing."

"Are you hurt bad?"

"I'll live."

They trudged off toward the courthouse.

NINE

—◆—

Sheriff Frank Horner took Thompson and Burditt into custody. Until he could complete his investigation, the question of bail was a moot point. The prisoners were locked in a cell on the top floor of the courthouse.

Thompson was permitted to contact his attorneys. A deputy was also dispatched to advise Catherine that her husband was under arrest. Within the hour, Luther Edwards and Jack Walton arrived at the county jail. They were allowed to meet privately with their client in a holding room normally reserved for court trials. An armed deputy stood guard outside.

Walton, who was the more experienced criminal attorney, took charge. He reminded Thompson that anything said fell under the attorney–client privilege, and could never be divulged. After a bit of coaxing, Thompson related the incidents of the day, from the time Burditt had walked into his office at the Iron Front. Walton and Edwards listened intently, and made copious notes. Walton finally shook his head.

"Your friends will be the death of you, Ben."

"And that includes me," Edwards hastily confessed. "I got you involved in that scrap with the cattlemen's association. Small wonder it didn't end as badly as tonight."

"You've got it all wrong," Thompson informed them. "A man has to stick by his friends when there's trouble. Otherwise, he's a poor excuse of a man."

"Let's leave that for now," Walton said. "I want to go back to what Burditt told you this afternoon. He was convinced that Wilson meant to kill him. Correct?"

"That's right."

"And you agreed to accompany him to the theater. To cover his back?"

"Yeah, that was the general idea."

"Even though Wilson had kicked him out of the theater last night. And with just cause."

"You're missing the point. Jim had to go back in there and face Wilson. If he didn't, everybody would think he was yellow."

"In other words, you went there knowing the situation could turn violent. You were prepared to kill to protect a friend. Is that a fair statement?"

"Fair enough."

"And that is exactly what happened. You killed two men."

"Not before they tried to kill me."

Thompson's left arm was cradled in a sling. Before the lawyers arrived, a doctor had been summoned to the jail. Upon examination, he proved to be suffering from a flesh wound, painful but easily treated. The doctor had pronounced him a lucky man.

Walton looked at him. "Do you understand what I'm driving at, Ben? A case could be made that you and Burditt went there to provoke a fight."

"That'll never hold water."

"On the contrary, the state will contend that it was calculated. Nothing less than premeditated murder. A hanging offense."

"What about all the witnesses?" Thompson countered. "They'll testify it was self-defense."

"I hope you're right," Walton said. "But you've put yourself in an extremely precarious position. The county attorney will almost certainly charge you with murder."

"How do we get around that?"

"We present *our* version of the truth. Hard as it sounds, we're fortunate you killed both Wilson and Mathews. Their version will never be heard in court."

"Sorry state of affairs," Thompson grumped. "You defend yourself and you wind up charged with murder. Things used to be different."

Walton nodded soberly. "I'm afraid we've entered the modern age. The old days are long gone."

"Don't worry, Ben," Edwards quickly added. "We'll get you off somehow."

A rap of knuckles sounded on the door. Sheriff Horner entered the room, closing the door behind him. "Thought you'd want to know I've turned Burditt loose. Everybody at the variety theater says he wasn't part of the shooting."

"What about Ben?" Walton asked. "Didn't they tell you it was self-defense?"

"Well, it's not quite that simple. We'll have to have a coroner's inquest and that'll tell us what's what. Until then, Ben stays in jail."

"How soon can a jury be impaneled?"

"Tomorrow," Horner said. "I stopped by Judge Tegener's house on the way back here. He ordered me to move things right along."

Judge Fritz Tegener was presiding justice over the Third District Court. Though irregular, he was empowered to order a coroner's inquest on a Saturday. "The sooner the better," Walton remarked. "But I have to say I'm curious. Why so expeditious?"

"Mark Wilson was a popular man with the sporting crowd. There's bound to be hard feelings, and the judge wants to put a lid on things. Either Ben's cleared, or he'll get bound over for preliminary hearing."

"Frank, I'm in the clear," Thompson said earnestly. "I was on my way out the door and Wilson tried to backshoot me. I was just defending myself."

Horner was a lawman of the old school. He subscribed to the theory that a backshooter, a coward by definition, deserved to be shot. Added to that was the fact that he considered Thompson a man of honor, and a passable friend. His brow wrinkled in a troubled frown.

"Ben, I hope to hell you beat it. But it's out of my hands now. We'll just have to wait and see."

The door opened and Catherine walked into the room. Horner and the two attorneys made their excuses, and quickly moved into the hallway. When the door closed, Catherine stepped into Thompson's free arm and they stood locked in silent embrace. He finally found his voice.

"Where's Bobby?"

"I left him with the neighbors."

"Does he know I'm in jail?"

"Not yet." She stepped back, tears welling up in her

eyes, inspecting his sling. "I thought my heart would stop when the deputy told me you'd been wounded. How bad is it?"

"Just a little nick," Thompson said lightly. "Doc Phelps told me he'd seen worse bee stings."

"I wish that's all it were. Are they going to let you out of here?"

"There's a coroner's inquest set for tomorrow. I just expect they'll turn me loose."

"Is it true—" she hesitated, searching his eyes— "two men?"

Thompson grimaced. "Katie, the way it worked out, I didn't have any choice. Things went to hell in a hurry."

She sometimes hoped he would change, finally hang up his gun. But then in reflective moments, she chided herself for wishful thinking. He was a prideful man when she married him, and he'd grown more so with age. She knew he would rather die than surrender his honor.

"Well, you're safe and that's all that counts. I'm sure the charges will be dropped."

Thompson touched her face. "I'm glad you came, even if I am in jail. I didn't want you worrying."

"Oh, Ben, you're such a fool sometimes."

She threw her arm around his neck and hugged him tightly.

Third District Court convened on Thursday, September 16. The spectator benches were packed, with people standing at the rear of the courtroom. The uptown sporting crowd, particularly the gamblers, were drawn to what promised to be a sensational hearing. One of their own was charged with murder.

For nearly two weeks, the newspapers had carried

the story on the front page. The coroner's jury had returned a finding of homicide, and Thompson had been bound over for preliminary hearing. Bail was set at $5,000, which was posted the same day, and he'd gone about business as usual while awaiting a court date. The oddsmakers were laying 5–3 on dismissal.

Catherine was seated in the front row. With her was Billy Thompson, who had traveled from Brownsville upon hearing of the shooting. He had arrived a week ago, full of confidence and good cheer, regaling them with stories of his adventures as a riverboat gambler. He expressed no concern whatever that his brother would beat the charges and walk out of court a free man. His conviction was based on the fact that he himself had done the same, several times.

Thompson was seated at the defendant's table, with his attorneys. Jack Walton radiated confidence, and Luther Edwards looked as if the result were all but a foregone conclusion. On the opposite side of the courtroom, George Upshaw, the county attorney, was seated with his assistant at the prosecutor's table. A vain man, Upshaw was short and slight of build, with sleek hair, muddy eyes, and a pencil-thin mustache. He had been quoted in the *Statesman* as saying Thompson would stand trial for first-degree murder. He looked like a fighting cock ready to be pitted.

"All rise!"

The bailiff's ringing voice brought everyone to their feet. Judge Fritz Tegener emerged from his chambers and walked briskly to the bench. He was a rotund German, the son of immigrants, noted for his pungent humor and his sometimes bizarre interpretation of the law. Every lawyer in Austin had at one time or another been dusted by his acerbic wit, and left to ponder the vagaries of the judicial system. He plopped down in his chair and nodded benignly to the spectators. His gaze settled on the advocates.

"Are we ready to proceed, gentlemen?"

Upshaw snapped to attention. "The state is ready, Your Honor."

Walton was only a beat behind. "We're prepared as well, Judge."

"Let's get on with it then."

Upshaw's first witness was the county coroner. His testimony dealt with the nature of the wounds suffered by Wilson and Mathews. On cross-examination, Walton asked if men who had sustained mortal wounds would still be capable of firing their weapons. Over Upshaw's strong objection the witness was allowed to answer the question. He thought it unlikely that the deceased had fired their guns after being wounded.

The next witness was Sheriff Frank Horner. His investigation, he testified, indicated that an altercation between Thompson and Wilson was the direct cause of the shooting. A waiter from the Capital Variety Theater was then called to the stand. He related that the incident began with a string of firecrackers being thrown on the stage. His recollection was that James Burditt was seated among the men who had thrown the firecrackers. Walton grilled him mercilessly on cross-examination, and the waiter finally reversed himself. He wasn't certain where Burditt had been seated.

Policeman Carl Allen was the next witness for the prosecution. He testified that Wilson had asked him to stay close to the theater on the evening of the shooting. Wilson expected trouble, he said, because Burditt had been ejected the night before. He went on to state that Burditt, following the incident with the firecrackers, had resisted arrest. Thompson, he recounted, had interfered with the arrest, and then, without provocation, struck Wilson when the theater owner tried to intervene. His recollection of who had fired the opening shot was vague; he had been knocked aside, and everything had happened too fast. His impression was that Thompson had been the first to draw a gun.

Thompson, watching from the defense table, was barely able to restrain himself. Walton reassured him with a pat on the shoulder, then proceeded to savage Officer Allen under cross-examination. He got Allen to admit that Thompson had *requested* Burditt's release, and promised to have him in court the following morning. Then, rattling Allen with a flurry of questions, he forced the admission that the blow struck by Thompson was the result of something said by Wilson. Allen pleaded a faulty memory as to the exact words; but conceded it might have been an insult. He refused to budge as to his vague recollection of who fired the first shot.

Jim Burditt was then called to the stand. Upshaw bullied and badgered, alleging that Burditt and Thompson had conspired to create a violent situation. His contention was that Burditt, through Thompson, planned to take revenge for having been roughly ejected from the theater. He attempted to extract a confession that Wilson's death was nothing short of premeditated murder. Burditt held his own in the verbal sparring match, flatly denying any thought of conspiracy, or intent to commit violence. On cross-examination, Walton subtly planted the seed that Burditt, far from seeking revenge, had actually feared for his own life. He had merely asked Thompson to guard his back.

George Upshaw informed the court that he had no further witnesses. Walton promptly called to the stand three theater customers, who were present at the time of the killings. Their testimony established that Wilson had fired first, while attempting to shoot Thompson in the back. The cross-examination by Upshaw was testy but futile; the men refused to alter their stories. Thompson was the last witness for the defense, and took the oath with his hand on a Bible. Walton approached the stand.

"Mr. Thompson, did you kill Mark Wilson and Charles Mathews?"

"Yessir, I regret to say I did."

"Would you tell the court why?"

Thompson squared his shoulders. "They did their level best to kill me. I fired in defense of my life."

"Mark Wilson fired on you first?"

"Yes."

"Charles Mathews fired on you first?"

"Yes."

"And only then did you return their fire?"

"That's how it happened."

Walton paused, playing for effect. "Tell me, Mr. Thompson," he said. "Why did you strike Wilson with your hand?"

"You'll pardon the language," Thompson said, glancing at the judge, who nodded. "Wilson called me a 'lying son-of-a-bitch'!"

"What prompted him to curse you?"

"I'd just told him what was clear to everybody in the theater. Namely, that he'd rigged it to have Jim Burditt arrested."

"And what did you do next?"

"Carl Allen got between us and I headed for the door. That's when Wilson turned loose with a shotgun."

"With your back to him?"

"Yes, with my back to him."

"On your oath, Mr. Thompson—" Walton struck a dramatic pose. "Did you conspire with James Burditt to commit murder? Did you go to the Capital Variety Theater with the intent of killing the deceased, Mark Wilson?"

"No, I did not."

"And did you fire on Mathews only after he had wounded you?"

Thompson's arm was still in a sling. Though the arm was healed, Walton thought the sling made an effective courtroom prop. As if on cue, Thompson gave the answer they had rehearsed.

"I've got the scar to prove he fired first."

"No further questions."

The cross-examination by Upshaw was wasted effort. Thompson calmly rebutted the questions, and Upshaw went back to his chair with a look of defeat. Judge Fritz Tegener announced that he saw no reason for lengthy review of the evidence. He would render an immediate decision.

"The court rules that the deaths of both Mark A. Wilson and Charles N. Mathews were justifiable homicide. Mr. Thompson, you are forthwith discharged. Bail will be remanded."

The courtroom erupted in cheers. Thompson shook hands with his attorneys, and pulled Catherine into a warm embrace. Billy slapped him on the back, whooping loudly, grinning like a jack-o'-lantern. As they made their way up the aisle, the spectators crowded around, offering congratulations. There was a mood of celebration in the air.

Outside the courthouse, reporters from the *Statesman* and the *Republican* waited on the steps. "Mr.

Thompson!" one of them shouted. "Do you feel vindicated?"

"Boys, I'll tell you, fresh air never smelled so good."

"What will you do now?"

Thompson smiled. "I think I'll stay out of variety theaters."

The spectators thronged around broke out laughing. Catherine clutched his arm, and Billy cleared a path through the crowd. As they walked off along the street, Thompson's smile quickly faded. His eyes took on a somber cast.

He wondered what he'd won, and the answer seemed all too clear. Nothing.

TEN

—⁂—

Thompson was seated in the parlor. Billy was standing in the dining room doorway, talking with Catherine. She was bustling around the kitchen, preparing a celebration dinner. The aroma of a roasting hen filled the house.

Through the window, Thompson saw Bobby out in the front yard. The boy was playing with a couple of his neighborhood pals, and the game they played was disturbing to watch. They were reenacting the variety theater shooting, and the other two boys were cast in the roles of Wilson and Mathews. Bobby was playing his father.

The game was a juvenile fantasy of a gunfight. Bobby would face off against the other boys, who pretended to draw pistols holstered at their sides. When they made their move, he would draw from what was clearly an imaginary shoulder holster. Their forefingers were extended, thumbs cocked like the hammer of a pistol, and shouts of "BANG! BANG!" drifted through the window. Bobby always won.

Thompson watched with a growing sense of concern. He thought the game was probably based on neighborhood gossip about the shootout. Yet to the boys it was just that—a game—played out with imaginary guns. They didn't understand that dead men, in real life, never got up to play the game again. The thing that troubled him most was that Bobby was cast in the role of hero, and there was nothing heroic about killing two men. He was sorely reminded of the old saying: like father, like son.

Earlier that afternoon, upon returning home, Bobby had greeted him with something akin to hero worship. Catherine and Billy were elated by the outcome of the court hearing, and their enthusiasm had spilled over onto the boy. Bobby had stayed with neighbors during the hearing, and he was aware that an adverse ruling could send his father back to jail. On being told the news, he'd flung himself on Thompson, wild with joy, overcome with relief. Anyone watching would never doubt that the boy idolized his father.

But now, looking out the window, Thompson was deeply concerned. Any father wanted the admiration of his son, relished the idea of being thought a hero. The difference was that few fathers killed men in gunfights and got their names in newspaper headlines. Or worried at the sight of their sons playing make-believe, and acting out what was too close to the truth. Notoriety, and killing men, was not the stuff of games.

Thompson leaned out the window. "Bobby, come on in now! Time to get washed up for supper."

"Be right there, Pa!" Bobby hurried toward the

porch, motioning to his friends. "See you guys later. Gotta go."

A moment later the boy burst through the door. His features were flushed with youthful exuberance. "Did you see us, Pa? I got 'em ever' time."

Thompson returned to his chair. "Yes, son, I saw you."

"Was that the way you got Wilson and Mathews? Was it?"

"Where'd you hear those names?"

"Aren't those the ones you shot, Pa? All the guys are talkin' about it. They're jealous as all get-out!"

"Jealous of what?"

Bobby beamed. "Their dads haven't killed nobody. They'd swap places with me in a minute."

Billy ambled in from the dining room. Thompson exchanged a glance with him, then looked back at the boy. "I want you to listen to me, son."

"Yeah, Pa, sure."

"There's no honor in killing a man. Nothing to be proud of or brag about. You understand me?"

"I dunno." Bobby appeared confused. "I mean, what's so wrong with it? You did it."

"Well . . ." Thompson rubbed his jawline, searching for words. "Sometimes another man comes after you with a gun, and you've got no choice. You have to defend yourself." He paused, underscoring the point. "But it's still nothing to be proud of."

"All the same, I'm proud of you, Pa. I'll bet Mom is, too."

"Son, I'm trying to tell you it's not an honorable thing. I don't want you bragging to your friends about me."

"I guess I see what you mean."

"We'll talk about it later," Thompson said gently. "You get yourself ready for supper. Comb your hair."

Bobby started toward the hallway. At the door, he turned and looked back at his uncle. "You ever killed anybody, Uncle Billy? The way Pa has?"

"Not just exactly, squirt." Billy managed to keep a straight face. "'Course, there's not many the equal of your Pa. He's strictly one of a kind."

"Boy, don't I know it! You oughta see him shoot bottles."

Bobby took the stairs two at a time. Thompson slowly wagged his head. "How do you tell him it's not right to kill people? He thinks I rode in on a white horse."

"You worry too much," Billy said. "Hell, he's just a kid, Ben. He'll grow out of it."

"Did we?"

"Did we what?"

"Grow out of it," Thompson said sternly. "I'm pushing forty and I've just put two men in their graves. I haven't learned a helluva lot along the way."

Billy laughed. "You're still kickin', aren't you? Better them than you."

"Maybe so, but I still feel like some Bible-thumpin' hypocrite. I hear myself telling Bobby 'do what I say, not what I do!'"

"I never saw a man so hard on himself. You got sprung today, big brother. Cheer up."

"Why don't you go help Kate? I'm not in a mood to talk."

"Guess I know a hint when I hear one."

Billy walked off through the dining room. Thompson slumped back in his chair, his eyes fixed on the ceiling.

All afternoon, since they'd left the courtroom, he had been wrestling with a problem. Watching Bobby and his pals playfully kill each other had only aggravated a sore spot. He was worn out with killing.

The root of the problem was Carl Allen. During the hearing, the policeman had lied under oath about the theater shooting. His testimony, when read between the lines, confirmed that he'd been in league with Mark Wilson. Yet Wilson was dead, and that left the question of why Allen would perjure himself for a corpse. Why would he still try to put a noose around Thompson's neck?

The answer, Thompson told himself, was Ed Creary. The city marshal had a score to settle, and he'd found the solution in a man with no backbone. Logic dictated that Creary had persuaded Allen—somehow intimidated him—into swearing false on the witness stand. Allen had no score of his own to settle, and perjury without purpose made no sense. The purpose was to get Thompson bound over on a charge of murder.

All of which raised a more troubling problem. Thompson had just told his son that there was nothing honorable in killing. Yet he asked himself now if he was too proud to overlook perjury and insult, a veiled threat. Or was it possible to follow his own advice?

He didn't want to kill Ed Creary.

Supper was not the celebration Catherine had planned. Thompson was quiet and thoughtful, almost withdrawn. His mind was elsewhere, and he scarcely joined in the conversation. He picked at his food with no great interest.

Billy tried to revive the spirit of the occasion. He joshed with Bobby and lavished praise on Catherine about her roast hen. Halfway through the meal, he launched into a rollicking story involving a one-eyed riverboat gambler on the Rio Grande. Catherine and Bobby dutifully laughed when the gambler was thrown overboard for dealing marked cards. Thompson merely nodded with a distracted smile.

By the time Catherine served angel food cake, there was little levity at the table. Thompson's mood seemed to have dampened the humor of everyone else, and they hurried through dessert in subdued silence. Bobby kept darting glances at his father, fearful that their earlier conversation had somehow spoiled the party. He finally asked to be excused, on the pretext that he'd just started building a new model ship. Billy, expressing great interest in the project, went along for a look.

Catherine hurried off to the kitchen. She returned in a moment with the coffeepot, and filled Thompson's cup. He spooned sugar into the cup, idly stirring as she took the chair closest to him. She noted his cake was only half eaten, and shook her head. She tried to keep her tone light.

"I never thought I'd see the day your sweet tooth failed you. You've hardly touched your cake."

"Best cake you ever baked," Thompson said mechanically. "I'm just off my feed tonight."

"Is your stomach bothering you?"

"No, my stomach's fine."

"Something else then?"

Thompson shrugged. "Sorry I rained on the parade. I wasn't in much mood to celebrate."

"Yes, I noticed," she said softly. "Do you want to talk about it?"

"You won't like it."

"Why not let me be the judge of that?"

A moment of brittle silence slipped past. Thompson stopped stirring his coffee, finally looked up at her. "Katie, I have to get out of town awhile."

"Why?" she said, openly surprised. "What brought that on?"

"I've decided I don't want to kill Ed Creary. If I stay, I likely will."

"Ben, I know you've never liked Creary. But why would you want to . . . harm him?"

"Creary tried to get me hung," Thompson said, his eyes suddenly cold. "You heard Carl Allen lie through his teeth in court today. That was Creary's work."

"Honey, I'm not following you," she said, startled by the anger in his voice. "What does Creary have to do with anything?"

"Why, that's simple enough. He saw a chance to settle my hash. He got Allen to perjure himself."

"Do you really believe he hates you that much?"

"No doubt about it," Thompson told her. "I've shamed him in public too many times to count. He meant to put me in a coffin."

"Perhaps it was all Carl Allen's doing. You said yourself he was part of Wilson's scheme."

"Allen's just a stooge. He wouldn't lie about me unless somebody held his feet to the fire. Creary's behind it."

"How can you be so sure?"

"I keep hearing a little voice in my ear. Call it a gut hunch or gambler's instinct, or whatever you want. I just know, that's all."

"I see," she said on an indrawn breath. "And you couldn't overlook it . . . this one time?"

"Time's what I need," Thompson said simply. "If I

stay here, I'd feel obliged to force Creary into a fight. I have to get away."

"Do you think that will change anything?"

"Maybe I'll learn to turn the other cheek. Time and distance might do the trick."

"Where will you go?"

"I've been thinking of Dodge City. I hear it's still a good stop for a gambling man."

She saw now that he'd thought it through. His mind was made up and nothing she could say would dissuade him. "How long will you be gone?"

"All depends," Thompson said, not sure himself. "However long it takes to get my mind straight. A month, maybe longer."

"What will happen to the club?"

"Joe Richter will look after things. I trust him, and he's sharp as a tack. I'll talk to him tonight."

She suddenly looked wistful. "When will you leave?"

"The sooner the better." Thompson reached out, took her hand. "I'll catch the morning train to Dallas and go on from there." He squeezed her hand. "You understand, don't you, Katie?"

"Yes, I understand. But I want you home early tonight. We have to say good-bye properly."

"Sounds like you've got something wicked in mind."

"Let's just say you won't get much sleep."

She rose from her chair and kissed him full on the mouth. Then, as though nothing unusual had happened, she began clearing the table. Thompson walked from the dining room to the parlor, and saw the glow of a cigar through the window. He moved into the hallway, opening the door, and stepped out onto the porch. Billy was seated in a rocker.

"You ought to have a word with Bobby," he said, puffing a cloud of smoke. "You weren't exactly the life of the party, and he thinks it was his fault. He needs to hear otherwise."

"I was too hard on him earlier," Thompson admitted. "I'll talk with him and make it right."

"What got you so down in the mouth?"

"You wouldn't understand if I told you. I'm catching the train for Dodge City tomorrow. How'd you like to come along?"

Billy straightened in the rocker. "You're a sackful of surprises. What's in Dodge City?"

"One way to find out," Thompson said. "Unless you're still set on being a riverboat gambler. Want to think it over?"

"Hell, I'm game for anything. But it's all sort of sudden, isn't it? I thought you'd took permanent root in Austin."

"Nothing here that won't keep for a while. I've got an itch to travel."

"How's Katie feel about that?"

"You ask too many questions."

"Well, you know, I am her brother-in-law. I have to look after her welfare."

"Just to set your mind at rest, I've got the home fires covered."

Billy gave him a lopsided grin. "By God, it'll be like old times again. You and me and Dodge City!"

"Wonder if the Comique and the Lady Gay, and all those other joints are still there. Things change in two years."

"I'll give you odds there's nothin' changed. They're probably shootin' up the South Side just like always."

Thompson grunted. "I sincerely hope not."

"Why do you say it like that?"

"I get all the gunplay I want here in Austin."

"Careful, Ben," Billy chided. "You're startin' to sound like you just got religion."

" 'All our yesterdays have lighted fools the way to dusty death.' "

"You quotin' scripture?"

"After a fashion," Thompson said. "It's a line from *Macbeth*."

"Who the hell's Macbeth?"

"I'll tell you about it on the way to Dodge."

ELEVEN

———≈≈≈———

Dodge City billed itself as "Queen of the Cowtowns." The Santa Fe railroad tracks bisected the town east to west, and to the south a wooden bridge spanned the Arkansas River. The business district was spread along a broad plaza north of the tracks.

Thompson and Billy stepped off the train shortly before eleven on the morning of September 24. The Western Trail, which had replaced the old Chisholm Trail for cattle drives, spiraled north from Texas to the bridge over the river. But there was no direct train route from Texas, and the trip required traveling to Kansas City and then doubling back to Dodge City. Their journey had consumed the better part of a week.

Fort Dodge, the nearest army post, was situated five miles east along the Arkansas. Until 1872, with the arrival of the railroad, Dodge City had been a windswept collection of log structures devoted to the buffalo trade. But then, hammered together with bustling industry, it had sprung, virtually overnight, into the rawest boom-town on the Western Plains. A sprawling hodgepodge of buildings, the town was neatly divided by the rail-road tracks.

The dusty plaza along Front Street was clearly the center of commerce and trade. Down at one end were the Dodge House Hotel, Zimmerman's Mercantile, and several smaller establishments. Up the other way were shops and the newspaper, bordered by cafes and various business places, including the Long Branch Saloon. Far-ther north, beyond the plaza, was the residential district of town.

Thompson rented them lodging at the Dodge House. A bellman lugged their bags upstairs, and got them quartered in an airy room overlooking the plaza. They unpacked and took turns at the wash basin, scrubbing off the accumulated grime and soot from their long train trip. Then, anxious to revisit old haunts, Thompson led the way out of the hotel. They walked back toward the railroad depot.

The sporting district, known simply as the South Side, was directly across the tracks. There, during trail-ing season, saloons, whorehouses and gambling dives pandered to the rowdy nature of cowhands. But at the railroad tracks, dubbed the Deadline, all rowdiness ceased. The lawmen of Dodge City, with a no-nonsense attitude toward troublemakers, rigidly enforced the or-dinance. Anyone who attempted to hurrah the respect-able part of town was treated to a night in jail.

Thompson thought it a sensible arrangement. The wages of sin on one side of the tracks and the fruits of commerce on the other. The neutral ribbon of steel in between served as a visible, and clearly effective, dividing line. The rule containing the wild-and-woolly cowhands to the sporting district seemed to work uncommonly well for all concerned. On the north side of the Deadline, the townspeople went about their business in relative peace.

The Lady Gay was one of the more popular watering holes. A combination saloon and gaming den, it was located across from the depot, on the corner of Second Avenue. As Thompson and Billy approached the boardwalk, a man dressed in whipcord trousers and a dark wool jacket crossed the street. He was lean and muscular, with a soup-strainer mustache, the bulge of a holstered pistol apparent beneath his jacket. He seemed lost in deep thought.

"I'll be damned!" Thompson said. "There's Jim Masterson."

"Jim!" Billy called out. "Hullo there, Jim. Wait up!"

Masterson turned at the sound of his name. His expression changed from quizzical to one of gladdened recognition. "Ben! Billy!" He rushed forward with his hand outstretched. "What the deuce are you doing in Dodge?"

"Long time, no see," Thompson said, returning his handshake. "We got lonesome for our old stamping grounds. Thought we'd pay a visit."

"You're a sight for sore eyes," Billy added. "We wondered who'd be here from the old crowd."

"Well, you got more than you bargained for," Masterson said. "Bat's comin' in on the noon eastbound. All the way from Tombstone."

"I was there!" Billy crowed. "Not more'n two months ago. He was dealin' faro for Wyatt Earp."

"Guess it's our lucky day," Thompson said jovially. "What brings Bat back to Dodge?"

Masterson frowned. "Boys, it's a long story and nothin' sweet about it. Let me buy you a drink."

They followed him into the Lady Gay. Though it was not yet noon, Thompson felt he couldn't refuse the offer of a whiskey. Over drinks, Masterson briefly explained why he'd summoned his brother from Arizona. After serving a term as town marshal, he and a man named Alonso Peacock had gone partners and bought the Lady Gay. Peacock, acting on his own, had hired a bartender named Updegraff, who was noted throughout the South Side for rough treatment of customers. Masterson promptly fired him.

The next day Peacock and Updegraff stormed into the saloon. An argument ensued, and within moments, all three men pulled their guns. As happened in so many cases, nerves undercut accuracy, and none of the shots took effect. But Masterson drove them into the street, and they beat a hasty retreat across the railroad tracks. For nearly two weeks, Peacock had avoided the Lady Gay, even though he was a full partner. Still, he and Updegraff were bent on revenge, and word of their threats had spread through town. Masterson had wired Bat in Tombstone.

"I see them around," he concluded. "But so far, they've kept their distance, and I send Peacock's cut of the receipts over to his house. I think they're waiting to catch me on a dark night."

"Sorry bastards!" Billy huffed. "So what happens when Bat gets here? You aim to force a fight?"

"Don't see any way around it," Masterson said. "Looks to me like it's fight or get bushwhacked. I told Bat as much in the telegraph I sent him."

"Count on me and Ben, too," Billy volunteered. "You've got our marker for that Nebraska business. Don't they, Ben?"

"Damn right," Thompson agreed. "Friends stick together."

A year ago, the summer of 1880, Billy was in Ogallala, Nebraska. He killed a man in a gunfight, and was himself seriously wounded. After a doctor treated him, he was confined to his bed in the local hotel, attended by a male nurse. The killing was ruled justifiable, but the dead man's friends were of another mind. Scornful of the law, they planned a lynching party in Billy's honor, once he was able to walk. They wanted him fit for his own hanging.

Billy, through his male nurse, managed to wire Thompson. Speed was essential, and Thompson wired Bat Masterson, who was living in Denver at the time. Without hesitation, Bat hopped a train to Ogallala, and arrived in the dead of night. He enlisted the aid of the male nurse and spirited Billy out of town aboard the midnight train. Had they been caught, his own life was at risk, but he refused all thanks. He told Billy it was the least a friend could do.

Today, reflecting on it, Thompson was struck by the irony of the situation. He'd left Austin to avoid more killing, and now, his first day in Dodge City, he was involved in yet another dispute. Still, putting irony aside, he thought it only fitting that he and Billy volunteer their services. Bat Masterson had done as much in Ogallala, and there was no greater debt than one owed a friend. Then, too, there was the matter of personal esteem, and respect. He admired the Masterson brothers.

For nearly a decade, in various Kansas cowtowns, he'd developed a lasting friendship with the Mastersons. Bat, a former buffalo hunter, had been elected sheriff of Ford County and earned a reputation as a tough lawman. Ed, the oldest brother, had served as marshal of Dodge City, only to be killed three years ago in a gunfight with Texas cowhands. A year later, Jim was appointed city marshal, and served with distinction until he quit to pursue business interests. Law and order in Dodge City was, to no small degree, the handiwork of the Mastersons.

"Who's sheriff now?" Thompson asked at length. "Anyone we have to worry about?"

"His name is Fred Singer," Masterson said derisively. "Fred's always a day late and a dollar short when it comes to law enforcement. His game is politics."

"Jim, it's no different in Austin. We've got a city marshal who's a disgrace to the badge."

"I often wonder—"

A train whistle cut him off. Masterson walked to a window on the north side of the saloon. The noon castbound rocked to a halt before the depot, and a man stepped down from the lead passenger coach. Masterson laughed out loud.

"There's Bat!" he said. "Just got off the train."

Thompson and Billy joined him at the window. Masterson suddenly stiffened, pointing at two men crossing from the South Side to the business district. His features were taut with anger.

"That's Peacock and Updegraff," he muttered furiously. "What the hell are they doing there?"

Thompson peered closer. "Did they know Bat was on the train?"

"I don't see how. But Bat damn sure knows them. C'mon, we'd better get out—"

His voice trailed off. Through the window, they saw Bat turn toward the South Side and stop abruptly as he

spotted Peacock and Updegraff. He shouted something
at them, and in the next moment, all three men went for
their guns. Bystanders scattered in every direction as
shots rang out across the street. Bat dove headlong
behind the rail embankment, and Peacock and Updegraff took cover behind a building just south of the
tracks. They traded shots in a flurry of gunfire.

Masterson hurled a chair through the window. He
drew his pistol, standing shoulder to shoulder with
Thompson and Billy in the open maw of the window-
frame. From the Lady Gay, they had an oblique field
of fire on the building south of the railroad tracks. Peacock and Updegraff ducked as slugs thunked into the
frame of the building around their heads. Caught in a
cross-fire, Peacock continued to exchange shots with
Bat. Updegraff turned to engage the assault from the
Lady Gay.

The men in the window fired in unison. None of
them would ever know whose shot took effect, but at
least one slug found the mark. Updegraff dropped his
gun, clutching at his chest, and slammed backward into
the building. As he slumped to the ground, Peacock's
nerves deserted him, and he sprinted west across Second
Avenue. Bat, still firing from the rail embankment, emptied his pistol in a rattling volley. Peacock disappeared
into an alley halfway down the block.

Masterson hurried toward the door. Thompson and
Billy followed along, and as they emerged from the
Lady Gay, they saw him grab Bat in a back-pounding
bear hug. Bat looked at them with a dumbfounded expression.

"Jesus Christ!" he said blankly. "Where'd you two
come from?"

"Texas," Thompson replied, shaking his hand. "We got here just in time for the fireworks."

"Well, you boys damn sure saved my bacon. I was pinned down with nowhere to go."

Billy pumped his arm. "What was it you yelled at them?"

"Hell, my mouth got ahead of my brain. Told 'em I knew they were heeled and let's get the fight on. Guess they took me serious."

A crowd began gathering on the boardwalks. Bat's suit was covered in dust from the rail bed, and a dent marred the crown of his derby hat. He was chunkier than his brother, solidly built, with pale eyes and a brushy mustache. He glanced around as a man with a star on his jacket approached them.

"Ford County's gone to hell," he said, eyeing the badge. "How'd you ever get elected, Fred?"

Sheriff Singer bobbed his head. "Bat, I'll swear, you're a regular lightnin' rod. I'm gonna have to arrest somebody for shootin' Updegraff."

"You're not arresting anybody, Fred. The son-of-a-bitch pulled a gun on me the minute I stepped off that train. Tell the coroner to rule it suicide."

"I got witnesses that'll say otherwise."

"Here's what I say," Bat informed him in an icy voice. "Before dark, Al Peacock will sell out to my brother. I guarantee it." He thumped the badge with his forefinger. "You cause Jim any trouble and you'll answer to me. Got it straight?"

Singer swallowed hard. "No need to threaten people thataway, Bat. You was a lawman yourself."

"I had to come a thousand miles to do your job for you. Peacock and Updegraff should've been arrested a

couple of weeks ago, when they pulled guns on Jim.
Why weren't they?"

"There wasn't any call to arrest them. Nobody was
hurt."

"You're full of it," Bat said, pushing past him. "Just
remember what I told you about Updegraff. He committed suicide."

Thompson and the others followed Bat into the
Lady Gay. The bartender brought glasses and poured
drinks all around. Bat hoisted his glass in a toast
and tossed off the whiskey. His mustache lifted in a
tight grin.

"Dodge City's gone to hell in a handbasket. Not like
the old days."

"You haven't changed," Thompson said with a
chuckle. "You're still up for a scrap."

"Look who's talking," Bat joked. "You and Billy
jumped right in when the guns went off. Guess we're
birds of a feather."

Jim Masterson laughed. "Damn good thing, too. We
owe you boys one."

"Hell you do!" Billy said. "Bat pulled my fat out of
the fire in Ogallala. We just returned the favor."

"Well, anyway," Bat observed. "We gave the good
folks of Dodge something to talk about. The newspapers will have a field day."

"So what's next?" Thompson asked. "You heading
back to Tombstone?"

"Ben, I think I've had my fill of dealin' faro. I believe I'll test the waters in Denver."

"Denver's nice this time of year. Never cared for it
when the snow flies."

"Why don't you and Billy join me?"

"Not a bad idea," Thompson remarked. "After today,

we've likely worn out our welcome in Dodge. How's it sound to you, Billy?"

"Lead the way," Billy said agreeably. "Here today, gone tomorrow, that's my motto."

Thompson smiled. "Looks like we're along for the ride, Bat. When do we leave?"

"Why, hell, anytime suits me. But I just suspect Billy's got the fix on things—gone tomorrow."

They drank a toast to Denver.

TWELVE

Dusk was settling over the land. Off to the west, the snowy spires of the Rockies rose majestically against a backdrop of fading light. The mountains towered skyward like an unbroken column of sentinels.

Denver was a center of finance and commerce. Originally a mining camp, the raw boomtown reproduced itself a hundredfold, until finally a glittering metropolis stood along the banks of Cherry Creek and the South Platte. By 1881, it was a cosmopolitan beehive, with a stock exchange, three railroads, and a population of thirty thousand. The city was unrivaled by anything on the Western plains.

Bat Masterson stepped out of the Brown Palace Hotel. He was accompanied by Thompson and Billy, dressed for an evening on the town. They had arrived early that afternoon, and there was a brisk scent of oncoming winter in the air. Thompson marked the date as October 1, a Saturday, and thought it might be a short stay. He had visited Denver on several occasions, once during the middle of a blizzard. He wasn't anxious to repeat the experience.

From the hotel, they turned downtown. Billy was a newcomer to Denver, and Masterson appointed himself as tour guide. For reasons lost to time, he explained, the sporting district was known as the Tenderloin. There, within a few square blocks of Blake Street, every vice known to man was available for a price. Saloons and gaming dives catered to the sporting crowd, and variety theaters featured headline acts from the vaudeville circuit. The nightlife attracted high rollers from all across the West.

One block over, on Holladay Street, was Denver's infamous red-light district. Billy, who hadn't had his ashes hauled in a while, was a rapt listener. Masterson observed that it was known locally as the Row. A lusty fleshpot of dollar cribs, girls posed in the windows, soliciting customers, available by the trick or by the hour. Hook shops dominated the Row, and newspapers wryly referred to the girls as "Brides of the Multitude." Yet there was no scarcity of high-class whores.

The parlor houses offered younger girls and a greater variety, all at steeper prices. Masterson, not unlike a civic booster of the risqué, noted that something over a thousand soiled doves plied their trade on Holladay Street. The expensive bordellos were the domain of the more exotic tarts, and Thompson was reminded of Guy Town in Austin. The ladies of the evening, though barred under the municipal code, were nonetheless a steady source of revenue. Their license fees were a large part of the city's budget.

Masterson next took them on a brief tour of Hop

Alley. A narrow passageway running between Larimer
and Holladay, it was Denver's version of Lotus Land.
Chinese fan-tan parlors vied with the faint, sweet odor
of opium dens, and those addicted to the Orient's heady
delights beat a path to a backstreet world of pipe dreams.
There was no taste too bizarre, and to a select clientele,
China dolls were available day or night. Hop Alley
managed to blend the exotic with the erotic.

Their tour ended at the Progressive Club. Masterson
noted that the gaming den was owned by Ed Chase, and
frequented by the top professionals. Chase was considered the czar of the Tenderloin, as well as Denver's un-
derworld element. He enforced his authority through a
gang of hooligans who collected weekly payoffs from
every dive in the sporting district. Vice was an orga-
nized business.

The rackets, Masterson commented, operated under
the protection of Denver's political machine. On the
first of every month one of Chase's thugs, carrying a
black bag, made the rounds at city hall. From the mayor
on down, every elected official in Denver shared in the
spoils. The payoffs were the grease of politics, a partnership of sorts with the sporting crowd. The Tenderloin operated without interference of any sort.

For all that, Masterson was quick to extol the virtues
of Ed Chase. The Progressive Club, he remarked, was
known for honest cards and a square deal. Thompson
thought the comment revealed more about Masterson
than it did Denver's vice czar. Despite his reputation as
a lawman, Masterson apparently had no qualms about
associating with a rackets boss. A square deal was now
more important than the law. The badge was history.

Thompson was impressed by the gaming club. A
large diamond-dust mirror was centered behind a

mahogany bar that dominated the front of the room. Opposite the bar were dice and roulette tables, faro layouts, and other games of chance. The walls were adorned with paintings of brazen women, and crystal chandeliers, blazing with light, were suspended overhead. A section at the rear was reserved for a grouping of six poker tables.

Masterson was clearly something of a celebrity. The bartenders greeted him by name, and several of the dealers waved from their tables. Ed Chase hurried forward from the rear of the bar, his features warmed by a smile. He was slim and angular, with iron-gray hair, impeccably attired in a charcoal gray suit and an elegant silk cravat. He extended his hand.

"Always a pleasure, Bat," he said cordially. "The last I heard, you were in Tombstone."

Masterson shook his hand. "A mining camp's no place for a civilized man. I decided Denver's the place for me."

"Well, whatever the reason, it's good to have you back."

"Ed, I'd like you to meet a couple of old friends. Ben Thompson and his brother, Billy."

"Gentlemen," Chase said, exchanging handshakes. "Welcome to Denver."

"They're from Texas," Masterson went on. "You and Ben have something in common. He owns a club in Austin."

Case nodded amiably. "I'm familiar with your name, Mr. Thompson. As is anyone who reads the *Police Gazette.*"

"Don't believe everything you read," Thompson said with a casual gesture. "I'd rather be known as a club owner."

"You're too modest, sir. Why, just last week, I read how you single-handedly took on two men. I admire grit."

Billy laughed. "Ben's got grit, awright. A bushel full!"

"And you, Mr. Thompson?" Chase said, glancing at Billy. "Are you a club owner as well?"

"Not for all the tea in China. I'm just another gamblin' man."

"That's why we came by," Masterson interjected. "Figured some high rollers might drift in later. We're interested in a game."

"Bat, there's always a game at the Progressive Club."

"Then you won't mind holding three chairs. We'll be back about nine or so."

"Why not stick around?" Chase said. "We could probably find you a game before nine."

Masterson grinned. "I've got a special treat in store for the boys. Thought I'd take them to see Lola Montana."

"No better way to start the night," Chase said agreeably. "Just between us, I prefer Lola Montana to poker myself."

"I'm damn glad to hear it," Billy said, with a broad smile. "Way Bat talks, she's hotter'n a three-dollar pistol. I was startin' to wonder."

"Take my word for it, she's the toast of Denver. You won't be disappointed."

Thompson watched the byplay with interest. He was struck by Chase's urbane manner, and thought it unusual for a man who ruled Denver's vice district with an iron fist. But even more, he suspected Ed Chase was prone to shade the truth.

Lola Montana couldn't be better than a game of poker. No one was that good.

Some while later Masterson led them through the doors of the Alcazar Variety Theater. The owner greeted Masterson with an effusive handshake, and personally escorted them to a table down front. A waiter materialized when he snapped his fingers, and he ordered a bottle of champagne. The bubbly, he told them, was on the house.

"Enjoy the show, Mr. Masterson," he said, rushing off. "Nice to have you back in Denver."

A man seated alone at a nearby table turned in his chair. "Masterson?" he called out in a loud voice. "Would that be *the* Bat Masterson?"

Masterson looked around. "Luke!" He grinned, moving forward with an outstretched hand. "I should've known you'd be here."

"I never miss a show. Why don't you and your friends join me?"

Thompson judged the man to be in his early thirties. He was tall, lithely built, with smoky blue eyes and light chestnut hair. A pistol in a crossdraw holster rode at belt level beneath his suit coat. Masterson quickly performed the introductions.

"Ben Thompson. Billy Thompson." He motioned them over to the table. "I'd like you to meet another old friend. This is Luke Starbuck."

"A pleasure," Thompson said, exchanging a handshake. "Your name is well known in Texas."

Starbuck smiled. "Yours is well known everywhere. I'm afraid we're grist for the mill with the *Police Gazette*."

"Well, you can't blame 'em," Billy said with a laugh. "You and Ben sell a lot of newspapers."

"Not by choice," Thompson remarked. "I wish they'd forget how to spell my name."

Starbuck nodded. "Amen to that."

Three private detectives in the West were widely recognized by the public. Charlie Siringo worked for the Pinkertons, and Harry Morse was headquartered in San Francisco. But Luke Starbuck, operating out of Denver, was regarded as the foremost manhunter of the day. He was reputed to have killed a dozen men.

The *Police Gazette* considered Starbuck front-page news. Among others, he'd been involved in the downfall of such noted badmen as Dutch Henry Horn and Billy the Kid. His fame as an investigator had spread throughout the country, and the attendant publicity had destroyed his anonymity forever. These days he operated undercover.

The house lights dimmed. A hush fell over the crowd as the curtains parted onstage. Lola Montana stood bathed in the cider glow of a spotlight. Her exquisite features were tilted in a woeful expression, and her clear alto voice filled the theater. She sang a heartrending ballad of unrequited love, her eyes misty.

The performance was flawless. Lola's voice was at once sultry and virginal, and she held the audience captivated to the last note. A moment slipped past, then the theater vibrated to wild cheers and thunderous applause. She took a bow, then another and another, and still the house rocked with ovation. She signaled the maestro.

The orchestra segued into a rousing dance number. A line of chorus girls exploded out of the wings and went highstepping across the stage. Lola raised her skirts, revealing a shapely leg, and joined them in a prancing cakewalk. The girls squealed and Lola flashed her underdrawers and the tempo of the music quickened. The audience went mad.

Thompson found his toe tapping in time to the music. There was a wanton exuberance to the routine, with Lola and the girls cavorting around the stage. Then the orchestra thumped into the finale with a blare of trumpets and a clash of cymbals. The chorus line, in a swirl of upraised skirts and jiggling breasts, went romping into the wings. The spotlight centered on the star of the show.

Lola Montana waved to the crowd. Then, bending over the footlights, she blew a kiss to Starbuck. She winked a bawdy wink, wig-wagging her behind, and strutted offstage. The audience roared with delight.

Starbuck looked embarrassed. When the curtain rang down, Masterson was still laughing. "I forgot to tell you boys," he said, glancing around the table. "Lola's the toast of the town, but she's Luke's woman. Doesn't say much for her taste in men."

"Look who's talking," Starbuck joshed him. "You'd give your eye-teeth to be in my place."

"Hell, I'd give my right arm!"

Billy poured a round of champagne. They toasted Lola Montana and congratulated Starbuck. Thompson nodded over the rim of his glass.

"You're a fortunate man," he said. "She's quite a lady. A real beauty."

Starbuck chuckled. "All I have to do is keep from getting shot. Lola doesn't much care for my line of work."

"How'd you get into the detective business?"

"I started out as a stock detective. One thing led to

another, and I quit chasing rustled cows. Got to where I just chase men."

"Well, you're good at it," Thompson said. "You must find it worthwhile."

"Yeah, I do," Starbuck admitted. "Not that it's the same as wearing a badge, you understand. But I reckon it takes all kinds."

"Don't let him kid you," Masterson interrupted. "Luke takes on the cases that most lawmen wouldn't touch. He just doesn't like to toot his own horn."

"You make too much of it, Bat."

"What about those payroll robbers? The ones you tracked to Hole-in-the-Wall? How many lawmen tagged along?"

Thompson was familiar with the case. Hole-in-the-Wall was an outlaw sanctuary in the wilds of Wyoming. Starbuck had gone in alone and come out alive, which said it all. No peace officer had ever ventured into the hideout.

"I got lucky," Starbuck said, uncomfortable with the conversation. "Lots of men could have pulled that off."

"Name one," Masterson countered. "I don't know anybody who would even try it. Go ahead, tell me I'm wrong."

Starbuck was saved by Lola Montana. She appeared from backstage, dressed in a low-cut gown, and walked to the table. The men jumped to their feet, offering her a chair, and poured her a glass of champagne. She immediately became the center of conversation.

Thompson thought she was even prettier in person. Her face was a perfect oval, her features expressive and animated, and her laughter was infectious. Yet her vivacity was largely lost on him, and he sat like an eavesdropper gone deaf. He was thinking of Hole-in-the-Wall.

Or more to the point, he was thinking about how men conduct their lives. He had met Luke Starbuck scarcely an hour ago; but the impression he got was distinct. Here was a man who challenged life, routinely went where others dared not go. A man not content with the ordinary.

The line from *Macbeth* popped into his mind. The line that had troubled him for over a month now, and wouldn't go away. A *tale told by an idiot, full of sound and fury, signifying nothing.* Or perhaps it was simply too little. Less than he was willing to accept.

Thompson told himself that his life was far from ordinary. Yet compared to the manhunter seated across the table, his existence bordered on the humdrum. Perhaps that was what had eluded him over the past month, the sense of challenge. The certainty . . .

The thought suddenly crystallized into words. The certainty that there was more to life than a fast gun and a deck of cards. A reason to believe that a tale signifying nothing was just a line in a stage play. Not a prophecy.

Nor was it an epitaph.

The answer was there all the time, and he wondered how he'd missed it. Distance sometimes cleared a man's perspective, opened his eyes. He saw it now.

He had to get back to Austin.

THIRTEEN

The engineer set the brakes with a racketing squeal. A moment later, belching clouds of steam, the train ground to a halt before the stationhouse. High in a cloudless sky, a warm noonday sun stood at its zenith. Passengers began debarking the train.

Thompson gathered his valise from the overhead luggage rack. Followed by Billy, he moved to the end of the coach and went down the steps onto the platform. Autumn was slowly settling across the land, and the trees along the river were tinged with color. He was reminded that he'd been away not quite a month. The date was October 11.

Before departing Colorado, he had wired Catherine their schedule. The train route had taken them through Raton Pass and into New Mexico, with connections eastward for Texas. All the way from Denver, Billy had badgered him for the reason behind their sudden departure. But he'd put Billy off with excuses, artfully skirting the truth. He first wanted to discuss it with Catherine.

There were carriages for hire outside the depot. On the way uptown, Thompson was more aware of the city than ever before, as though seeing it from a new perspective. By now Billy was disgruntled with asking questions, and sat wrapped in silence. The ride took them past the state capitol, and Thompson again warned himself that politics was a dirty game. He thought he would need help.

Upon arriving home, Catherine met them at the door. Her eyes were bright with excitement, and she kissed Thompson soundly on the mouth. Billy accepted a peck on the cheek, and she closed the door as they dropped their bags in the hallway. She looked them over with a happy smile.

"I'm so glad you're back," she said gaily. "You'd better prepare yourselves when Bobby gets home from school. He's wild to hear about your adventures."

"Don't know as I'd call it that," Billy said grumpily. "Your husband's not a man to light long in one spot. We spent most of our time on trains."

Thompson waved him off. "Billy took a shine to Denver. He wanted to stay longer."

"Longer!" Billy croaked. "We was only there one night."

"One night?" Catherine repeated with surprise. "Why did you leave so quickly?"

Billy cocked an eyebrow. "You'll have to ask your husband that. He's kept it a big, dark secret."

"Goodness, that sounds mysterious."

"Ben's a mystery, all right. Maybe you can get him to talk."

Catherine laughed. "I've never had any problem before."

"Lemme know when you hear the lowdown. Think I'll get myself cleaned up and presentable. What I'm wearin' could stand up all by itself."

Billy hefted his bag, walking to the stairs. Thompson hooked his hat on a coatrack, took Catherine's arm, and steered her into the parlor. He waited until he heard Billy moving around upstairs, then lowered himself into a chair. Catherine gave him a curious look.

"What is it?" she said. "I've never known you to keep secrets from Billy."

Thompson motioned her to the sofa. "Billy can wait. I wanted to talk to you about it first."

"I'm on needles and pins. What's so important?"

"Katie, I've decided to run for city marshal. I figured you ought to hear it before anyone else."

Catherine sat perfectly still. Her mouth ovaled in a tiny gasp, and her eyes were round with shock. "Are you serious?" she finally managed. "I thought you detested politics."

"I do," Thompson affirmed. "It's the dirtiest game around."

"Then why would you get involved? What on earth gave you the idea?"

"Well, it's hard to explain. I've been troubled by things for a couple of months now. Not satisfied with the way things are."

"What things?" she asked. "Are you talking about Ed Creary and the police force?"

"No, I'm talking about me," Thompson said. "I'm trying to tell you I'm not satisfied with myself. I want my life to count for something."

"I don't understand, sweetheart. You have a family

and a successful business. You're respected by the people who matter. Doesn't all that count?"

"'Course it does. But when you boil it all down, I'm still just a gambler. I want to be known for more than that."

She looked dazed. "How does being a peace officer accomplish anything?"

"Folks remember the good ones," Thompson said with conviction. "Not that I'll ever be a Lee Hall, or any of the other Ranger captains. But I'll make a good city marshal."

"You want to be remembered, is that it?"

"Katie, I'm not looking to have people build statues of me. I just want my life to count."

Catherine suddenly saw it. He wasn't talking about what others thought of him. Nor was he concerned with immortality, statues erected in his honor. He was talking about what he thought of himself.

A moment passed while she came to grips with the idea. All in a rush, she realized that he considered his accomplishments inadequate, shy of some personal benchmark. He wanted to do something singular with his life.

"You know something?" she said, reaching out to touch his hand. "I think you'll make the best marshal Austin ever had."

Thompson squeezed her hand. "With you backing me, how can I miss? I'll give this town some real law and order."

"You haven't much time, and Ed Creary is a smooth politician. The elections are less than a month off."

"You're right on both counts. I've got to get busy."

The city charter mandated a general election every year. The race for mayor, as well as for aldermen and the marshal's post, would be decided on the first Monday in November. Thompson had three weeks to win an election.

Something he hadn't told Catherine was in the back of his mind as well. On the way home from Colorado, he'd decided that Creary's attempt to get him hanged deserved a special form of retribution. Instead of killing Creary, he would humiliate him in public, by defeating him in the political arena. The sweetest revenge was in disgrace, not death.

"Where will you start?" Catherine said. "There's so much to do."

"The mayor hates Creary worse than the Devil hates holy water. That's the place to start."

"Do you think he'll drop Creary from the ticket?"

Thompson grinned. "I'm damn sure gonna find out."

She thought he'd never looked more confident of anything.

"Jesus H. Christmas!"

"I figured that's how you'd feel."

"You want to be a *lawdog?* You're off your rocker."

"There's worse things."

"Name me one!"

Billy paced to the edge of the porch. Thompson had brought him outside to break the news. He knew it would cause fireworks, and he meant to have it resolved before Bobby came home from school. Catherine, wisely, had retreated to the kitchen.

"Listen to yourself," Thompson said. "Bat Masterson was a lawman, and you never had a better friend. Am I right or not?"

"That was Kansas," Billy sulked. "This is home ground, Ben. Texas!"

"So what?"

"So it's a whole different ball of wax. Lawmen in Texas get their heads twisted on crooked. They think a badge makes them God."

"Well hell, Billy, it's not contagious. Don't you think I can keep my head on straight?"

"You lay down with dogs, you get up with fleas. That's the moral of that story."

Thompson understood his brother's bitterness. Billy was thirty-six years old, and he'd been running from the law half of his life. The Rangers had chased him from the Rio Grande to the Red, and treated him none too gently whenever he was caught. He had never been convicted of a crime, but that was the result of Thompson's bankroll and the clever attorneys hired in his defense. He held all Texas lawmen in contempt.

"Hear me out," Thompson said. "A badge won't change me one iota, even if I wore it the rest of my life. You ought to know me better than that."

"Kee-rist," Billy moaned. "Don't you see, it's just the thought of it. A lawdog in the family."

"You'd better get used to the idea. I'm going to run and I intend to win."

"You made up your mind before we left Denver, didn't you? Why'd you wait till now to tell me?"

"We both know you've never kept a secret in your life. You would've spilled the beans the minute we walked in the house. I figured Katie deserved to hear it first—from me."

"What'd she say about you wearin' a badge?"

"She's behind me a hundred percent. Which is a damn-sight more than I can say for you."

Billy stalked to the end of the porch. He stared out at College Hill, absently watching students cross the campus. A prolonged moment slipped past, and finally he turned back to Thompson. He lifted his shoulders in an elaborate shrug.

"What the hell," he said with a dismal smile. "Katie's got more sense than both of us put together. I'll tag along."

"Glad you came around," Thompson said, relieved. "Family has to stick together, especially brothers. I'll be needing your help."

"What kind of help?"

"A city marshal can't operate a gaming parlor. The voters would consider it a conflict of interest."

"Yeah?" Billy said, his expression guarded. "And . . . ?"

"I want you to run the Iron Front," Thompson said with a grand gesture. "We'll go partners, just like I always talked about. Split it down the middle."

"Nice try, but no sale. I never was one to be tied down, and nothing's changed. You'll have to find somebody else."

"I'd rather keep it in the family. Besides, it's high time you settled down. You're not getting any younger."

Billy grinned. "You might as well save your breath. I'm headed back to the Rio Grande and the riverboats. I like it on the border."

"Billy, you disappoint me."

"Just think of me as the black sheep in the family. You always said I was shiftless and no-account."

"I'll be damned if I ever said any such thing!"

"You won't hurt my feelings . . . it's true."

"Pa!"

The shout brought them around. They saw Bobby racing across the street, a load of school books under his arm. He scampered up the steps, dropping the books, and threw himself at his father. His eyes were like saucers.

"You're back!" he yelled. "I missed you somethin' awful, Pa."

"Well, I'm home now, son."

"For keeps?"

Thompson smiled. "For keeps."

Late that evening Thompson stepped off the streetcar. He waved to Billy, who was on the scout for *filles de joie,* and headed for a parlor house in Guy Town. The streetcar trundled off down the tracks.

Thompson crossed the intersection at Congress Avenue. He was reconciled to the fact that Billy had rebuffed his offer with casual indifference. His brother preferred the gypsy life, and he'd never held out any great faith that a partnership was in the cards. He proceeded along Mulberry Street.

The alternative, he told himself, was probably the best bet anyway. He'd worked out a contingency plan on the train from Denver, all too aware that Billy was a wayward spirit. He had been truthful when he'd said he would rather keep it in the family. But on the other hand, business was business.

The Iron Front was crowded for a Monday night. After nearly a month's absence, Thompson was greeted with more than customary good cheer. The dealers and bartenders gave him the high sign, and the club's patrons eagerly ganged around to shake his hand. He was flattered by all the attention.

Joe Richter hurried forward. "Good to see you, boss," he said with genuine warmth. "When'd you get back?"

"Just this afternoon," Thompson replied, accepting his handshake. "How'd things go while I was away?"

"I don't like to brag—"

"Go ahead, brag."

"—But you'll like what you see when you check the books. We're up six percent over normal."

"Joe, that's damn good work," Thompson said, openly pleased. "You do better when I'm gone."

"No way, boss." Richter tried for a modest tone. "We just hit a streak, that's all."

"Let's go back to the office. You won't be missed for a minute. I've got some news for you."

"Why sure, whatever you say."

In the office, Thompson took a seat behind the desk. He waved Richter to the only other chair in the room, and proceeded to outline his plans. Richter suddenly got attentive when he spoke of declaring his candidacy for city marshal. He finished with a reference to the conflict of interest issue.

"So it's a problem," he said. "Nobody would stand for the marshal operating a gaming parlor. I'd get roasted by the newspapers."

"Boss, I'm damn near speechless," Richter said in a serious voice. "You're not thinking of selling the Iron Front, are you? I'd hate to find myself out of a job."

"I was thinking the other way 'round, Joe. How'd you like to be a partner?"

"Are you joking?"

"I never joke about money."

"Well, I like that idea a whole lot. What d'you have in mind?"

"Here's the deal," Thompson told him. "You run the Iron Front and I'll run the town. Your partnership gets you ten percent of the net."

Richter held his gaze. "Fifteen percent sounds more like it."

"Don't get greedy, Joe."

"I'm worth it."

"Tell you what I'll do," Thompson said, poker-faced, "Twelve percent and that's my last word on it. Deal?"

"Done," Richter said with a pearly grin. "You won't regret it, boss."

They shook hands on it. Thompson started toward the door, then stopped. "One last thing."

"What's that?"

"Don't call me 'boss' anymore. That handshake just made us partners. From now on, it's Ben."

"Whatever you say—Ben."

Thompson led the way through the door. A poker game was in progress at the rear of the club, and he briefly considered taking a chair. Then, just as quickly, he discarded the notion. He needed a good night's sleep.

Tomorrow he planned to start the bandwagon rolling.

FOURTEEN

~~~·⚊⚊⚋⚋⚊~~~

Early the next morning Thompson walked into City Hall. He was attired in a dark suit, with a sedate cravat, the stovepipe hat fixed squarely on his head. He looked the very picture of an affluent businessman.

Sueann Mabry, the mayor's secretary, looked up from her desk. A spinster, she had plain dumpling features and her hair was pulled severely behind her head in a tight chignon. She greeted him with prune-faced civility.

"May I help you, Mr. Thompson?"

"Good morning, Sueann," Thompson said, doffing his hat. "I'm here to see the mayor."

"Oh?" Her voice was tinged with mild reproach. "Do you have an appointment?"

The anteroom was empty. Thompson had purposely arrived early, before the day's schedule became too hectic. He smiled, shook his head. "Ask the mayor if he can spare a moment. Tell him I'm the bearer of good tidings."

Sueann Mabry gave a rabbity sniff. She disapproved of anyone involved with the sporting crowd, even an uptown club owner. Yet she knew the mayor often played poker with Thompson, and counted him a friend. She rose from behind her desk.

"Please wait here."

She moved to the door of an inner office. She knocked lightly, then stepped inside and closed the door. A moment later she reappeared, her features neutral. She nodded crisply. "Mayor Wheeler will see you."

"Thank you, Sueann," Thompson said pleasantly. "By the way, I was admiring your dress. You ought to wear that color more often. Very nice."

She blushed, batting her eyes. She stepped aside, waiting until he entered the office, and closed the door. Tom Wheeler stood behind his desk, wagging his head with amusement. He motioned Thompson to a chair.

"You should be ashamed of yourself. Sueann will think you're flirting with her."

"No harm in paying a lady a compliment. I doubt she ever gets one from you."

"Touché," Wheeler said, chuckling. "I hadn't heard you'd returned to town. Have a good trip?"

Thompson lit a cheroot. "I spent some time in Dodge City and Denver. Enjoyed it, but I'm glad to get home."

"Well, I'm glad to see you back. Our weekly poker games aren't the same without you."

"I missed them myself. But I didn't drop by to talk poker. I'm here on another matter."

"Oh?" Wheeler said curiously. "Something official?"

"Yeah, after a fashion," Thompson acknowledged. "I plan to run for city marshal in the November elections. I'm here to ask for your support."

Wheeler's mouth dropped open. "Marshal?" he stammered. "You're pulling my leg."

"Never more serious in my life. How's the idea strike you?"

"Why would you run for marshal? I never heard you express any great love for lawmen."

"Tom, I have to level with you. I've decided I want to do more with my life than shuffle cards. I think I'll make a damn good peace officer."

"I've no doubt you would."

Thompson puffed on his cheroot. "You've said yourself you'd like to dump Creary. Here's your chance."

"Ed Creary's no problem," Wheeler observed. "So far the party hasn't endorsed anyone. We're letting him sweat it out."

The politics of Austin was ruled principally by Democrats. The Republican Party, for more than a decade, had been shunned by Texas voters. During the Reconstruction Era, following the Civil War, the scalawags and carpetbaggers had left a bitter legacy. These days, though the Republicans fielded a slate of candidates, it was virtually a lost cause. Few of them ever got elected to office.

"You *are* the party," Thompson remarked. "When you say frog, everybody squats. So if Creary's not the problem, what is?"

Wheeler looked uncomfortable. "You have a certain reputation, Ben."

"That's true, and I plan to turn it to my advantage in the election. Who better to police the town than a man who won't take guff off anybody? I'll give troublemakers a real dose of law and order."

"Yes, I'm confident you would. But that doesn't offset the other problem."

"What other problem?"

"In politics, perception is everything. You are perceived—rightly or wrongly—as one of the sporting crowd."

Thompson grinned around the cheroot. He took it from his mouth and exhaled a perfect smoke ring. "As of last night," he said, "I became the silent partner in the Iron Front. No one will be able to accuse me of conflict of interest."

"What does that mean," Wheeler asked—"silent partner'?"

"I'm not a gambler anymore. I won't be playing poker at the Iron Front, or anywhere else. Joe Richter will run the club from now on."

"You've given up poker . . . for good?"

"Tom, I've cut the cord with the sporting crowd. You're looking at a new man."

"I'm frankly amazed," Wheeler said, stunned. "I find it hard to believe."

"Believe it," Thompson said earnestly. "I'm a reformed gamblin' man."

"You must want the job of marshal pretty bad."

"Once I make up my mind, that's it. I mean to win this election."

Wheeler nodded soberly. "The question is, will it be good for the ticket? There's a lot at stake."

"You're talking about getting yourself reelected."

"I am indeed! Nothing is a given in this town."

The city founders believed that long terms of office

fostered corruption and unscrupulous political alli-
ances. To avoid shady dealings, they drafted a municipal
charter that mandated a one-year term for the mayor,
the aldermen, and the city marshal. The result was a
frequent change in the roster of those who governed the
city, and a constant shifting of loyalties. There were no
political dynasties in Austin.

There were ten wards, with an alderman elected
from each ward. The city council was composed of the
mayor and the aldermen, with the mayor positioned to
break a tie vote. The list of aldermen might include
contractors, grocers, lawyers, real estate agents, livery-
men, and usually one saloonkeeper from Guy Town, the
Third Ward. The diversity tended to keep everyone
halfway honest, and made for contentious bedfellows.
Wheeler, who governed the factions through diplomacy,
was seeking a third term.

"Look at it this way," Thompson said. "Everyone in
town knows Creary is taking payoffs from the dives.
I'll campaign on a pledge to make the sporting crowd
toe the line. Wouldn't you rather endorse an *honest*
marshal?"

Wheeler was silent a moment. "Let's not kid ourselves," he finally said. "Creary will still run, and he
has supporters. He'll just turn Republican."

"I don't care if he changes his name to Santa Claus.
I'm telling you I'll win, Tom. You can take it to the
bank."

"By God, I believe you will. I really do."

"You'll support me then?"

"Here's my hand on it."

"You're shaking hands with Austin's next marshal."

"Is that what you saw in your crystal ball?"

Thompson grinned. "Just call me a prophet."

* * *

The balance of the morning was spent calling on potential supporters. Thompson's first stop was the Mercantile National Bank, where he spoke with the president, James Shipe. His next stop was the county courthouse.

By noon, he had secured the endorsement of Shipe as well as Sheriff Frank Horner. The banker, who was impressed by Thompson's sincerity, readily climbed aboard the bandwagon. The sheriff required considerably more persuasion, but he finally came around. He agreed that an honest city marshal would be a welcome change.

Thompson was encouraged by their support. Shipe was one of Austin's most prominent bankers, and an influential voice within the business community. Horner was the county's chief law enforcement officer, known for his integrity and his unbending attitude toward criminals. Their backing, along with that of the mayor, would rapidly broaden the base of support. All that remained was the newspapers.

The *Statesman* was located near the corner of Congress Avenue and Beach Street. Shortly after the noon hour, Thompson walked into the office of John Cardwell. A lifelong resident of Austin, Cardwell was the editor and publisher, widely respected for his objective reporting of civic affairs. He was a man of distinguished bearing, with gray hair and the eyes of a sage. He knew where the skeletons were buried in Travis County.

Thompson presented his case in a forceful manner. Apart from the need for impartial law enforcement, he underscored the support he'd garnered by the mayor, the sheriff, and James Shipe. He planned to announce his candidacy in tomorrow's paper, and he made no pretext about the purpose of his visit. He wanted the endorsement of the *Statesman*.

Cardwell listened with an impassive expression. He never once interrupted, staring across the desk, his fingers steepled, until Thompson finished talking. His features were inscrutable.

"You make a persuasive argument," he said. "Certainly no one questions your honesty."

"I appreciate the sentiment, Mr. Cardwell."

"Did you ever meet Wild Bill Hickok?"

"Yes," Thompson said carefully. "We met in the Kansas cowtowns."

"Unfortunate thing," Cardwell mused. "How he was assassinated, I mean. But in any event, he was considered to be an honest lawman. Wouldn't you agree?"

"That's what I always heard."

"Even so, he enforced the law with his guns. Summary justice without the benefit of the courts. Would that be a fair statement?"

"Fair enough."

"So here's my question to you, Mr. Thompson. Would you turn out to be Austin's Wild Bill Hickok?"

Thompson held his gaze. "I believe a gun is the last resort, Mr. Cardwell. All the more so when it involves a peace officer." He paused for emphasis. "I advocate law and order, not summary justice."

"Excellent answer," Cardwell said approvingly. "You're certain to be asked that question during the campaign. I think you'll do quite well."

"Does that mean you'll endorse me?"

"Oh, you can definitely count on the support of the *Statesman*. I agree, it's time to send Ed Creary packing. Long past time!"

Across town, Thompson's message was received

with less enthusiasm. George Harris, editor and publisher of the *Republican*, gave him a chilly reception.
The masthead of the newspaper had nothing to do with
the Republican party, but Harris was nonetheless vitriolic in his opposition to Mayor Wheeler. A reformer by
nature, he supported the clergy's efforts to abolish Guy
Town and drive the sporting crowd from Austin. He
wanted nothing to do with the mayor's candidate for
city marshal.

Thompson figured one out of two wasn't all that bad.
The *Statesman* was the older paper, with larger circu-
lation, and its editorial policy reflected the popular
views of the public. He would have preferred the *Republican* in his corner as well, but he wasn't displeased
with the outcome. He'd started the morning a candidate
without affiliation or support, and he now had the backing of key players in Austin's political arena. All in all
he thought it had been a pretty good day.

Early that afternoon, when he arrived home, he was
in a splendid mood. As he came through the door, he
saw Billy's valise on the floor in the hallway. He found
Catherine and Billy in the parlor, and his mood evapo-
rated on the instant. Billy was ready to travel.

"What's this?" Thompson said. "Leaving without
saying good-bye?"

Billy shrugged. "We were never much on good-byes.
Figured I'd be gone by the time you got home."

"You might have told me this morning."

"Guess it slipped my mind. I was still half asleep
when you left."

Thompson let it pass. "You headed back to Brownsville?"

"Yeah, it's the riverboats for me," Billy said lightly.
"I'm catching the three o'clock train."

"Why not stay on a few days? What's the rush?"

"A rolling stone gathers no moss. Gotta keep movin'."

Billy kissed Catherine on the cheek. Then he turned, wringing Thompson's hand with a crooked grin, and moved into the hallway. A moment later the front door closed, and they watched from the window as he walked toward the corner. His stride was brisk, almost a swagger, the valise swinging from his hand. He looked like a man in a hurry to get somewhere.

Catherine sighed. "I always hate to see him go. He's such a loveable scamp."

"That's Billy," Thompson agreed. "Blink your eyes and he's off again."

"Well, anyway," she said softly, linking her arm in his. "How did things go downtown?"

"Katie, I think you'd better get used to a lawman in the family."

"You've announced your candidacy?"

"Wait till you see tomorrow's paper."

The announcement appeared the following morning in the *Statesman*. The print was big and bold, spread over a half page, and went directly to the point. There was no mistaking the message.

To the Good People of Austin:

    A number of our leading citizens have convinced me to become a candidate for the office of City Marshal. I can truthfully say that the difficulties of the independent life I have led were the result of an impulse to protect the weak from the aggressions of the strong. I am thoroughly acquainted with the character of Austin and her citizens, and I propose to restore honest law enforcement to our streets. If honored with election

to this important post, my whole time and attention shall be devoted to official duties, and no law
abiding member of our community shall regret
the choice. Upon these terms I invoke the support
of all my fellow citizens.

Your obedient servant
Ben Thompson

FIFTEEN

—◄◄◄◅◦◮►►►—

The announcement created a furor. By the next day Austin was divided into two camps. One faction applauded Thompson's candidacy for city marshal. The other roundly condemned him as an opportunist.

The clergy was particularly vocal. The Austin Ministers Association was an organization composed of preachers and priests from every church in the city. On Wednesday morning, the association convened an emergency session and issued a statement to the newspapers. The pastors denounced Thompson as unfit for public office.

Opposition from a sector of the business community was no less strident. Alexander Wooldridge, president of the Austin National Bank, quickly formed a coalition of prominent businessmen. A civic leader and philanthropist, Wooldridge had been instrumental in founding a public school system, and was generally credited with bringing the University of Texas to Austin. His opposition served to buttress the outrage of the clergy.

The furor was offset to some extent by statements of support issued by Mayor Wheeler and Sheriff Horner. James Shipe, reacting to Wooldridge's outcry, rapidly formed a coalition of his own. By late Wednesday morning the business community was split down the center, with the town's leading bankers spearheading the factions. John Cardwell, true to his word, came out in staunch support of Thompson. His editorial in the *Statesman* went to the heart of the issue.

> Mr. Ben Thompson announced himself a candidate for City Marshal in yesterday's issue. He is well and favorably known to everyone in the city, and is in every way worthy of the confidence and support of the people. Mr. Thompson is a formidable competitor for the office, and if elected will serve the people faithfully. This paper endorses his candidacy with every certainty that he will bring a new sense of law and order to the streets of Austin.

The *Republican* fired a broadside of its own. George Harris proved to be a man of his word as well. His editorial was scathing, and personal.

> The decent people of Austin reel under the shock of Ben Thompson's candidacy for public office. Thompson is a notorious shootist and mankiller, long aligned with the tawdry element of Guy Town. The mere thought of Thompson empowered with a badge is repugnant to this editor and to all people who respect the law. We urge good-minded

voters to cast their ballot for City Marshal Ed Creary, who was betrayed by the Democrats and will now run on the Republican ticket. Elect a God-fearing man, not a mankiller.

The editorial enraged Thompson. His normal reaction to such insults would have been to call Harris out, force a fight or an apology. Yet mudslinging was common to politics, and any rash act on his part would add credence to the slurs. All morning, he'd stalked through the house, muttering to himself, stumped for a proper response. When Catherine called him for the noon meal, he came to the table with no great appetite. His mind was on matters other than food.

"Dammit anyway!" he grumbled, cutting into a slab of beefsteak. "I'd like to box his ears till he's bloody. That's the least he deserves."

Catherine seemed unperturbed. "You knew politics was a shabby business. You have to play the game by their rules."

"That doesn't make it any easier to swallow. Where's the man get off saying I'm aligned with Guy Town? That's just a flat-out lie."

"Perhaps you should arrange an interview with the *Statesman*. You're entitled to tell your side of the story."

"Yeah, maybe so." Thompson chewed thoughtfully on a hunk of steak. "But how the deuce do I take on the churches? No one wins fighting with preachers."

"I'm afraid that's a lost cause," she said with a teasing smile. "Particularly since you haven't set foot in a church since we were married. You'd be very much like a fish out of water."

"I suppose I'll leave the churches to Ed Creary. What

was it the *Republican* called him, a 'God-fearing man'? Wonder if they know he takes payoffs from the parlor houses."

"Well, at least Governor Roberts has taken a neutral position. The *Statesman* said he declined to comment on local affairs."

"Guess I got lucky there," Thompson conceded. "You'll recall he wanted me arrested over that dust-up with the cattlemen's association. Maybe the mayor put a bee in his ear."

She took a sip of coffee. "You really should count your blessings, sweetheart. Some of the most influential men in town have taken your side."

"I need more than 'some.' I need a majority."

"You've only just begun. I'm sure you'll win them over. Give it a little time."

"Katie, time's in short supply. I've got nineteen days till election."

Thompson paused, a bite of steak speared on his fork. His gaze became abstracted, and he stared off into the middle distance. A ghost of a smile touched the corner of his mouth.

"What is it?" she asked. "You look very . . . devious."

"I'm thinking, nothing ventured, nothing gained."

"You're talking riddles. Ventured how?"

"What was it you said, I have to win them over?"

"Yes, that's right. And . . . ?"

Thompson smiled. "Time to beard the lion in his den."

The Austin National Bank was located on the corner of Colorado and Mesquite. Directly across the street was the State House grounds, and the capitol building. The legislature was in session, and the broad plaza swarmed with activity. The lawmakers were returning from a leisurely noon meal.

Alexander Wooldridge watched the activity from his desk. His office fronted the bank building, with a large window looking out onto the capitol grounds. The office was lavishly appointed, furnished with wing-back chairs and a sofa crafted in lush morocco leather. The walls were lined with oil paintings, and the massive desk appeared carved from a solid piece of walnut. The room seemed somehow appropriate to the man.

The banker was in his late forties. Tall and slim, his bearing was ramrod straight, a posture of worldly self-assurance. He wore a frock coat with dark trousers, and a dull gray cravat discreetly pegged with an onyx stickpin. The watch chain across his vest was woven in intricate strands of gold. He was a commanding figure of a man, his salt-and-pepper hair offset by eyes the color of slate. He gave the impression he could see through walls.

Wooldridge was one of the movers-and-shakers in Austin. Apart from the bank, and his personal wealth, he was on a first-name basis with the governor and a great number of the legislators. A year ago, his prestige in the community had persuaded voters to tax themselves in a referendum to support the local school system. His lobbying efforts, along with a large philanthropic endowment, had resulted in legislation directed at higher education. Governor Oran Roberts had praised his role in the creation of the University of Texas.

Today, staring out the window, Wooldridge was absorbed by the sight of the legislators. He planned an even more aggressive lobbying campaign to secure funds for expansion of the university. A light knock interrupted his reverie, and he turned from the window. His secretary, Myrtle Peppard, waited just inside the door.

"Mr. Wooldridge," she said nervously, "that Ben Thompson is outside. He insists on seeing you."

"Did you tell him I was busy?"

"Yessir, but he won't listen. He demanded that I give you the message."

"Demanded, did he! Very well, Myrtle, show him in."

Wooldridge thought it typical of a man he considered a ruffian. He respected James Shipe, who was his sole rival in business affairs and civic matters. But he could only speculate as to why a fellow banker would endorse an infamous gunman for public office. He wondered as well as to the purpose of this unannounced visit.

Thompson walked through the door like he'd foreclosed on the bank. "Mr. Wooldridge," he said with open charm, "I appreciate you seeing me. It's most kind of you."

"Not at all." Wooldridge accepted his handshake, motioned him to a chair. "What can I do for you, Mr. Thompson?"

"I won't waste your time fencing around. I've come to ask how I can win your support in the election for City Marshal. Anyone who knows me will tell you I'm the best man for the job."

"You certainly don't suffer from lack of confidence."

"That's never been one of my faults. You're a man of some confidence yourself, Mr. Wooldridge. There ought to be a way we can find common ground."

Wooldridge assessed him with icy calm. "You no doubt read the editorial in today's *Republican*. I share those sentiments, Mr. Thompson." He paused, his features sphinx-like. "You are who you are."

"And no apologies for it." Thompson rocked his hand, fingers splayed. "I've killed a few men in my time. But I never fired on a man who hadn't fired on me first. Wouldn't you say that's an enviable quality for a peace officer?"

"I won't be drawn into debate. You are a professional gambler and a member of the so-called sporting crowd. Your interests are not in the best interests of Austin."

"How do you arrive at that conclusion?"

"Let me pose a question," Wooldridge said. "We have a cancer in our community known as Guy Town. I propose the eradication of evil and vice in every form. As our city marshal, would you work to that end?"

Thompson returned his stare. "Except for the churches, most folks find no harm in Guy Town. Until they do, I'll enforce the law and keep a lid on things. I'm not in the business of policing people's morals."

"Then we are at an impasse, Mr. Thompson. I cannot support a man who condones vice. Anything else?"

"No, that pretty well covers it. Thanks for your time, Mr. Wooldridge."

Thompson rose from his chair. He walked to the door, not altogether sure he'd been right about nothing ventured, nothing gained. The truncated conversation had merely rubbed salt into a festering sore. Alexander Wooldridge was a cleric without the collar. A reformer.

He thought he'd better move fast. Damn fast.

Sueann Mabry started when he came through the door. Thompson waved her down, moving past her desk with a breezy smile. He proceeded on to the inner office, rapping once with his knuckles, and stepped inside. He found the mayor hunched over a stack of correspondence.

"Afternoon," he said with cheery vigor. "How goes the paperwork?"

"Don't ask," Wheeler grumped. "You seem in high spirits for a man who got roasted by every preacher in town. Not to mention the *Republican*."

"God loves saints and sinners alike. But since you brought it up, that's why I'm here. I just met with Alexander Wooldridge."

"You what—?"

"Thought you'd be interested," Thompson said, dropping into a chair. "I had some notion of winning him over to the cause. You might say he was too polite to laugh."

"That's Wooldridge," Wheeler said quickly. "One oar in the water with the legislature and the other with the churches. He's a regular diplomat."

"No, Tom, he's a reformer. He wanted to know if I would back a movement to close down Guy Town."

"What did you say?"

"I told him it's not the city marshal's job to police people's morals. I figured it would be a waste of breath to ask him what he thinks of Ed Creary."

"You figured right," Wheeler commented. "He'll oppose you to get at me. He knows Guy Town will never be closed down while I'm in office. I'd rather keep vice under control than have it go underground."

"You took the words out of my mouth," Thompson said. "All the same, I'm glad I called on Wooldridge. He gave me a real eye-opener."

"How so?"

"We're up against some solid citizens. Wooldridge

and his business cronies are in thick with the churches. We've got to fight fire with fire."

Wheeler eyed him dubiously. "I'm not sure I like the sound of that. What's on your mind?"

"A rally," Thompson said, gesturing wildly. "Torches, lots of speeches, a band and a big crowd. Our own evangelical meeting—spread the gospel."

"And what sort of gospel are we preaching?"

"Law and order. No more special treatment for the sporting crowd, and no more payoffs. Honest law enforcement."

Wheeler considered a moment. "That could reflect badly on me. As mayor, I could be held accountable for Creary's payoff scheme."

"You saw the light!" Thompson said zealously. "You caught on to his crooked dealings and you dumped him. You'll look like the hero."

"By God, you've got a point. I did dump him!"

"And you damn well deserve the credit."

"Not a bad angle," Wheeler said, toying with the idea. "Of course, our opposition could turn the tables on you. All that stuff about being too quick with a gun. They'll have stooges planted in the crowd."

"I'll handle it," Thompson said with conviction. "I'm the man for the job because *nobody* in the sporting crowd wants trouble with me. Austin will have the safest streets in Texas. That's my new campaign slogan."

Wheeler laughed. "Ben, you're starting to think like a politician."

"I have Alexander Wooldridge to thank for that. He taught me a lesson about the rules of politics."

"I wasn't aware there were any rules."

"Offhand, I'd say there's two."

"Which are?"

"Anything goes . . ."

"And?"

"No holds barred."

Mayor Tom Wheeler thought that summed it up perfectly. He thought as well that Ben Thompson was a quick learner. Politics could be reduced to a fundamental truth.

No holds barred was the name of the game.

SIXTEEN

The rally was held on Saturday, October 16. Shortly before seven that evening, the Austin Fire Brigade Band marched from the firehouse to the capitol. A large crowd was already gathered on the state house lawn.

Mayor Tom Wheeler had pulled out all stops. For the past three days, full-page advertisements for the rally had appeared in the *Statesman*. Flyers promoting the event had been plastered on lampposts and buildings from the railroad depot to the uptown business district. Aldermen from nine wards had spread the word, and turned out their constituency in force. The only dissenter was the alderman from the Third Ward, Guy Town.

By seven o'clock fully a thousand people were congregated on the state house lawn. Thompson stood with the mayor and the aldermen at the intersection of Congress Avenue and Mesquite. They were joined by James Shipe and Sheriff Frank Horner, who were on the roster of speakers for the evening. Policemen were posted on street corners around the plaza, and several sheriff's deputies were in attendance. Conspicuous by his absence was City Marshal Ed Creary, newly endorsed by the Republican Party.

Catherine and Bobby, along with the mayor's wife, were in the vanguard of the crowd. The evening was chilly, and Catherine wore a fashionable Eton jacket, with the left sleeve pinned to the coat. Bobby was all eyes, barely able to contain himself, caught up in the excitement of the buzzing throng. As dark settled over the plaza, torches were lighted, and a flickering blaze reflected off the capitol. Colorful placards, mounted on short poles, bobbed over the heads of the crowd. The theme of the signs, in bold letters, was LAW AND ORDER.

On signal from the mayor, the bandleader raised his staff. Trumpets blared and the band broke out in a thumping rendition of John Philip Sousa's *The Washington Post March*. The stirring air filled the plaza, and the band, resplendent in brass-buttoned uniforms, quick-stepped onto the street. Formed in ranks of four, Wheeler and Thompson, along with Shipe and Horner and the aldermen, strode off behind the band. The assembled townspeople massed in a long column to the rear.

The torchlit parade circled the state house grounds. Onlookers ganged the sidewalks, and as the band marched past, hundreds more rushed to join the column. On the south edge of the plaza, having looped the capitol, the band wheeled left on Mesquite. Still more people tagged along, and by the time the parade approached City Hall, the crowd had swelled to almost two thousand people. The bandleader, walking backward, pumped his staff and the band segued into *Dixie*. The column jammed into the intersection of San Jacinto.

A tall platform stood raised before City Hall. The wooden structure was festively decorated with red, white and blue bunting, and the seal of the City of Austin was painted on the front of the speakers' podium. Wheeler and Thompson, followed by the other dignitaries, mounted a flight of stairs at one side of the platform. Streetlamps paled in the blaze of torches as the crowd pressed closer and the men arrayed themselves on line behind the mayor. He walked directly to the podium, and the band thumped to a halt. The crowd fell silent.

"People of Austin!" he boomed, his arms outstretched. "We come here tonight to celebrate our city's march toward a progressive new era. An era of law and order—for all!"

Wheeler went on to review the positive measures undertaken during his administration. He dwelled at length on the improved waterworks, the construction of a new grade school, and a reduction in property taxes. Then he turned to the subject of law and order, the reason for tonight's rally. He acknowledged official corruption in Guy Town—readily confessed his inability to police the police—and laid out a plan for the abolishment of unscrupulous graft. His voice ringing, he extolled the virtues of the man who would bring honor to the badge—Ben Thompson. A marshal for the new era!

The crush of spectators roared approval. Wheeler postured a moment, then brought James Shipe to the podium. The banker spoke of his long association with the candidate, a friendship founded on honesty and moral values. He noted that all of Austin's aldermen—with the exception of the one who represented the sporting crowd—were present to welcome Thompson aboard the Democrat bandwagon. After another burst of applause, he was followed to the podium by Sheriff Frank Horner. The lawman was succinct and blunt, relating problems caused for the county by poor law enforcement in Guy Town. He heartily endorsed Thompson as a man equal to the job—and worthy of the badge.

Mayor Wheeler then performed a resounding introduction of the candidate. The crowd gave Thompson a wild and boisterous ovation as he walked to the podium. He stood staring out over the throng with a broad grin, his arms raised in the universal sign of victory. The applause gradually faded, and as the onlookers quieted, his features took on a somber cast. His voice was strong and forceful, confident.

"I pledge to you that as your next city marshal I will bring law and order to our streets. And in particular, I will enforce the law without favoritism in the gaming parlors, saloons and *other* establishments in Guy Town!"

The crowd understood that "other establishments" was a delicate reference to whorehouses and prostitution. There were snickers among the men, and imperceptible nods of approval among the women. Thompson then went to the heart of the accusations leveled by his opposition, what he termed "character assassination." As marshal, he declared, he would never resort to "gun law" unless confronted by armed and deadly criminals. His so-called reputation, he asserted, would work to the benefit of Austin. The rougher element would be deterred from violence.

A murmur of agreement rippled through the onlookers. Thompson next tackled accusations charging him with conflict of interest. "Any man who knows me," he announced, "knows that my word is my bond. All personal ties to gambling will be severed for however long I wear a badge. You have my oath on it." With wry amusement, he then broached allegations that he was a member of the sporting crowd. "I will not be tarred with that brush," he said forcefully. "I have no obligation to anyone—man or woman—among the sporting class. Guy Town will declare a day of mourning the day I am elected marshal."

"What're you gonna do?" someone yelled contentiously. "Shoot 'em if they don't walk the straight and narrow? You're a gunman, not a lawman!"

Thompson expected hecklers. He was surprised the rally hadn't been interrupted before now. Yet he was determined to handle agitators with humor. He looked down at the man with an indulgent smile.

"I won't have time to shoot anybody," he said amiably. "I'll be too busy marching tinhorns and grifters off to jail. You might be my first customer."

The spectators hooted with laughter. Thompson quickly launched into a ringing denunciation of the current marshal, Ed Creary. He remarked that crime was at an all-time high, citing figures for the last year. Nine murders, with four as yet unsolved. Assault and robbery and burglary at record levels. But not one arrest in an entire year for disorderly houses and bunco games. Streetwalkers and crooked gamblers, he thundered, enjoyed immunity from the law. A free ride for those who greased the palm of the city marshal.

"Let's call a spade a spade," he went on. "Graft and payoffs are an open secret in Guy Town. Ed Creary's a crook with a badge."

Thompson paused, one arm thrust overhead. "Elect

me marshal and Austin will have the safest streets in Texas. I promise you honest law enforcement!"

The crowd erupted in cheers. The band thumped to life and people shouted themselves hoarse. A sea of LAW AND ORDER placards danced and jiggled in the light of the torches. Mayor Wheeler joined Thompson at the podium, their arms raised in victory, laughing and waving to their supporters. Flash-pans popped as newspaper photographers caught the image in a frozen moment.

The excitement of the rally gradually faded. Within a matter of minutes, as Wheeler and Thompson shook hands with the dignitaries, the band marched off under the cadence of flutes and drums. The majority of the crowd straggled along, still carrying their torches and placards, talking quietly among themselves. Only a few supporters remained behind for a handshake with the candidates.

The newshounds were waiting as Thompson descended the steps from the platform. A reporter for the *Republican* pushed forward. "Mr. Thompson, you've brought serious allegations against Marshal Creary. Do you have any proof?"

"The court of public opinion," Thompson responded. "Lots of people in Guy Town will tell you anything you want to know about payoffs. All you have to do is ask."

"I asked if you have proof."

"And I told you where to find it."

"Hardly the same thing," the reporter countered. "Abraham Lincoln once said: Deception is the distinguishing characteristic of snake-oil peddlers and politicians. You're starting to sound like a politician, Mr. Thompson."

Thompson forced a laugh. "Whatever else I am, I don't accept bribes. That'll be a welcome relief from Ed Creary."

"Mr. Thompson," the reporter for the *Statesman* broke in. "You pledged to make the streets of Austin the safest in Texas. What are your plans for that?"

"A good peace officer is johnny-on-the-spot. He stops trouble before it has a chance to get started. That's how our police department will operate in the future."

"Are you satisfied the officers on the force will be able to handle the job?"

"I'm satisfied they will when I become marshal."

Thompson ended it on a positive note. He waved the reporters off, and moved to where Catherine waited with Bobby. The youngster stared up at him with something approaching awe, for once reduced to silence. The mayor was hosting drinks for the aldermen at the Austin Hotel bar, and Thompson was expected to attend. He first wanted to see Catherine and the boy safely on the streetcar. They walked toward Congress Avenue.

"I thought it went splendidly," Catherine said, taking his arm. "You're quite the speaker, Mr. Thompson."

Thompson chuckled. "Tom Wheeler's been coaching me for two days. I felt like a ventriloquist's dummy."

"Fiddlesticks! Those were your words, not his, and the crowd loved it. You were very . . . genuine."

"In politics, sincerity counts for more than substance. I'm liable to end up a cynic yet."

"You will not," she protested. "That's why you've received such favorable support. People know you would never engage in trickery."

"That's my finest attribute," Thompson said, gently mocking her. "A square deal, even in politics."

Bobby tugged at his sleeve. "Pa, what'd that reporter fellow mean? The one talkin' about Abe Lincoln?"

"You know what a snake-oil peddler is, don't you, son?"

"Why sure, Pa, that's one of them medicine shows. Where they sell stuff for whatever ails you."

"Do you believe their cures work?"

"Mom says it's all hokum."

"Well, according to the reporter, Abe Lincoln said the same thing about politicians. They lie to people."

"Yeah . . . ?" Bobby looked perplexed. "How come they called him Honest Abe then? A president's a politician, isn't he?"

Thompson ruffed his hair. "There's an exception to every rule, and Lincoln proves the point. Even if he was a Yankee."

"So that means you're like Honest Abe, doesn't it? You don't tell lies."

"Son, just between us, I'm pretending to be a politician. I wouldn't be one for a million dollars."

"I figgered that's what it was, Pa."

Bobby ran ahead to the corner. Thompson shook his head, and Catherine squeezed his arm. "You're terrible," she said, trying not to laugh. "He'll never trust a politician again."

"Then I've taught him a good lesson, Katie. Anybody who makes public speeches shouldn't be taken at his word—except for me and Honest Abe."

"You really are a prankster."

"Yes, that too."

Thompson put them on the streetcar. He waved as

the driver clanged the bell and the mule plodded off along the tracks. Then he turned back downstreet, and walked toward the Austin Hotel. As he approached the corner, he saw Ed Creary and policeman Carl Allen standing in the aureole of light beneath a lamppost. His mustache lifted in a tight smile.

"Good evening, Ed," he said without a trace of humor. "You missed the rally."

"I heard about it," Creary said, jerking his chin at Allen. "Carl told me you were on your high horse. Like you were preachin' the Sermon on the Mount."

"Well, we know Carl's a liar, don't we? Perjured himself after taking an oath on the Bible. Didn't you, Carl?"

Allen blanched. "That wasn't the—"

"Button your lip," Creary snapped. "Let's get down to cases, Thompson. You're spreadin' hogwash about me."

Thompson stared at him. "What hogwash is that?"

"All this stuff about Guy Town and payoffs. I want it stopped."

"And if it's not?"

"I'll tend to you," Creary said roughly. "One way or another, you'll get yours."

"Are you threatening me, Ed?"

"You take it any way you want."

Thompson's eyes went hard. "I'd hate to kill my only opponent for public office. The voters might think I acted in haste."

"Goddamn you!" Creary bridled. "You don't scare me."

"Walk away or pull your gun. I'm through talking."

The men stood enveloped in a cone of silence. Creary seemed to be debating the odds, whether two against one would take the play. Then, as though dissuaded of the notion, he turned on his heel. Allen hurried after him.

Thompson watched until they rounded the corner. He realized that he'd almost broken his promise to himself. A shaky promise, but nonetheless well meant.

He still didn't want to kill Ed Creary.

SEVENTEEN

———≈≈≈≈———

Thompson lathered his face from a soap mug. The steel of his straight razor glinted as he stropped it back and forth on a leather strap hanging from the wall. He tested the edge on his thumb and began shaving.

A shaft of sunlight flooded the bathroom window. He studied himself in the mirror and thought it was a fine day for an election. The date was Monday, November 1, and the polls would open in less than an hour. Gingerly, careful not to nick himself, he worked the razor across his jawline. He wanted to look his best.

Some minutes later, reeking of bay rum, he walked back to the bedroom. He moved to the armoire, opened the double doors, and surveyed his suits. After a moment, he selected a dark jacket with a matching vest and gray trousers. A white shirt, hand-stitched from Egyptian cotton, and a striped cravat completed his outfit. He began dressing.

The past two weeks seemed lost in a blur of activity. Since the night of the rally, he had campaigned relentlessly, gladhanding voters all over town. He had appeared as guest speaker at various fraternal orders and the weekly luncheons of several business organizations. A major appearance had been the monthly meeting of the Confederate Veterans Society, where his record during the war assured a warm reception. He'd hammered away on the issue of law and order wherever he spoke.

No less determined, his opposition had continued its smear campaign. Ed Creary and the Republican Party had lambasted him at every opportunity. Their attacks were personal and vitriolic, and centered on his notoriety as a mankiller. The gunfight two months ago at the Capital Variety Theater had been bandied about endlessly; their argument stressed the folly of licensing a shootist with a lawman's badge. Yet Creary kept his distance, and avoided any chance of a confrontation like the one he'd provoked the night of the rally. He seemed content to vindicate himself at the ballot box.

Finished dressing, Thompson paused before the full-length mirror on the armoire. He subjected himself to critical inspection, noting that the holstered Colt was concealed by the drape of his jacket. The pistol was an unwitting reminder that a personal showdown with Ed Creary was as remote as the stars. Creary might backshoot him, or arrange his murder, but even that seemed improbable. A lifetime of assessing men and tight situations left him with no real concern. He thought Creary was all wind and no whistle.

A final tug of his jacket satisfied him that he would pass muster. Turning away from the mirror, he went out of the bedroom and moved along the hallway. Bobby had darted in earlier, wishing him luck with the election, and hurried off to school. The boy was jumping with excitement, loudly confident that by the end of the day his father would be the new city marshal of Austin. Thompson privately agreed, for he thought the youngster was on the money. He planned to win it going away.

Downstairs, he found Catherine in the kitchen. She was radiant, brimming with enthusiasm, her vitality all but infectious. Over the past three weeks she had become his most ardent supporter, obsessed with the idea of him wearing a badge, She alluded to it only in an oblique manner, and yet there was never any doubt that she shared his vision. A means to a new life, something more than a gambler, the honor of public office. She desperately wanted him to win.

"Don't you look elegant!" she said, kissing him on the cheek. "You'll be the best-dressed candidate in town."

"I figured I ought to look the part."

"And never with better reason. It's your big day."

Thompson took a seat at the table. She brought a platter with beefsteak and eggs, and a basket of fluffy buttermilk biscuits. As he began loading his plate, she poured him a steaming mug of coffee. He broke the yolk on an egg.

"That's some breakfast," he said, nodding at the platter. "You'd think I was a lumberjack."

"A man needs to fortify himself on election day. You probably won't get another bite until the polls close."

"I just suspect you're right. Tom Wheeler says it's important to be out and about shaking hands. He calls it 'pressing the flesh.'"

"You're certainly my choice," she said brightly. "I wish I could vote for you."

Thompson slathered butter on a biscuit. "One of these days women will have the vote. I'd say it's just a matter of time."

"Well, the important thing is to get you elected. I can't wait to see your new badge!"

"Careful now, let's not get overconfident. I haven't won it yet."

"You will," she said with conviction. "And don't play Mr. Modest with me. You know very well you're the front-runner."

"I don't know any such thing." Thompson took a bite of steak, waved his fork. "Any gambler's superstitious by nature, and that includes me. Never count the pot till you've seen the last card."

"Yes, but you're forgetting something, sugar. As of tonight, you won't be a gambler anymore. You'll be a marshal."

"Katie, I hope to hell you're right. I want it so bad it makes my teeth ache."

"Then eat your breakfast and stop worrying. You already have it won."

"What makes you so sure?"

She smiled an enigmatic smile. "I've seen the last card."

The polls were located in the Knights of Pythias Building. A fraternal order devoted to charitable causes, the organization donated space each year for the city elections. It was considered neutral ground.

The weather was crisp and clear. A bright morning sun edged higher in the sky as Thompson approached the building. Tom Wheeler was talking with several of his cronies on the front steps. He hurried forward with a hearty smile.

"There you are, Ben!" He pumped Thompson's arm with vigor. "I started to wonder if you'd forgotten it's election day."

"I thought the polls didn't open till eight."

"A politician is always johnny-come-early. You want to be the last face the voters see before they cast their ballot."

"Press the flesh," Thompson said genially. "Wasn't that how you put it?"

"Absolutely," Wheeler replied. "We'll make a politician of you yet."

"I'd rather be marshal."

"A rose is a rose by any other name. Even a marshal has to cultivate the political garden."

Thompson nodded. "How are things looking?"

"Tiptop," Wheeler said cheerily. "I have every confidence it'll be a clean sweep. We'll skunk the Republicans again."

Wheeler was rabid on the subject of the Republican Party. Like all Texans, he had suffered the injustices committed by Yankee occupation forces during the Reconstruction Era. With Republican puppets in the state house, Texas hadn't been readmitted to the Union until 1870. His political career in large part stemmed from dark memories.

The past few weeks had done nothing to alter old animosities. The *Statesman* and the *Republican*, like battleships under full sail, had exchanged daily broadsides. Yet the *Republican* editorials had been charged with acrimony and malice, vilifying Democrats in slanderous terms. Wheeler had been singled out for having thrown his support to Thompson in the marshal's race. He was still steaming from the rough treatment.

A large crowd was gathered outside when the doors opened at eight o'clock. Thompson and Wheeler and the Democratic candidates for aldermen waited on the steps, shaking hands and offering a last word of encouragement. The polling station was located in a cavernous room on the ground floor, with monitors from both parties to supervise the election. A steady stream of voters began filing into the building to cast their ballots.

The Republican candidates were working the crowd as well. They kept to the other side of the steps, ganged in a loose phalanx, wringing hands like drowning men. Ernest Cramer, the mayoral contender, was a chunky man with a waxish grin and heavy jowls. His manner was agitated, somehow jittery, and he shifted nervously from foot to foot. Not unlike his cohorts, he seemed to be playing a role, and doing it badly. He looked like a loser.

Ed Creary was the last to make an appearance. His features were gaunt, with dark circles under his eyes, as though he'd awakened late for the party. He wore his marshal's badge on his suit jacket, and he waded into the flurry of handshaking with a bogus smile. His one hope was that Democrats would forego partisan politics and vote for an experienced lawman. His problem was that everyone in town now believed he was a crook. He seemed like a man waiting for bad news.

Alexander Wooldridge arrived with a group of clergymen. He studiously ignored the Democrats, and greeted Creary with a warm handshake. The preachers flocked around, careful to ignore the Republicans for fear of offending their Democratic parishioners. Yet they offered their good wishes to Creary, bestowing a public blessing despite his unsavory links to Guy Town. They were impervious to the irony of the situation, or perhaps simply unmindful. A crook, in their view, was the lesser of two evils. There was no redemption for a shootist.

A moment later James Shipe came up the steps. He exchanged a barbed glance with Wooldridge, and shook his head with a satiric look. Then he walked directly to Wheeler and Thompson, greeting them with jaunty good humor. "Mr. Mayor. Ben," he said, extending his hand. "Let me be the first to congratulate you."

"Jim, you're a little premature," Wheeler said. "They've just now opened the doors."

"Now or later, it's all the same. You'll come away with the keys to City Hall."

Thompson chuckled. "What did your tea leaves say about a badge for me?"

"I'm no swami, you understand. But I'm a prognosticator of impeccable credentials. You are our next city marshal, Ben."

"Tell me that when the polls close."

"Speaking of the polls," Wheeler said, "why, don't we cast our own votes? No time like the present."

Shipe cocked his head. "Who do you plan to vote for?"

"The process of the ballot is secret. But I think it's safe to say I'll vote for myself—and Ben."

"And will you vote for yourself, Ben?"

Thompson laughed. "I sure as hell won't vote for Ed Creary."

"The question is, who will?"

They sauntered unhurriedly into the Knights of Pythias Building.

* * *

The lights burned bright in City Hall. Thompson was seated in the mayor's office, staring out the window into the darkening night. Wheeler's gaze was fixed on a wall clock, which ticked inexorably toward nine. Neither of them had spoken in the last half hour.

All day they had worked the election crowds. When the polls finally closed at seven o'clock, they stopped by a café for a quick supper. Then, walking back to City Hall, they made small talk while awaiting a count of the ballots. Their vigil was now into the second hour.

"Nearly nine," Thompson said, breaking the silence. "How long's it usually take?"

"Depends on whether there's a recount—"

The door burst open. Buddy Hubbart, the mayor's brother-in-law and the city tax assessor, walked in with a horsey smile. "Won it by a landslide!" he crowed. "You carried every ward, Tom."

Wheeler beamed. "How about Ben?"

"Creary only took the Third Ward," Hubbart said, nodding to Thompson. "You just got yourself elected marshal."

"I'll be damned." Thompson looked relieved. "Who cares about Guy Town anyway? They knew I wouldn't take payoffs."

"Congratulations, Ben." Wheeler offered him a firm handshake. "You're going to make a fine lawman."

"I couldn't have done it without you. I'm obliged for your support."

"Keep the sporting crowd in line and we'll be even. You've got a free hand to do whatever you want in Guy Town."

"Don't give it another thought," Thompson assured him. "Cardsharps and grifters are at the top of my list."

"That's the ticket." Wheeler turned back to his brother-in-law. "How'd we do with aldermen?"

"Nine out of ten," Hubbart said. "Lost the Third Ward to a Republican. All this law and order talk scared off the sporting crowd."

"Damned ingrates!" Wheeler cursed. "After all I've done to put the quietus on the reformers. Ben, I want you to teach them a lesson. Understood?"

Thompson nodded, "I'll figure out a way to rap their knuckles."

"Well, enough of that for now. We're the big winners tonight and *that* calls for a celebration. Let's find the rest of the boys."

The election eve party was held in the bar at the Austin Hotel. Wheeler was surrounded by the aldermen, his City Hall cronies, and a large contingent of Democratic supporters. Everyone was quick to congratulate Thompson, praising his victory, and there was a round robin of toasts to the winners. The party got progressively louder and more drunken.

Thompson ducked out shortly before midnight. He caught the last streetcar of the evening, with just himself and the driver aboard. The ride to College Hill cleared his head of whiskey fumes, and gave him time to reflect on his new position. By now the initial rush of elation had turned to a sense of deep satisfaction. He'd carried the vote, and with it, the trust of the people of Austin. He quietly resolved to bring honor to the badge.

Catherine was waiting when he came through the door. He saw by the expression on her face that she'd already heard the news. She put her arm around his neck, hugging him fiercely, and kissed him full on the mouth. Her voice was husky with emotion.

"Welcome home . . . Marshal."

"Marshal," Thompson repeated with a chipper grin. "Got a good ring to it, doesn't it? How's it feel to be the wife of a lawman?"

She looked into his eyes. "I've never been more proud in my life."

"Katie, I'm not the least bit tired. You up to a celebration?"

"I'm up to anything tonight."

"You're liable to get more than you bargained for."

"Braggart."

She slipped into his embrace with a musical laugh.

EIGHTEEN

A week later Thompson was sworn in as city marshal. The ceremony took place in the mayor's office, early on Monday morning. Horace Warren, the city court judge, administered the oath.

By law, new office-holders were sworn in a week after their election. Mayor Wheeler and his secretary, Sueann Mabry, were witnesses to the ceremony. Judge Warren had Thompson raise his right hand and place his left hand on a Bible while repeating the oath. He was charged to uphold the laws of the City of Austin and the State of Texas.

Traditionally, the city marshal wore civilian clothes. But Thompson was attired in a uniform he'd designed himself and had tailored over the past week. The color was navy blue, with brass buttons on the jacket and a five-pointed star for a badge. The cap was round and flat, with a leather brim and gold braid, and a laurel-wreathed CITY MARSHAL affixed on the front. He looked the part of a modern police officer.

"Congratulations," Judge Warren said upon completing the oath. "I wish you every success in your new position."

"Thank you," Thompson replied with a broad smile. "You won't see me in your court anymore—except in an official capacity."

"You are welcome in my court anytime, Marshal. Allow me to compliment you on your uniform."

"Seemed only right, since the men are required to wear uniforms. Why should the marshal be the exception?"

"Indeed," Warren said, nodding approval. "You'll set a fine example."

Sueann Mabry shyly offered her congratulations. When she and Judge Warren went out, Wheeler closed the door. He looked around at Thompson. "I wanted to wish you my personal best, Ben. What's your first order of business?"

"I'll meet with the men and officially take charge. How do I go about relieving Ed Creary?"

"I'm happy to say he saved you the trouble. He sent word he'd vacated office as of last night. I suspect he wanted no part in the changing of the guard."

"Good riddance," Thompson said. "Just so you know, I plan to fire Carl Allen. I won't have a perjurer on the police force."

Wheeler appeared dubious. "That's certain to draw criticism. People will think you're settling a personal score."

"I've been criticized before. He lied under oath in a court of law. He's not fit to be a police officer."

"Why not wait a week or so? Your first day on the job makes it look like sour grapes."

"No, it won't wait," Thompson informed him. "I campaigned on a promise of *honest* law enforcement. I expect you to back my play."

"Don't concern yourself about that," Wheeler said hastily. "You're the marshal and you call the shots. Do whatever you have to do."

"Tom, I appreciate the vote of confidence. Let me get to work."

"Keep me advised on things."

"You can depend on it."

Thompson walked down the hall. The police department was located at the rear of the building, near a back door. Outside, a recessed stairway led to the city jail, a holding pen and six cells which occupied the basement. Locally, it was referred to as "The Tomb."

The graveyard shift was going off duty as Thompson entered the squad room. There were twelve men on the force, rotating shifts on a weekly basis. Six men worked the night shift from four in the afternoon to midnight, when Guy Town was at its most troublesome. Four men were assigned to days, and two usually sufficed for late night patrols. Half the force was present for the morning change of shifts.

The men snapped to attention on a barked command from Sergeant Lon Dennville. As the highest-ranking officer on the force, he ran the office and was on call, night or day, in case of an emergency. He welcomed Thompson to the department, and formally introduced him to the six officers present. One of them, just off the graveyard shift, was Carl Allen.

"While the men are here," Dennville asked, "would you like to say anything, Marshal?"

"I'll keep it short," Thompson said, looking from man to man. "You're experienced law officers and you know what's expected of you. Do your job and we'll get along just fine. Come see me if you have any problems."

The men wore blue uniforms and black helmets, and went armed with revolvers as well as billy clubs. All of them knew Thompson and his reputation, and none of them doubted he was about to impose stricter law enforcement on Austin. They stared straight ahead, shoulders squared, waiting to be dismissed. Dennville glanced at Thompson.

"Anything else, Marshal?"

"That's all for now, Sergeant. I'd like to see you and Allen in my office."

Thompson moved to a private office at the rear of the squad room. When he entered, he stopped just inside the door, clearly surprised. A handsome walnut desk, polished to a sheen and obviously new, was positioned before the window. Behind it was a tall judge's chair, crafted in oxblood leather, and equally new. Dennville paused in the doorway.

"Courtesy of the mayor," he said. "He thought the city could afford a new desk for the new marshal."

"Well, Sergeant, he sure picked a beauty."

Thompson took a seat in the oxblood chair. He ran a hand across the gloss of the desktop, and smiled in appreciation. Then, glancing up, he saw Allen standing behind Dennville. He motioned them into the office.

"I'll give it to you straight," he said, fixing Allen with a hard stare. "You're a liar and a perjurer, and a disgrace to the uniform. You're fired, as of right now."

"You've got no right," Allen said lamely. "Creary forced me to testify against you. I was just following orders."

"So here's your last order. Put your badge on this desk and make yourself scarce. You're off the force."

"You're gonna be sorry, Mr. Big Shot."

Thompson rose from his chair. "I won't ask you again. Hand over the badge."

Allen swallowed, his Adam's apple bobbing up and down. He unpinned the badge from his tunic and carefully placed it on the shiny desk. His eyes black with hatred, he turned and walked out the door. Thompson looked at Dennville.

"Any objections?"

"Not from me," the sergeant said. "You've made yourself an enemy, though. He's a regular little weasel."

"To hell with him," Thompson said dismissively. "Before the day's out, I'll make lots of enemies. So will you."

"How so?"

"I've always respected you, Sergeant. From all I've seen, you're on the square and you get the job done. Are you up to some rough work?"

Dennville looked quizzical. "What sort of rough work?"

"We're going to put out the word in Guy Town."

"And what's the word?"

"Don't step over the line . . . ever."

Guy Town was a world apart. A circus of sorts, it was a place where grown men came to play. Some were attracted by the gambling, and others by women. Whiskey simply fueled the merriment.

Early that afternoon Thompson and Dennville proceeded along Cypress Street. They were both known to the sporting crowd, though Thompson rarely ventured into Guy Town. Dennville, on the other hand, was there on a nightly basis, enforcing a rough brand of justice. He was intolerant of drunks and rowdies, and often led the police into fist-swinging melees common to the red-light district. He was considered an artist with a billy club.

Thompson in a police uniform was a sight that drew stares. Having denounced the sporting crowd during the elections, he was now looked upon as a Judas. For years, though he was an uptown gambler, he had been regarded as one of the fraternity. But his campaign for law and order and his election as marshal, had put him on the opposite side of the fence. Worse yet, he'd exposed the payoffs from dives, and threatened the established order of vice. Things would never be the same in Guy Town.

The sporting crowd was no great mystery to Thompson. Essentially they were outcasts, preying on the unwary and the gullible with no more scruples than an alley cat. Within the fraternity there were petty squabbles and jealousies, and incessant bickering for position in the hierarchy. Yet there was solidarity as well, for they saw themselves as a small band pitted against the world. Their ranks were forever closed to outsiders.

Thompson's plan was simplicity itself. There was a pecking order in the sporting crowd, with some more influential than others. However independent, gamblers, saloonkeepers, and whorehouse madams looked to their own for leadership. For the most part, those with the most successful operations assumed a dominant role in the hierarchy. The place to start, Thompson informed Dennville, was at the top of the heap. Their first stop was the Lone Star Gaming Parlor.

The owner was Ned Parker. A heavyset man, he operated one of the roughest dives in town. His dealers were skilled sharpers, and the object of the drill was to fleece the customers without getting caught too often. Anyone who objected was dealt with swiftly and harshly by the bruisers who worked for Parker. Until a week ago, he had been a paying client of Marshal Ed Creary. His crooked games had never drawn police scrutiny.

The Lone Star was a large boxlike room devoted solely to gaming. A long bar traversed one wall, and on the opposite side were faro and twenty-one layouts, and two dice tables. Everyone in the room paused as Thompson and Dennville came through the door, and walked directly to an office at the rear of the bar. They entered without being announced.

Ned Parker was seated behind a desk. The stub of a cigar was wedged in the corner of his mouth, and the chair creaked as he leaned forward. His beady eyes flashed with anger. "You boys oughta learn to knock."

Dennville closed the door. Thompson crossed to the desk and stopped. "Ned, I'm here with bad news," he said with a faint smile. "I was sworn in just this morning."

"So what?" Parker said, puffing a cloud of smoke. "You think I'm impressed with your fancy uniform?"

"You will be before I leave. I've come to put you on notice."

"Notice of what?"

"The rules have changed," Thompson said. "I don't take payoffs and you're through running crooked games. Break the rules and I'll close you down."

"Don't make me laugh," Parker retorted. "You'd have to shut down every joint in Guy Town."

"No, you're wrong there, Ned. The others will fall in line when I close your doors."

"I thought you were handing out all that horseshit to get yourself elected. Are you on the level?"

"Take me at my word," Thompson said evenly. "One complaint about crooked cards and I'll slap a padlock on this place. You wouldn't like it in jail."

Parker munched his cigar. "You've been a sporting man your whole goddamn life. You tellin' me you suddenly got religion?"

"I was a gambler," Thompson said, ignoring the gibe. "I was never a crook."

"I ought to sue you for slander."

"You wouldn't win that one, either. Get straight and stay straight. That's the message."

"What about the other joints?" Parker demanded. "You deliverin' the same message to them."

Thompson smiled. "You'll deliver it for me, Ned."

"Why would I do a fool thing like that?"

"To protect yourself and the Lone Star. Why give them the edge when your games are straight?"

"I haven't said I've bought the sermon myself."

"Then you'd better start wearing warm clothes. I'm told it gets downright frosty in the city jail."

Thompson left him to ponder the thought. The next stop was a parlor house on the corner of Cedar and Colorado. The bordello was operated by Blanche Dumont, herself an institution in Guy Town. Her career spanned two decades, and her house was the most elegant in the district. The other madams considered her the virtuoso of the flesh trade.

The reception room was decorated in French Rococo, with silk damask draperies and a massive crystal chandelier. The girls were voluptuous and genteel, and a pearly-toothed black man coaxed the latest tunes from a sparkling white piano. Blanche Dumont, who was built like a pouter pigeon, wore a gown that barely restrained her breastworks. She greeted Thompson with coquettish trepidation.

"Marshal Thompson," she said, her bosom heaving. "And my dear friend, Sergeant Dennville. I do so hope this is a social call."

"Afraid not, Blanche," Thompson replied pleasantly. "We're here on official business."

"Oh, that sounds so . . . dire."

"Not if you give me a little cooperation. I'm here to ask a favor."

"Aren't you the charmer?" she said with a coy smile. "How could I refuse a gentleman anything?"

Thompson suppressed a laugh. "Blanche, I want you to use your influence with the other madams. Deliver a friendly warning."

"Oh, dear me . . . a warning?"

"Tell them I won't tolerate any high jinks. I expect them to run orderly houses and stop rolling drunks. Anybody who crosses me will be on the next train out of town."

"Well, I'll try," she said, fluttering her eyelashes. "Of course, I can't promise anything. Some of the ladies are : . . indiscreet."

"You're a persuasive woman," Thompson said. "I depend on you to convince them, and no diddling around. Let's get the word out by tonight."

"You are the insistent one, aren't you?"

"I treat my friends right, Blanche. You help me and I'll help you. Do we understand one another?"

"Oh, goodness yes, perfectly."

Outside, a wintry sun was tilting westward. Dennville shook his head as they turned toward Congress Avenue. He laughed a low, chuffing laugh.

"You've got a way with the ladies, Marshal. All the whores will be talking tonight."

Thompson chuckled. "I'd say we've done a good day's work."

"And I'd give a nickel to hear what the sporting crowd says."

"I just suspect it'd singe our ears."

They walked off through the streets of Guy Town.

NINETEEN

‒‒‒‒‒⊪⋓⫙‒‒‒‒‒

"I really think you should go."

"Katie, I'd feel like a hypocrite."

"You're a public official now. You have a responsibility to set an example."

"The roof would probably collapse when I walked in the door. God doesn't look kindly on heathens."

"Oh, that's monstrous!"

Catherine turned from the mirror. They were in the bedroom, and she'd worked herself into a snit. She was dressed for Sunday morning church services, and her color was high. For all her cajolery, Thompson refused to budge, dodging every argument with maddening equanimity. She thought he was shortsighted and obstinate.

"Honestly, Benjamin!" she said waspishly. "You're so exasperating sometimes."

Thompson knew he was in trouble. She never called him by his full name unless she was in a temper. He tried to shrug it off with a smile, watching as she gathered a cabriolet bonnet and pinned it atop her hair. She wore a satin Princess Polonaise dress, very much in vogue, and complimentary to her figure. He gave her a slow once-over.

"You're looking mighty pretty today. I always liked you in purple."

"Magenta!" she corrected him sharply. "And don't you dare try to flatter me. I won't be patronized."

"Guess I'm in the doghouse, huh? All because of a little thing like church."

"What am I going to tell Reverend Jones? I promised him you would attend services today."

Reverend Clarence Jones was pastor of the First Methodist Church. His prominence in the community was magnified by his position as chairman of the Austin Ministers Association. His devotion to universal brotherhood was such that even the Baptists spoke kindly of him.

"Whoa now, Nellie," Thompson said suspiciously. "Why would you be talking about me with Preacher Jones?"

"You needn't be crude," she said, fussing with her hat. "You could at least call him 'Reverend.'"

"And you needn't try to slip off the hook. Since when have I become a topic of discussion with a preacher?"

"Since you became marshal, if you must know. You've been in office a week, and people are already starting to say nice things about you. Reverend Jones made a point of asking me if you would attend services."

"Did he?" Thompson said gruffly. "After he did his damnedest to get me defeated in the election. The man's got brass, I'll give him that."

Catherine sighed. "You might give him the benefit of the doubt. Perhaps he realizes he made a mistake."

"Was that what he said?"

"Well, no, not just in those words. But he said he'd been hearing good things about you."

"Yeah?" Thompson inquired skeptically. "Like what?"

"You know," she murmured, trying to say it without saying it. "How you've made things better . . . downtown."

"You're talking about whores and such? Guy Town?"

"No one uses those terms in polite society."

"Katie, I'm the city marshal, remember? I don't have a lot of dealings with polite society."

"Well, anyway, you've made an impression on the right people. I'm sure they realize they misjudged you."

Thompson's first week on the job had been notable by its relative calm. His detractors fully expected him to shoot someone, leave the streets littered with bodies. Instead, a lull seemed to have settled over Guy Town, even the rowdies wary of clashing with the police. The word slowly got around that Thompson had issued a stern warning to the sporting crowd.

"Won't you reconsider?" Catherine asked. "I mean, after all, Reverend Jones did ask for you. Doesn't that tell you something?"

"Maybe too much," Thompson said dryly. "Jones and the rest of the preachers want to start a reform movement. I won't let myself get drawn into it."

"Ben, for goodness' sake listen to yourself. Do you really think the reverend has ulterior motives?"

"I think preachers are just like anyone else. They'll play along to get along—and get what they want."

"Now you're starting to sound cynical."

"No, just practical."

"Bobby and I will be late for church. I have to go."

"I'll see you off."

Thompson was dressed in his uniform. He'd planned to stop by the office, even though it was Sunday, and check on the men. He strapped his gun on over his tunic, and followed her out the door. She led the way downstairs.

Bobby was waiting in the hall. His hair was slicked back, and he wore a brown herringbone suit with a matching cap and checkered bow tie. He looked around as they came down the stairs, and a moonlike grin spread over his face. He seemed to squirm with excitement.

"I knew Ma would talk you into it. Boy, won't Reverend Jones be surprised!"

"Not today, son," Thompson said. "I've got business that needs tending."

"Aww, darnit all, Pa! I wanted everybody at church to see you in your new uniform."

"Maybe we'll do it another time. Today's not a good day."

"Yeah, but all the guys'll be there. I was countin' on it, Pa!"

"You heard your father," Catherine broke in. "We'll just have to go without him. It can't be helped."

"What'll I tell the guys?"

"Tell them your father was called away by duty."

Thompson took a woolen shawl from the coatrack and draped it over Catherine's shoulders. She gave him a sheepish smile, aware that her conspiracy with the boy had been uncovered. He grinned, squeezing her arm, and she kissed him on the cheek. As he opened the door, Bobby jumped back with surprise. Clell Miller, one of the police officers, stood with his hand raised to knock.

"Sorry about that, Marshal. Didn't mean to scare nobody."

"No harm done," Thompson said. "What can I do for you?"

Catherine slipped past them. "We have to run or we'll be late. Come along, Bobby."

The boy reluctantly followed his mother out the door. As they went down the front steps, Thompson looked back at Miller. "What's the problem, Clell?"

"Sergeant Dennville sent me to fetch you. We've got a disturbance at Dora Kelly's house."

"What sort of disturbance?"

"One of her whores stiffed a customer. The sarge figured you'd want to know."

"Clell, he figured exactly right. Let's go."

Sergeant Dennville was seated at his desk in the squad room. A man who looked to be in his early twenties was slumped in a nearby chair. His left eye was a rainbow of purple and black.

Dennville glanced around when Thompson and Miller came through the door. He rose from behind his desk as they crossed the room, his expression one of sober amusement. He motioned to the young man.

"'Morning, Marshal," he said. "This gentleman is Amos Barber. He'd like to file a complaint."

The young man got to his feet. His left eye was almost swollen shut, discolored from the eyebrow to the cheekbone. He nodded with a hangdog look of shame. "Sorry to get you out on a Sunday, Marshal."

"Don't worry about it," Thompson said. "That's quite a shiner you've got there. Who slugged you?"

"The bouncer at Dora Kelly's place. I wanted my money back and we got in a big argument. She finally sicced him on me."

"You wanted your money back from Dora Kelly?"

"No, the girl," Barber said. "Her name was Frankie."

"Frankie Howard," Dennville added. "She's one of Dora's whores."

Thompson nodded. "How did the girl come by your money, Mr. Barber?"

"Well—" Barber hesitated, averting his gaze. "She got me drunk and I spent the night in her room. When I woke up this morning, my wallet was empty. She robbed me."

"And that's when the trouble started?"

"All hell broke loose. I called her a thief and she called me a liar, and Dora Kelly sicced her bouncer on me. Threw me out of the place."

"How much money did you lose?"

"Everything I had in my wallet—eighteen dollars."

"We can recover your money," Thompson said. "But you'll have to testify against the girl in court. Are you willing to press charges?"

"Court?" Barber winced, clearly uncomfortable. "Will my name get put in the papers? I can't afford to lose my job."

"Where do you work?"

"I'm a teller at the First National Bank. Mr. Wooldridge wouldn't stand still for one of his employees being caught in a—parlor house. He'd fire me on the spot."

"Yeah, he's the sanctimonious sort, isn't he?"

"Marshal, he's hell on wheels when it comes to Guy Town. I'm a single man, but that wouldn't even matter. He'd still give me the boot."

Thompson considered a moment. He thought it ironic that Alexander Wooldridge was even remotely involved with a whorehouse robbery. His first instinct was to let it appear in the newspapers, and embarrass the man who had scorned him during the elections. But his responsibility was to the law, and somehow ensuring that the young bank teller wasn't made the scapegoat. He looked at Barber.

"Maybe there's a way to keep it out of court. You'll still have to file a complaint."

"Anything you say, Marshal," Barber quickly agreed. "Just so it doesn't get in the papers."

"You wait here," Thompson said. "Officer Miller will keep you company. Sergeant Dennville, you come with me."

"Yes, sir."

A short while later Thompson and Dennville entered the bordello operated by Dora Kelly. As they came through the door, a hulking bruiser of a man stopped them in the hallway. He was stoutly built, with mean eyes and the flattened nose of a prizefighter. He barred their path into the parlor.

"We're closed," he said in a surly voice. "Come back tomorrow."

"Stand aside," Thompson ordered. "I'm here to see Dora Kelly."

"She ain't seein' nobody today."

"Save yourself some grief, tough guy. Out of my way."

"You don't scare me, Thompson. What'll I get, a night in jail? Fuck off."

Thompson hardly seemed to move. The Colt appeared in his hand and he laid the barrel across the bouncer's skull with a mushy *thunk*. Stunned, the man wobbled backward, trying to raise his clenched fists, and Thompson struck him again. He went down, out cold.

Dora Kelly stormed across the parlor. She was a lumpy woman, with henna-dyed hair, and the look of a harridan. Her eyes burned with fury.

"You sorry bastard!" she screeched. "What d'you mean hittin' Sam like that!"

"You're under arrest, Dora." Thompson holstered his pistol, stepping over the bouncer. "You and one of your girls, Frankie Howard."

"You kiss my fat ass, Ben Thompson. Arrest for what?"

"Larceny, robbery, and running a bunco game. And felonious assault on the young fellow your goon worked over this morning."

"That's a pack of lies!" she fumed. "You won't never make it stick."

Thompson grinned. "We'll let the judge decide who's telling the truth. I calculate you ought to get five years, maybe ten."

"Wait a minute now, don't get crazy on me. I'll square it with the kid, even double his money. Give him free nookie the rest of his life. How's that?"

"You should have listened to Blanche Dumont. She warned everybody I wouldn't tolerate rough stuff."

"C'mon, have a heart for chrissakes!"

"Here's the only deal you'll get," Thompson said. "You and Frankie be on the evening train for Dallas. Otherwise, you're headed for prison."

"Jesus Christ!" she bellowed. "You're runnin' me out of town?"

"Dora, you're closed down as of right now. I'll have this place padlocked before the sun sets. You're through in Austin."

"You goddamn shitheel! Who gives you the right to play God?"

"I'm done talking," Thompson said sharply. "Catch a train or go to jail. What's your pleasure?"

"Some choice," she snapped. "I'll catch the train."

"Couple of other things."

"Christ, what now?"

"Take your friend along." Thompson said, jerking a thumb at the bouncer. "I want him out of Austin."

"Sam goes wherever I go. What's the other thing?"

"I'll have the eighteen dollars you took off young Mr. Barber."

She pulled a wad of cash from the pocket of her housecoat. After peeling off several bills, she slapped them into his hand. Her features were set in an angry scowl.

"I hope you burn in hell."

"Don't miss your train, Dora."

Thompson stepped over the bouncer, who was leaking blood on the carpet. He went through the hallway and out the door, followed by Dennville. On the street, they walked toward the corner in silence. Dennville finally gave him a curious sidewise look.

"You're better with a pistol than I am a billy club. Where'd you learn that trick?"

"In the Kansas cowtowns," Thompson said. "Bat Masterson calls it 'buffaloing' a man."

"Neat work," Dennville said with admiration. "Same goes for Dora, too. We're better rid of her."

"You might say Dora was an object lesson."

"What's an object lesson?"

"A demonstration that we're serious."

"Nobody's ever gonna doubt that."

Thompson was pleased with the morning's work. He thought the story would be all over the sporting district by nightfall. A story with a moral.

Get straight or get out of town.

TWENTY

—◆—

The story quickly made the rounds. All over Guy Town, madams and cardsharps realized that Thompson was in dead earnest. Anyone who bent the law was certain to become acquainted with the city jail. A serious infraction would likely result in a one-way train ticket.

On Monday, the newspapers offered differing versions of the incident. The *Statesman* dryly reported that Marshal Thompson had "exported Dora Kelly and one of her lady boarders to climes farther north." The *Republican* commented that "Our new marshal now operates a kangaroo court, with himself as judge and jury." No one questioned he would skirt the letter of the law when it suited his notion of justice.

By the following Saturday, the sporting crowd was of mixed emotions. On the one hand, Thompson rejected any alliance with the reformers, whose goal was nothing less than the abolition of Guy Town. On the other, he enforced his own moral code with harsh measures, rigidly intolerant of anything that smacked of underhanded schemes. He upheld the right of men to gamble, carouse, and fornicate within certain bounds. He punished anyone who stepped across the line.

Thompson normally went home for supper. He found that the hours of a lawman were somewhat similar to those of a gambler. All forms of crime, from simple burglary to armed robbery, were more prevalent once the sun went down. Not surprisingly, he'd discovered that Saturday was the busiest night of the week for a peace officer. Saturday was payday for workingmen, and with money in their pockets, Saturday night was their night to howl. He skipped supper at home to tend to business.

On Saturday, November 20, he was seated in his office. He'd returned around six o'clock from an early supper in a nearby café. Sergeant Lon Dennville was now at supper, and Clell Miller was manning the squad room. There were five officers on the streets, with four of those assigned to patrol Guy Town. Later, Thompson and Dennville would tour the sporting district, appearing unannounced in gaming dives and saloons. Their presence generally served to put the rowdier element on notice.

Over the past two weeks Thompson had become fast friends with Lon Dennville. Their relationship was still one of chief lawman and second in command; but an easy trust now existed between them. Dennville, little by little, had opened up and revealed how the department had operated before the election. Ed Creary, he noted, had kept to the office, rarely venturing onto the streets, particularly on a Saturday night. He'd made it a practice to show up after a troublesome situation had been quelled. Usually just in time to provide a quote for the newspapers.

Thompson was hardly surprised. His assessment of the former marshal had always been that of a man who left the dirty work to others, and took the credit. Nor was he overly amazed when Dennville explained how the system of payoffs from the dives had operated. Carl Allen made the weekly collections, and Creary ordered the other men on the force to overlook irregularities and crooked games. The men detested Creary, with the exception of Allen, and their honesty had never been put to the test. Creary kept all of the graft for himself, with a token payment to Allen.

Thompson once asked Dennville why he hadn't quit the force. Dennville explained that he had a wife and three children, and political corruption was no reason for them to go hungry. He'd signed on as a policeman seven years ago, serving under four different city marshals in that time. Slowly, by steering clear of politics, he had worked his way through the ranks, finally being promoted to sergeant. Out of the four marshals, Creary was the only crook and Dennville had turned a blind eye to the payoffs. He thought Creary would never be elected to a second term.

Still, reflecting on the past two weeks, Thompson was somewhat less sanguine. Without hard proof, the mayor and the city council would never have turned on Creary. To indict the man they had supported for office, particularly on the basis of rumor, would have been to indict themselves. When Thompson decided to run for election, they'd found a solution that made them look good with the voters. Otherwise, Ed Creary might be sitting in the marshal's office tonight.

Dennville rapped on the door. "Not interrupting anything, am I?"

"Nothing monumental," Thompson said. "I was thinking about Ed Creary."

"What about him?"

"How the election could have gone the other way. It was my word against his about the payoffs. There was no proof."

"There was no evidence," Dennville amended. "The sporting crowd knew it, and they're the worst gossips in the world. That was enough for the voters."

Thompson lit a cheroot. "Good thing, too," he said, exhaling smoke. "Otherwise I'd be dealing poker tonight."

"Guess where Creary is tonight?"

"You sound like you know something I don't."

"The Lone Star," Dennville said soberly. "Ned Parker hired him to ride shotgun on the gaming operation. How's that for a joke?"

"Pretty sad," Thompson observed. "Creary's got no taste for trouble. Why would Parker hire him?"

"Parker's bouncers can handle any trouble. I think Creary's just window-dressing."

"I don't follow you, Lon."

"Former marshal, defender of the law, all that stuff. A testimonial that the games at the Lone Star are straight."

"That won't wash," Thompson said. "We just agreed everybody knows Creary was accepting payoffs. Why would anyone take his word on straight games?"

Dennville shrugged. "Maybe any window-dressing's better than none at all. Maybe Parker hired him out of charity. I haven't got the answer myself."

There was a protracted moment of silence. Thompson stared off into space, puffing thoughtfully on his cheroot. He knew Ned Parker to be a cagey operator, slick and shrewd. A man who never acted without purpose.

"Maybe we're missing the message," he said at length. "What if Parker wanted to show the sporting crowd he's not impressed with me or my badge? What better way than to hire Ed Creary?"

"Yeah, I suppose," Dennville said doubtfully. "But we'd still close him down if he's running crooked games. What's the point?"

"Parker's always got something up his sleeve. What you see isn't necessarily what you get."

"So what do we do?"

Thompson stood. "Let's head on down to Guy Town."

"We were anyway," Dennville said. "Do I hear the wheels turning? You got something in mind, Marshal?"

"You check out a few saloons, and I'll stop by the Lone Star. Just to pay my regards."

"Are you talking about Parker or Creary?"

"I'll know when I get there."

The Lone Star was packed. On a Saturday night men from throughout Travis County traveled to Guy Town. Their pilgrimage was in pursuit of women, liquor, and games of chance. The sporting crowd invariably sent them home with hangovers and empty pockets, no wiser for the experience. The dives were always mobbed on payday.

Thompson walked through the door shortly after seven o'clock. The evening was off to a fast start, with men ganged three deep at the bar. The gaming layouts were crowded as well, knots of men chasing fortune with more abandon than skill. A whoop of laughter went up as someone rolled a winner at a dice table.

All around the room, men turned as Thompson moved past the gaming layouts. His uniform drew attention, and his name was known throughout the county. The election, and his campaign to bring honest gambling to Guy Town, had won him many friends. Few men understood how the games were rigged, but every man wanted a fair shake. His election as marshal was widely applauded.

Halfway through the crowd, Thompson paused and watched the action at a twenty-one layout. The dealer was aware of his scrutiny, and nervously dealt a hand around the board. His apparent interest in twenty-one was actually a dodge, for his attention was focused on a faro layout at the next table. Out of the corner of his eye, he watched the dealer finish out an entire deck of cards. He detected no sleight-of-hand.

Ed Creary was standing at the end of the bar. He watched Thompson while Thompson pretended to watch the twenty-one game. His eyes were guarded as Thompson turned away and moved on through the crowd, pausing briefly at one of the dice tables. He suspected the purpose of the visit was not gambling; but rather his newly announced position with the Lone Star. He tried to appear indifferent when Thompson approached the bar.

"Well, Mr. Creary," Thompson said expansively. "I understand you've found gainful employment. How's it going?"

"No complaints," Creary said stiffly. "So far, it beats politics."

"I wasn't aware you had any experience at gambling. How'd you come to land the job?"

"Are you asking out of personal curiosity?"

Thompson made an offhand gesture. "Just like to keep tabs on who's who in Guy Town."

"I'm the house manager," Creary told him. "Not that it's any of your business."

"Last time we met you were hot under the collar. Sounds like you're still carrying a grudge."

"Take it any way you want. I don't owe you an explanation."

"Not as long as you obey the law."

The door to the office opened, Ned Parker looked from one to the other, his expression cloudy. He nodded to Thompson. "What brings you around, Marshal?"

"Thought I'd give you a pat on the back," Thompson said with some irony. "From the looks of things, you're operating on the square. How's it feel to be legit?"

"Nobody ever said I wasn't."

"Nobody except me. But like they say, that's water under the bridge. You're on the right track, Ned."

"Glad you approve," Parker remarked. "Anything else on your mind?"

"No, just that I see you've hired Mr. Creary. You'll make a good team."

"Why don't I believe you mean that?"

"You're a suspicious man, Ned."

"Marshal!"

Gabe Ewing, one of the city policemen, pushed through the crowd. His mouth hung open, revealing a gold tooth, and he was breathing heavily. He skidded to a halt.

"Sergeant Dennville wants you muy pronto! There's a brawl over at the Cosmopolitan."

"Anybody hurt?"

"Will be unless they're stopped. Gawddamn cowboys got into it with the railroad men."

"Let's go."

Thompson hurried toward the door. Outside, Ewing followed him at a fast clip, angling across the street. The Cosmopolitan, far less elegant than its name, was a hangout for railroad workers. Ewing quickly explained that a bunch of drunken cowhands had invaded the saloon, apparently looking for a fight. The railroad men jumped to defend their territory.

Downstreet, Thompson stopped before the open doors of the Cosmopolitan. Dennville and three policemen were busting heads with their nightsticks, trying to wedge a path into the melee. The saloon was a wreck, tables and chairs upturned, and the backbar mirror shattered. Cowhands and railroad workers pounded away in a slugfest, grunting and cursing in a riotous donnybrook. The floor was littered with dazed and bloodied men.

Thompson stepped through the doors. He pulled his pistol, holding it overhead, and fired three shots into the ceiling. The roar of the Colt bracketed off the walls, the echo deafening in the confined quarters of the room. Everything abruptly stopped, men frozen with their arms cocked to throw a punch and others locked in a stilled wrestling match. The combatants stared toward the door, slowly separating, their eyes fixed on the uniformed man with a gun. A leaden silence settled over the saloon.

"Fun's over!" Thompson shouted, wagging the snout of his pistol. "You boys back off and stand easy. *Now*."

Warily, their eyes on the gun, the men broke apart. The cowhands congregated near the bar, assisting their fallen comrades to their feet. The railroad workers collected their own wounded and gathered along the opposite wall. They stood loosely bunched, staring daggers at one another, reduced to bloodied silence. Not a man among them was unscathed.

Dennville walked forward. "Wish I'd thought of a gun. You damn sure got their attention."

"What happened?" Thompson asked.

"You know cowboys," Dennville said with disgust. "Saturday night's a complete loss unless they find a fight. They busted in here, just itching for trouble."

"What about the railroad men?"

"They didn't have much choice in the matter. It was a fight or run."

Thompson looked at the cowhands. "You boys are under arrest and let's not hear any back talk. Everybody outside . . . right now."

Dennville and his men spread out along the bar. They herded the cowboys, fourteen in number, through the front doors. A few minutes later they had them formed in columns of twos, somewhat like a squad of battered soldiers. They stood slump-shouldered in the center of the street.

"Hold on a goddamn minute!"

A large, gangly man came hurrying up the sidewalk. He was stuffing his shirt in his trousers, breathing hard. He slammed to a halt before Thompson.

"What's going on here, Marshal?"

"Who are you?"

"Floyd Ollinger," the man said. "I own the Circle O spread outside Round Rock. These are my boys."

Thompson nodded. "You look like you got caught with your pants down, Mr. Ollinger."

"Well, hell, I was over at Blanche Dumont's house. Somebody busted in and told me my boys was in a fix."

"Your boys are headed for jail."

"What's the charge?"

"Drunk and disorderly, breach of peace, and resisting arrest. I'll likely think of something else by the time we get them locked up."

Ollinger groaned. "Ain't there some way besides jail, Marshal? I'd gladly pay for any damages."

"No, sir, no other way," Thompson said. "Austin is the state capital, not a cowtown. You ought to teach your boys the difference."

Dennville marched the squad of cowhands toward Congress Avenue. Thompson nodded curtly to the rancher and walked off behind the column. A reporter was standing at curbside, scribbling furiously in his notepad. He had his story for the night in Guy Town.

The *Statesman* ran it in the Sunday morning edition. A bold headline was centered below the fold on the front page.

CITY MARSHAL DECLARES
AUSTIN NOT A COWTOWN;
ARRESTS COWBOY TOUGHS

TWENTY-ONE

On Tuesday morning Thompson left the house around nine o'clock. He was attired in a Prince Albert suit and stovepipe hat, with a fur-collared chesterfield topcoat. He walked toward the streetcar stop at the corner.

The sky was overcast, dingy clouds drifting on a sharp northerly breeze. Yet he was in a chipper mood, his stride brisk and his shoulders squared. Over breakfast, he'd read a report in the *Statesman* on the Saturday night incident in Guy Town. The fourteen cowhands had been held in jail until their hearing yesterday morning in city court. Judge Horace Warren had fined them fifty dollars each and assessed a thousand dollars in damages.

Floyd Ollinger, the rancher who employed them, had paid heavily for a night on the town. The *Statesman* reported that he had shelled out almost two thousand dollars, including court costs, to secure the release of his crew. Thompson had received congratulations from the mayor, the sheriff, and a brief but laudatory note from the state house. Governor Oran Roberts commended him on a job well done, and his knack for the succinct phrase. Austin was indeed no longer a cowtown!

In celebration, Thompson had given himself the day off. Since being sworn in, slightly more than two weeks ago, he'd gone into the office every day, including Sundays. He felt he deserved a break, and in any event, he was on call in case of an emergency. Dennville was fully capable of handling routine matters, and knew where to reach him if he were needed. He had let personal affairs slide since taking office, and he couldn't put it off any longer. He planned to check the books at the Iron Front.

Downtown, he stepped off the streetcar at Mulberry and Congress Avenue. People were by now accustomed to seeing him in uniform, and he drew bemused stares from by-passers as he proceeded along the street. A few minutes later he entered the Iron Front and found the usual morning ritual already under way. The bartenders were busy stocking shelves for the noon hour rush, and a handyman was wiping down the gaming tables with a clean, damp cloth. Joe Richter was seated at the desk in the office.

"Ben!" He got to his feet with a wide grin and an effusive handshake. "I never see you anymore—except in the newspapers."

"My wife says the same thing," Thompson observed amiably. "I spend most of my time these days in Guy Town."

"Yeah, I read the *Statesman*. That was some free-for-all Saturday night. Sounds like you and your police were really outnumbered."

"Well, like the fly walking across the mirror said: It all depends on how you look at it. We had them surrounded, Joe."

Richter chuckled. "I notice you're not in uniform. Don't tell me you're playing hooky?"

"Took the day off," Thompson said. "Thought I'd have a look at the books. How are we doing?"

"By golly, Ben, I hate to toot my own horn. But things are downright zippy, and that's a fact. We're already ahead of last year."

"I should've made you a partner before now."

"Hey, better late than never. I've got no complaints."

Thompson found nothing to quibble about either. Richter got him seated at the desk and left him alone to inspect the bookkeeping ledgers. He spent an hour running figures, and finally sat back with a mild look of wonder. The date was November 23, and the Iron Front was ahead of last year by almost $12,000. All that with still a month to go before the end of the year. He told himself it was an early Christmas.

"Where's the sonovabitch that calls himself City Marshal?"

Thompson looked up with a scowl. The man in the doorway was strikingly handsome, with wavy straw-colored hair and eyes like steel-blue agates. He wore a fringed buckskin jacket and an ivory Stetson, with a brace of pistols snugged tight in a buscadero rig. The jingle-bobs on his spurs chimed musically as he stepped into the office. Thompson broke out in laughter.

"King Fisher!" he said, clasping the other man's hand. "How long's it been?"

"A year, maybe two or three. I heard these idjits up here elected you marshal. Figgered I had to see it with my own eyes."

"You came all the way to Austin for that?"

"Naw," Fisher said with a sly smile. "Got myself appointed deputy sheriff of Uvalde County. How's that for laughs?"

"I think God played a joke on somebody."

"What the hell, every dog gets his day."

King Fisher was an unlikely lawman. A rancher, his spread was near the town of Eagle Pass, some two hundred miles southwest of Austin. His checkered life had made him a legend of sorts along the border with Old Mexico. He was known to have killed seven men in gunfights, and he'd been arrested several times on charges of rustling and murder. Yet he had been acquitted in the most sensational trials ever held in Uvalde County.

Thompson considered Fisher one of his closest friends. In their wilder years, they had gambled up and down the border, on both sides of the Rio Grande. When Thompson went on to the boomtowns, traveling the gamblers' circuit, Fisher established a ranch outside Eagle Pass. He'd prospered, marrying his childhood sweetheart, and fathered four daughters. But he was still marked as a dangerous man, quick to take insult. Thompson had often thought they were peas from the same pod. And now they both wore badges.

"So what brings a big lawman like yourself to Austin?"

"Delivered a prisoner," Fisher said. "Some dimdot robbed a bank in Fort Worth and hightailed it for the border. We caught him in Piedras Negras."

"Did you now?" Thompson said, arching an eyebrow. "I seem to recall Piedras Negras is on the other side of the river. How'd you square that with the Mexicans?"

Fisher grinned. "I've got a deal with the chili peppers. They look the other way when I cross the river and nobody gets hurt. Works out real good."

"Why didn't you take your prisoner on to Fort Worth?"

"Well, you can just imagine, the Rangers got their bowels in an uproar when they heard the news. This half-assed bandit outruns 'em and outsmarts 'em, and I nail him without a hitch. They wired orders to drop him off here."

Thompson sobered. "I remember you never had much use for the Rangers. Small wonder they got bent out of shape."

Captain Lee Hall, among other Rangers, had arrested Fisher over the years. Every time, he'd managed to slip out of their net by convincing a jury he was an upstanding citizen. The Rangers thought of him as the one who got away.

"I've quit worryin' about the Rangers," Fisher said breezily. "Let 'em tend to their knittin' and I'll tend to mine."

"Will you be in town for a while?"

"Got in on the mornin' train and I'm headed back on the afternoon train. Jack Harris invited me to stop off in San Antone."

"Don't play cards with him," Thompson warned. "He's too slick by half."

Fisher looked surprised. "I figgered you and him would've patched things up by now. You still on the prod?"

"I'm not one to forget a man who rooks me. Trouble was, I couldn't prove it."

Harris owned a gambling hall and variety theater in San Antonio. A year ago, on a visit there, Thompson had gotten into a dispute with Harris over cards. He was still embittered by the experience.

"You ought to kiss and make up," Fisher said jokingly. "I'll tell him to send you a love letter."

"That'll be the day," Thompson said, waving it off. "Look here, why don't I treat you to a steak for lunch? Then I'll put you on your train."

"Hell, I never turn down a free meal. We'll kick around old times."

"Like the time that señorita's old man invited you to a shotgun wedding?"

"Jumpin' Jesus, don't remind me!"

Their laughter carried into the club as they walked from the office. Thompson's chipper mood was brightened even more by the appearance of an old friend. A friend from what was now the good old days.

They swapped stories over thick steaks charred blood-red in the center.

Early that evening the men began wandering into the Iron Front. Mayor Wheeler and James Shipe were the first to arrive, followed in short order by the law partners, Luther Edwards and Jack Walton. Will Cullen, the liquor wholesaler, came in a little after eight.

The men gathered in the private room at the rear of the club. Their weekly poker game, revived shortly after the elections, was no great secret. Thompson gambled nowhere else, and he felt he'd upheld his promise to the voters. The game, in his opinion, was a social affair, more recreation than gambling. He had to work at not winning.

A cider glow from the overhead lamp lighted the table. The walls, paneled in dark hardwood, gave the room a certain elegance, and a sideboard was stocked with liquor. The men took their customary chairs after pouring themselves a drink, ready for an evening of friendly rivalry. James Shipe, since he was a banker, acted as the game's banker. He exchanged chips for cash.

Thompson shuffled, his hands deftly working the cards. He dealt around the board, flipping the cards face-up on the table. The first man to catch an ace would have the opening deal, and tonight that was Luther Edwards. He called five-card stud, again shuffling the cards, and allowed Wheeler, who was seated on his right, to cut the deck. The men anted a dollar.

"Damnedest thing," Cullen said as he peeked at his hole card. "I've gotten used to seeing Ben around town in his uniform. He looks like somebody else in a suit and tie."

"King bets three." Walton, who was high on the board, tossed in three chips. "Now that you mention it, I prefer the uniform. It gives him an air of . . . dignity."

"Look who's talking," Thompson retorted, calling the bet. "Maybe we ought to require lawyers to wear uniforms. You boys could use some dignity."

"Ouch!" Walton said, pulling a face. "I think I got hoisted on my own petard."

Shipe folded his hand. "Don't let him kid you, Ben. You're doing a fine job and everybody here knows it. You're the talk of the town."

"And the newspapers," Wheeler said, dropping chips into the pot. "Even the *Republican* can't find fault with the police department. That in itself is an achievement."

"Have to raise," Edwards said. "Bump it three."

Everyone paused to inspect his hand. He had a jack showing, and he gave them a crafty smile. Cullen folded his cards. "Just goes to show you about lawyers. Dealt himself a pair of jacks."

"Luther likes to bluff," Walton said, throwing in a handful of chips. "Your three and raise you five."

"I'm convinced." Thompson turned his up card face-down. "I doubt you're both bluffing."

Wheeler studied on it a moment. Then, with a reluctant sigh, he dropped out. Edwards and Walton, the two attorneys, were the only ones left in the hand. They played the next three cards, betting and raising, enjoying themselves immensely. At the end, Walton turned up a king high, still certain his partner was bluffing. Edwards won it with a pair of jacks.

"How 'bout them apples!" he crowed. "Dealt myself a winner."

"Your time's coming," Walton joshed him. "I'll get you before the night's over."

Thompson watched the byplay with amused interest. He knew their style of poker, and he'd read them and their cards from the outset. Edwards was a conservative player, who rarely bluffed. By contrast, Walton regularly bet and raised on the come, chasing a winning hand. He thought it fortunate that their livelihood was derived from the practice of law. Poker was not their game.

Cullen began shuffling the cards. Shipe, who was seated to Thompson's left, glanced around. "That was quite a story in the *Statesman*. Judge Warren really stuck it to those cowboys."

"Hooray and hallelujah!" Wheeler cackled. "That two thousand went straight into the city treasury. At this rate, Austin may have its first surplus in years." He laughed humorously. "Keep those fines coming, Ben."

"Take it easy on crime, though," Walton said with mock concern. "You're liable to put us lawyers out of business."

"The governor thinks different," Thompson said. "I got a real nice note from him yesterday."

"What—" Wheeler blurted out. "You got a note from Oran Roberts?"

"Just a few lines about those cowboys. He said something like 'a job well done.' "

"I'll be a monkey's uncle," Wheeler muttered. "Nobody in City Hall ever got a note from Oran Roberts. You're the first."

Edwards chortled out loud. "You're just a bunch of bureaucrats. Ben's jailing rowdies and posting whores out of town. The governor knows who deserves credit."

"Don't make too much of it," Thompson interjected. "I told you, it was a little note. Maybe ten lines."

"That's not the point," Wheeler said. "Oran Roberts is a skinflint with compliments. Consider it high praise."

"Whatever you say," Thompson said, uncomfortable with the attention. "We sort of got off track here, gents. Let's play poker."

Cullen called five-card draw. A sizeable pot developed, and Shipe won it with three fours. The game shifted back and forth throughout the evening, with no heavy winner. But between hands, the talk was of the note from Governor Oran Roberts. No one thought it anything less than remarkable.

By the end of the evening Thompson was worn out with the talk. He was gratified by the esteem of men he respected, particularly these men. But he felt himself too much in the limelight, and purposely folded several strong hands. There was room for more than one winner among friends.

He managed to lose a hundred for the night.

TWENTY-TWO

———◆———

A tawny sun flooded the land. The sky was clear and there was a crisp wind out of the north. The warmth of the sunlight took the bite out of the air.

Lute Walker drove a farm wagon south toward Austin. Seated beside him was his wife, Selma, wrapped in a woolen greatcoat against the morning chill. Their team of horses, a roan and a blaze-faced sorrel, puffed frosty snorts with every breath. Winter was upon the hilly countryside.

The Walkers were black landholders. Their farm was located some ten miles northeast of Austin, along Bluebonnet Creek. They were in their forties, married for nearly seventeen years, and to their great regret, childless. Selma was barren.

Every Saturday the Walkers drove into town. Like farmers from all over Travis County, they came to town once a week to stock provisions and visit with their friends. These brief trips were especially rewarding for the Walkers; their few friends were widely scattered around the county. They were the only colored people on Bluebonnet Creek.

Today's trip was even more meaningful. It was the first Saturday in December, and there were plans to be made for the Christmas season. Every year a special service was held at the Evangelical Baptist Church of Austin, the largest black church in the county. People drove for miles to attend a pageant celebrating the birth of Jesus.

Lute and Selma were former slaves. Following the Civil War, when they were freed, their first act was to enter into wedlock. Then, quickly departing a cotton plantation in Eastern Texas, they traveled west in search of the Promised Land. The Union government offered them forty acres and a mule to start them on the path to freedom. They settled in the hill country outside Austin.

Those were unusual times for freedmen in Texas. The summer of '65, the Union Army of Occupation took charge of the state with an iron hand. Union commanders held the power of life and death; their word was law, without appeal or mitigation. The verdict of a military tribunal was final, and former Confederates were treated to harsh justice. Black men, for the first time in their lives, were equal before the law.

Carpetbaggers swarmed into Texas from the North. Loyal Unionists, northern born, they occupied the civil posts vacated by the rule of occupation. Next came the scalawags, southern-born turncoats, swearing allegiance to the Union in return for a license to steal. Between them they held every government office of importance, from governor to county judge. Their dictates were enforced by the bayonets of federal troops.

Yet it all ended in March 1870. Texas was readmitted to the Union, and the occupation forces went on to other duties. Carpetbaggers and scalawags were turned out of office, and native Texans once more governed the Lone Star State. For black freedmen, it was as though the clock had been set back to bleaker times. They were reduced to second-class citizens, denied the vote; no longer equal before the law. They were niggers again.

Lute and Selma Walker nonetheless prospered. By watching every nickel, they were able to purchase another forty acres from a disenchanted freedman. The land was bountiful, and while they would never be wealthy, they were comfortable. Devout Christians, they gave thanks at Christmas by providing for the less fortunate. Their meeting today with Reverend Titus Lacy was for that very reason. No needy family would go wanting on the day Christ was born.

Halfway into town the steady drum of hoofbeats sounded to their rear. Lute Walker looked over his shoulder and his brow squinched in a tight frown. Two riders, cowhands from the Box B Ranch, were rapidly gaining on the wagon. One was Clint Buchanan, a burly man with a mean streak and a hair-trigger temper. The other was Ross Taylor, tall and lanky, no less loutish than his partner. They were known to Walker, and best avoided. He glanced at his wife.

"Keep your mouth shut," he warned. "Don't pay no 'tention to what they say. Let me do the talkin'."

Selma sniffed. "I got no truck with white trash."

"You mind me now, woman!"

The cowhands reined in alongside the wagon.

Buchanan leaned forward on his saddlehorn. "Well, looky who we got here. Where you headed, Rufus?"

"Jes' into town," Walker said, gripping the reins tightly. "Got things to do."

"High and mighty, ain't you?" Buchanan growled. "Never a 'yes, sir' or a 'no, sir' or any other kind of sir.' You're talkin' to a white man, boy."

"Whyn't you jes' let us be, Mistuh Buchanan? We don't want no trouble with you folks."

"Hell, you're the one causin' all the trouble. Ain't that right, Ross?"

"Damn sure a fact," Taylor agreed. "What we got here is a coon that don't know his place."

Ethan Bullock, owner of the Box B, had been trying to buy Walker's farm for years. He loathed the idea of a black man farming eighty acres that abutted the southern quadrant of his rangeland. Neither the offer of money nor petty acts of harassment had altered the situation. He routinely encouraged his men to bedevil the Walkers.

"Helluva note," Buchanan said in a surly voice. "You oughta show a little respect, Rufus. Nobody likes a smart-ass coon."

Selma Walker jerked around. "Git on away from here, white trash. Go on, *git!*"

"You hear that?" Buchanan bellowed. "Sorry bitch called us white trash."

Taylor flushed. "I never could stand an uppity nigger. We gonna take that, Buck?"

Buchanan pulled his pistol. "Stop that gawddamn wagon! Do it or I'll plug you."

Walker hauled back on the reins. Buchanan and Taylor, waving their pistols, forced the couple to dismount from the wagon. Then, while Buchanan covered them, Taylor jumped into the wagon and drove off. They stood watching their wagon and team disappear down the road.

Buchanan rode away, leading Taylor's horse. He called back over his shoulder. "So long for now, blackbird!"

"Lordy," Walker muttered, fixing his wife with a look. "Told you to mind your mouth."

"I don't take nothin' off no white trash!"

"Well, you done done it now, woman."

Lute and Selma Walker trudged off toward Austin.

Thompson was seated in his office. He'd just returned from the noon meal and he felt comfortably stuffed. So far it had been relatively quiet for a Saturday, with only one incident in Guy Town. He knew that would change by nightfall.

The sound of voices drifted in from the squad room. He heard the deep rumble of a man's voice and the strident tones of a woman in some distress. A moment later Sergeant Dennville appeared in the doorway with a black couple. He ushered them into the office.

"Marshal Thompson," he said, motioning them forward, "this is Mr. and Mrs. Walker. Thought you ought to hear their story. They've been robbed."

"Come right in, folks," Thompson said, indicating chairs before his desk. "Have a seat and tell me what happened."

"Thank you kindly." Selma Walker seated herself and her husband took the other chair. "We been walkin' more'n three hours. I'm plumb wore out."

"I wouldn't wonder," Thompson said sympathetically. "Whereabouts were you robbed?"

Lute Walker cleared his throat. " 'Bout five miles out on the Phlugerville Road. Took our wagon and team."

"What about your money?"

"No, suh, Marshal, they wasn't after money. Them boys jes' set on makin' trouble."

"Why would they do that?"

"'Cause they trash!" Selma Walker said hotly. "Ol' man Bullock all the time sic 'em on us. Wasn't the first time."

"Ethan Bullock, the rancher?" Thompson asked. "Are you saying you know these men?"

"We knows 'em," Walker intoned heavily. "Couple of cowhands what works for the Box B. Clint Buchanan and Ross Taylor."

"So they've hoorahed you before?"

"Couldn't hardly count the times. Bullock wants our land and we ain't gonna sell. He jes' keeps on pushin' and pushin'."

Thompson despised a bully. He could never tolerate the strong using force to intimidate the weak. The fact that the Walkers were colored only made it worse. There was no practical way for them to fight a white man. The times were against them.

"We'll find these men," Thompson promised. "Would you be willing to testify in court? That's the only way we can bring charges."

"We surely will," Selma Walker affirmed. "The likes of them belongs in jail."

Walker looked concerned. "What about our wagon and team, Marshal? We ain't fixed to buy another."

"We'll do our best, Mr. Walker. You have my word on it."

"Lordy mercy," the woman said, turning to her husband. "How we gonna git home, Lute? I cain't walk no more."

"Don't you worry," Walker assured her. "Reverend Lacy find us a way home. We *be fine*."

Thompson rose. "Let me know where you'll be, Mr. Walker. Just in case we find your wagon."

"We come back here before we leave town. I appreciates all you done, Marshal."

"No thanks necessary, Mr. Walker. Glad to be of service."

Dennville showed them out of the office. He returned a moment later. "I was thinking maybe we should notify the sheriff. They were robbed outside the city limits."

"Good idea," Thompson said. "Send Miller over to the courthouse. Tell Sheriff Horner we're working on it."

"How do you want it handled?"

"I'd like you to take a tour of Guy Town. It's Saturday, and those cowboys probably headed for the nearest saloon. Or maybe one of the whorehouses. Try to get a line on them."

Dennville nodded. "Do you want them arrested?"

"No," Thompson said firmly. "Way it sounds, we've got ourselves a couple of hardcases. Come get me if you find them."

"You think they'll fight?"

"Lon, I never try to second-guess cowboys. They're apt to do anything."

"I'll go have a look around."

Dennville turned out of the doorway. Thompson lit a cheroot and leaned back in his chair. He puffed a wad of smoke, reflecting on the Walkers and their long hike into town. No one deserved to be treated that roughly.

He thought the men responsible belonged on a rock pile.

* * *

The whorehouse was located on Live Oak Street. A favorite with cowboys, it was three blocks west of the stockyards. The girls, priced to please, were two dollars a pop.

Directly across the street was a saloon. Dennville waited inside by a fly-blown window, watching the bordello. Tied to a sturdy rack outside the house were four saddle horses and a team hitched to a farm wagon. The team matched the description given to him by the Walkers.

Upstreet he saw Thompson round the corner with Gabe Ewing. He'd sent Ewing, one of the officers on the day shift, to notify the marshal. As they walked toward the saloon, he moved to the door and stepped outside. He jerked a thumb at the whorehouse as they halted on the curb.

"Our boys are over there," he said. "I went around to the back door and talked with Sallie Dagget, the madam. She identified them as Clint Buchanan and Ross Taylor."

Thompson stared across the street. "You'd think they would've ditched the wagon and team. Wonder what was in their minds?"

"Well, like you said, never try to second-guess cowboys. Maybe they figured black folks wouldn't report a robbery."

"How many men in the house?"

"Just four," Dennville replied. "When I talked with Sallie, they were all upstairs with girls. That was about thirty minutes ago."

"So they could be downstairs by now."

"I'd say that's a safe bet."

Thompson nodded to Ewing. "Gabe, I want you to cover the back door. We'll come through the front and try to take them without a fight. Watch yourself if they make a run for the alley."

"I'll be waitin' if they do, Marshal."

Ewing hurried toward the corner. Thompson gave him five minutes, then led Dennville across the street. They entered the front door into an alcove that opened onto the parlor. Two girls, dressed in filmy housecoats, were drinking with two men at a small bar along the opposite wall. An older woman, seated on a sofa by the window, looked around at Dennville. Her head bobbed imperceptibly at the two men.

"Everybody stand easy," Thompson said in a stern voice. "Clint Buchanan? Ross Taylor?"

"That's us," Buchanan said brusquely. "What about it?"

"You're under arrest for robbery of a wagon and team."

"You gotta be shittin' me. We took that wagon off ol' Tarbaby Walker. Wasn't nothin' but a joke."

"Your joke misfired," Thompson told him. "Armed robbery's a prison offense. Drop your gun belts."

"No goddamn way!" Buchanan snarled. "I ain't gonna be arrested over no nigger."

"Me neither," Taylor said, backing away. "You just leave us the hell be."

"Hold it," Thompson ordered. "Don't do anything stupid."

"We ain't ascared of you, Thompson."

"Drop your guns—*now.*"

Buchanan ducked low behind the bar. Taylor grabbed one of the girls, an arm around her neck, using her as a shield. Thompson drew his pistol, his attention fixed on the bar. Dennville advanced on the girl and Taylor, gun in hand.

Buchanan popped up from behind the bar. He eared the hammer on his Colt in a metallic whirr, and fired. The slug nicked the doorjamb in a spray of splinters and flecked paint. Thompson feathered the trigger and Buchanan's head exploded in a mist of brains and bone matter. He dropped as though struck by a thunderbolt.

The girl squirmed aside, kicking Taylor in the leg. He yelped, clawing at his holster, and brought his six-gun level. Dennville, pistol extended at arm's length, shot him in the chest. A bright dot stained his shirtfront and he stumbled backward, legs tangled. He pitched to the floor on his back.

Sallie Daggett fainted. She slumped sideways on the sofa, her mouth ajar. One of the girls froze, her eyes blank, and the other sank to her knees, head buried in her hands. The acrid stench of gunsmoke, permeated with the odor of blood and death, filled the room. No one moved.

Dennville slowly lowered his pistol. He stared at the dead men with a look of numbed shock. His face was knotted with revulsion.

"Jesus," he said quietly. "They knew they couldn't win. Why'd they fight?"

Thompson grunted. "Some men won't be convinced."

"Convinced of what?"

"Not to get killed."

TWENTY-THREE

On Monday morning, Thompson arrived at the office early. He was carrying copies of the *Statesman* and the *Republican*, which he hadn't taken time to read at breakfast. The shooting was headlined in each of the papers.

Dennville and the other officers greeted him as he moved through the squad room. The graveyard shift was being relieved by the day shift, and half the force was momentarily present. The men watched with guarded respect as he went through the door of his office.

Their attitude toward Dennville had altered as well. Until Saturday, the sergeant had never killed a man in the line of duty. Like most police officers, he'd rarely had occasion to pull a gun, relying instead on a nightstick. Yet he had acquitted himself well in the shootout, and the men treated him with newfound respect. He was something of a celebrity in the squad room.

Thompson took a seat behind his desk. After lighting a cheroot, he unfolded the *Statesman*, the date on the masthead December 6. He'd purposely avoided reading the article at breakfast, wary of further exciting Bobby. The youngster was already bursting with pride that his father had killed a man while wearing the badge of city marshal. The article was less sensational than Thompson had expected.

A straightforward accounting of the gunfight was first presented. The paper called it an unfortunate incident, brought on by two unruly cowboys already wanted for robbery. There was a brief report of how the cowboys had stolen a wagon and team at gunpoint from an unarmed colored man and his wife. Thompson and Dennville were commended for their courage under fire and their devotion to duty. The article went on with accolades for the police department.

Austin had never been more orderly. Since the election, our community had enjoyed one of the dullest months in police circles in a long time, all due to stricter law enforcement. Every law-abiding citizen should consider it a worthy tribute to City Marshal Ben Thompson and his officers.

Underscoring the point, the article then related statistics from the police blotter. For the past month, there had been no murders or assaults, and only one burglary within the city limits. The offenses were minor in nature, ranging from vagrancy and intoxication to keeping a disorderly house and disturbing the peace. All told, the number of arrests totaled only seventy-seven, a further reflection on the efficiency of the new city marshal. The article ended on a laudatory note.

Thompson next turned to the *Republican*. George Harris, the editor, was at some pains to stress Saturday's gunfight. His article dwelled on the virtual certainty of violence and bloodshed when a "shootist" occupied the office of city marshal. Yet, once he'd vented his spleen, he reluctantly admitted the overall drop in the crime rate. He attributed this to a general fear of Thompson, rather than efficient police work. Still, he was unable to distort what remained the central fact. Austin's streets were safer under the new marshal.

All in all, Thompson was satisfied with the coverage. He'd fully expected Harris to again raise the specter of a "shootist" wearing a badge. But when he put aside the *Republican*, he thought it had cost the editor dearly to recognize in print the reduction in crime. The article contained little in the way of praise, and that in itself was hardly surprising. He was nonetheless pleased with the token acknowledgment of a job well done. Hard facts were difficult to ignore.

Dennville rapped on the door. "You've got a visitor—Alexander Wooldridge."

"I'll be damned," Thompson said, somewhat startled. "Show him in, Lon."

A moment later Wooldridge entered the office. His normally stern expression seemed somehow tempered. "Good morning, Marshal," he said evenly. "I trust I'm not intruding."

"Not at all," Thompson replied, motioning him to a chair. "What can I do for you, Mr. Wooldridge?"

The banker got himself seated. "I've read those articles," he said, nodding at the newspapers on the desk. "I'm here to make a confession."

"Confession?"

"Thompson, I've always considered myself a

forthright man. I want you to know that I now believe
I misjudged you."

"Did you?" Thompson said, unwilling to let him off
the hook. "Are you talking about me, personally, or my
work as a peace officer?"

Wooldridge shifted uncomfortably in his chair. "I
opposed your election for what I considered sound reasons. I see now that my concerns were misplaced.
You've done an excellent job."

"I have to admit I'm curious, Mr. Wooldridge. Why
the sudden change of heart?"

"Simply put, I was wrong. Austin has benefited by
your election to office. I felt obligated to say as much."

"How about this?" Thompson said, tapping the *Republican* with his finger. "George Harris claims I'm still
a 'shootist' with a badge. Doesn't that bother you?"

"Not greatly," Wooldridge observed. "You once said
to me that you'd never shot a man who hadn't fired on
you first. The death of those cowboys was regrettable,
very sad indeed. But I now take your point."

"That's good to hear, and I appreciate the sentiment.
I know it wasn't easy for you to come here."

"I never allow pride to stand in the way of principle.
You deserved an apology."

"Let's just say all's well that ends well."

"One other thing." Wooldridge hesitated, his features
solemn. "I'm in your debt for that unsavory affair with
Amos Barber. Your discretion saved me a good deal of
embarrassment."

The name rang a bell. Thompson abruptly remembered the young bank teller who had been robbed and
beaten in a whorehouse. His brow arched in question.

"How'd you find out about Amos Barber?"

"There's little in Austin I don't know about."

"Did you fire him?"

"Nooo," Wooldridge said slowly. "But I daresay Mr. Barber won't be visiting Guy Town again. In a manner of speaking, he's seen the light."

"I'm glad to hear it," Thompson said. "He just got in with some bad company. No harm done."

"Yes, thanks to you, Marshal."

Wooldridge got to his feet. They exchanged a handshake and the banker walked toward the door. Thompson dropped back into his chair, still somewhat surprised by the unannounced visit. Dennville entered the office.

"Just call me nosy," he said. "What the deuce did he want?"

"Absolution."

"For what?"

"Deceit and deception."

"Who'd he deceive?"

Thompson smiled. "Himself."

There was another surprise awaiting Thompson that evening. Bobby met him at the door when he came home for supper. The boy was jumping with excitement.

"Uncle Billy's here!" he yelled. "He brought me some real Mexican spurs!"

Catherine and Billy were seated in the parlor. Thompson moved across the room as his brother rose from the sofa. Billy wrung his hand with a broad grin, inspecting the uniform. He cocked one eye in a wry look.

"I didn't hear any music," he said jocularly. "Where'd you leave your band?"

Thompson laughed. "You're looking at the latest thing in police uniforms. Designed it myself."

"You could've fooled me. You're tricked out fine enough to lead a parade."

"Pa! Pa!" Bobby demanded. "Lookit here!"

The youngster proudly displayed a pair of Mexican spurs. The shanks and heel bands were in bright silver, engraved with an intricate leafy pattern. The hand-tooled leather straps were decorated with silver conchas, and the rowels resembled spiked buzzsaws. Bobby's eyes danced with merriment.

"You ever see anything like that, Pa? Uncle Billy brought 'em all the way from Mexico."

"They're dandy, all right," Thompson said, properly impressed. "We'll have to get you some fancy boots."

"And a horse!" the boy whooped. "Will you get me a horse, too, Pa?"

"I'll have to think about that. A horse is a big responsibility."

"Awww, criminy, Pa! What's boots and spurs without a horse? Pleeeze!"

Catherine rose from her chair. "Let's leave your father and Uncle Billy to talk. You can help me with supper."

"C'mon, Ma." Bobby's face fell. "Lemme stay with them."

"You heard me, young man. No back talk."

"Yes 'um."

The boy put on a woebegone expression. He followed his mother through the dining room, still carrying the spurs. Billy watched after them a moment, slowly shaking his head. He grinned.

"Guess we know who rules the house. Katie don't take no sass."

"She's a caution," Thompson said, seating himself in an armchair. "Where'd you get the spurs?"

"Took 'em off a dead Mexican."

"You killed a Mexican?"

"Just joshing," Billy said with a lopsided smile. "'Course, I can't say the same for you, Mar-*shal*. Heard about them cowboys the minute I stepped off the train."

"Couple of damn fools," Thompson said gruffly. "I gave them every chance to surrender. They made a fight of it."

"Well, cowboys never had a lick of sense. Otherwise they wouldn't be cowboys."

"Those two sure fit the ticket."

Billy looked at him. "How's it feel to be a lawdog?"

"Have to say I like it," Thompson admitted. "Wearing a badge has its own rewards. I sleep good at night."

"You always was good at whatever you did. Even if it is a strange line of work for a Thompson."

"Are you still shamed to have a lawman in the family?"

"Hell, I don't tell nobody," Billy said with a glint of amusement in his eyes. "You think I want to get booted out of the sporting crowd?"

"Always got a snappy comeback," Thompson said amiably. "So what brings you to Austin?"

"Lost my taste for the riverboats. Damn things just go back and forth, back and forth."

"Don't try to kid an old kidder. You've got another dose of itchy feet, don't you? Where are you headed now?"

"Leadville," Billy said. "Figured I needed a change of scenery."

"From the Rio Grande to the Rockies? Yeah, I'd say that's a change."

"You know the gamblin' man's motto—follow the money."

Leadville was located deep in the Colorado Rockies. A strike of unsurpassed magnitude made it the silver capital of the world. The population now exceeded forty thousand and the monthly payroll of $800,000 was the largest of any mining camp in the West. There were reportedly two hundred gaming parlors, all operating seven days a week.

"Whyn't you come along?" Billy said. "Chuck that badge and get back to the sportin' life. We'll have ourselves a whale of a time."

"You're a bad influence," Thompson said with mock solemnity. "I've got a police force to run and a town to look after. Austin couldn't get along without me."

"God, listen to the man! I see you've learned to toot your own horn. Hope your hat still fits."

"Don't worry yourself on my account. You're the one who needs a keeper."

"Here we go again," Billy hooted. "I get along just fine, thank you all the same. Nobody's yet clipped my wings."

"Christmas isn't far off," Thompson said. "Why don't you stay over till after the New Year? You'll find plenty of poker games right here."

"Never give up, do you? I'll have to pass on the invite. Gotta keep movin'."

"You'll freeze your butt off in the Rockies. There's probably ten feet of snow."

"So there's nothin' to do but gamble till springtime. What more could a man ask?"

Catherine served a sumptuous pot roast for supper. Over a second serving, Billy entertained them with tales of the El Dorado called Leadville. He told them, swearing he had it on good authority, that $100,000,000 in ore was taken from the mines each year. Bobby listened, entranced and wide-eyed, all the way through dessert. He went to bed clutching his Mexican spurs.

Later, in their bedroom, Catherine asked Thompson if the tales were really true. He assured her that Billy was only exaggerating by five or ten million. Then, as he began undressing, he recounted the morning visit by Alexander Wooldridge. He considered it a good omen for the future.

"Way I see it," he concluded, "Wooldridge will support me in next year's election. I'm all but guaranteed a second term."

"Why of course you are!" she exclaimed. "With or without Wooldridge, you're certain to win. You're the best marshal Austin ever had. Everyone says so."

"Not everyone, but close enough. I might end up wearing a badge a good while."

"You'll wear it as long as you want it. I just know you will."

Thompson went to sleep a contented man. His one concern was his brother, who seemed infused with gypsy blood. Yet he understood the pull of wanderlust. The lure of the sporting life.

He sometimes dreamt of the old days.

TWENTY-FOUR

~~~III/III~~~

Austin basked beneath a mellow January sun. The sky was clear all the way to the horizon, just a hint of winter in the air. Friday morning crowds, encouraged by a break in the weather, filled the streets.

Thompson emerged from City Hall at noon. He stood for a moment, surveying the street, watching the press of shoppers move along the sidewalks. After several days of cold drizzle, the warm sun had brought people jamming into the business district. He idly wondered how long the good weather would last.

A week ago Austin had ushered in 1882. The crowds today somehow reminded him of the revelers on New Year's Eve. He'd kept the entire police force on duty that night, with most of them assigned to Guy Town. By midnight, the city jail had been overflowing with boisterous drunks and scrappy cowhands. He was relieved that New Year's came only once a year.

Never introspective, Thompson was nonetheless an astute observer. As a gambler, he'd read men's faces, their actions and mannerisms, at a card table. He was vaguely aware that he now employed somewhat the same technique on a crowded street, or whenever he inspected a Guy Town dive. Hardly two months as a peace officer, and yet he viewed the world from a different perspective. He looked at people with the eye of a lawman.

"Surveying your kingdom, Marshal?"

Thompson turned at the sound of the voice. He saw John Walton coming down the steps of City Hall. The attorney was carrying a leather briefcase, his features amused. He motioned out into the street.

"You look like a general inspecting his troops. What do you see out there?"

"Law-abiding citizens," Thompson said with an ironic smile. "Just the sort to put you lawyers out of business."

"Never happen," Walton retorted. "We've been defending the innocent since Roman times. Julius Caesar would've gotten off with a good lawyer."

"So who'd you get off today, counselor? I take it you've just come from court."

"Yes, another morning under the memorable jurisprudence of Judge Warren. He makes up the law as he goes along."

"Don't let him hear that," Thompson advised. "Was your client anyone I know?"

Walton looked rueful. "Your men caught him burgling the Beach Street Pharmacy. Ollie Crawford."

"Otherwise known as the dumbest thief in Travis County. He was rifling the cash drawer in the dark of night—with a lighted candle."

"I regret to say Ollie's no mental giant. Defending him requires an innovative legal argument."

"I'll bet it did," Thompson said. "What was your defense?"

"Mental impairment," Walton replied with a straight face. "I argued that a burglar who works with a candle falls under the legal definition of lunacy. I pled for a short, and hopefully instructive, stay in the mental asylum."

"How did that go over with the judge?"

"I'm delighted to say he bought it."

"You're joking," Thompson said dubiously. "He sentenced Crawford to the asylum?"

Walton beamed. "He said, and I quote: 'Anyone that stupid had to be crazy.' He gave him six months."

"I'll be damned. You're even cagier than I thought, John. Not to mention devious."

"Duplicity is the trademark of a criminal attorney. Although I don't get to practice my trade much these days. You've scared off all my clients."

"Just doing my job."

That statement hardly told the tale. After two months in office, Thompson had reduced the crime rate to an all-time low. The burglary by Ollie Crawford was the only serious offense in the last thirty days. Guy Town was relatively quiet, and hard cases routinely bypassed Austin. No one wanted to incur the displeasure of the city marshal.

"Tell you what," Walton said with some levity. "You're bad for business, but I'm the forgiving sort. What say I spring for lunch?"

"You're on," Thompson agreed. "How about Delmonico's?"

"Sounds good to me."

Thompson led the way up Mesquite Street. Delmonico's was something less than its name, a café of solid fare and low prices. But it was handy for the noonday meal, only a half block away, and frequented by the City Hall crowd. The Blue Plate Special was twenty cents.

Upstreet, Thompson pulled open the door. Then, as he was about to wave Walton through, he noticed a commotion from the direction of Congress Avenue. He looked closer and saw Gabe Ewing scattering people right and left as he sprinted along the sidewalk. The policeman skidded to a halt.

"Fire!" he bellowed. "Marshal, the capitol's on fire. Look there!"

Thompson turned toward Congress Avenue. State House Square opened off the near corner, and the capitol dome was visible in the distance. The buildings across the street blocked his view of the capitol itself; but he saw clouds of thick, black smoke spiraling skyward. He grabbed Ewing's arm.

"Did you sound the fire alarm?"

"They're on the way," Ewing said, bobbing his head. "Figured I oughta come get you."

"Head back to the office," Thompson ordered. "Tell Dennville to roust out the night shift and call in the patrol from Guy Town. I want every man on the force, pronto. Get moving!"

Ewing took off for City Hall. Thompson, with Walton at his side, ran toward Congress Avenue. When they rounded the corner, they saw the capitol sheathed in roiling flames. The fire appeared to have started on the ground floor, and then spread rapidly to the upper stories. Dense black smoke all but obscured the dome.

Thompson's first reaction was that it looked worse than it actually was. The state house was constructed of limestone blocks, and the building had always seemed impervious to fire. But as he looked closer, he saw that the inside of the capitol was a raging inferno. The interior walls were constructed of wood, most of them heavily paneled, and the rooms ignited like kindling. The three-story structure was quickly engulfed in flame.

From downtown, he heard the clang of a fire bell. He turned as the horse-drawn engine hurtled northward on Congress Avenue. A dozen or more firemen clung to the engine, their long coats flapping, hard-crowned helmets covering their heads. The driver brought the engine to a grinding halt, sawing at the reins, barely able to control the horses. The engine rocked to a stop at the corner of Mesquite and Congress Avenue. The capitol building was almost a hundred yards across the square.

Fully a thousand people lined the streets surrounding the state house grounds. The capitol had been evacuated, and buildings around the square quickly emptied as frightened shoppers hurried outside. Thompson was aware of more people crowding onto the square, drawn by the sight of the capitol wreathed in flames. Angry shouts attracted his attention and he spotted Dennville bulling a path through the throng. The onlookers gave way reluctantly, jostling and shoving, their eyes fixed on the fire. The sergeant finally broke clear, trailed by four policeman. He halted in front of Thompson.

"We're it for now," he said. "I sent somebody to fetch the night watch."

"Here's what we'll do," Thompson told him. "Post one man to patrol each side of the square. I want those people kept back from the fire."

"Four men aren't much for that job."

"They're all we've got. When the others show up, put them where they're needed most. You roam the square and jump on trouble spots."

Dennville gazed out at the crowds. "Some of those people won't want to move. They're here to see the fireworks."

"Use your nightsticks," Thompson commanded. "Bust their knees if they won't cooperate. Just keep them back on the sidewalk."

"Where will you be?"

"Over by the fire engine. I'll take care of the crowd there myself. Let's get moving."

Dennville rushed off with Ewing and the other officers. Thompson, still trailed by Walton, walked to the southwest corner of the square. The firemen were frantically attaching hoses to water hydrants on opposite sides of the street. Onlookers were ganged close around, watching the operation with ghoulish interest. Thompson waded into their ranks.

"Get back!" he shouted roughly. "Give these men room to work. Off the street!"

The crowd edged back onto the sidewalk. One man was slow to move, and Thompson took him by the collar. He lifted the man on tiptoe and danced him to the curb. The spectators broke out laughing as he dropped the man in the gutter.

"You folks stay clear!" he called out. "Let the firemen do their job."

The firemen began reeling off hoses from the engine. A man was stationed at each of the hydrants, waiting with a single-headed lug wrench. Within a matter of moments, the hoses were played out to their full length. The lines were still some fifty yards shy of the capitol building.

The fire chief rapped out an order. At each of the hydrants, the men cranked their wrenches, throwing open the valves. The hoses swelled, undulating with the rush of water, and the firemen wrestling the nozzles braced themselves. A jet of water burst from the hoses with a sharp *pop.*

The water arched in a rainbow under the noonday sun. The firemen planted their feet, raising the nozzles, trying to direct the stream onto the fire. But their hoses were stretched taut, and they were still fifty yards from the capitol building. The water pressure from the hydrants was inadequate for the distance.

The firemen struggled valiantly, muscling the hoses forward another foot or so. Yet the hydrant pressure was simply too low to hurl a forceful stream into the middle of the square. By the time the water reached the fire, it diminished into a weak spray, and turned to steam as it made contact with the flames. The firemen were reduced to little more than spectators.

Thompson, like the crowds lining the square, watched with a look of disbelief. For the first time, he noted a congregation of government officials gathered on the opposite corner. Among them were Governor Oran Roberts, Sheriff Frank Horner, several state legislators, and Mayor Wheeler. He saw Harry Burke, the fire chief, rushing toward them with an expression of impotent rage. He hurried across the street.

"I warned you!" Burke shouted, halting before the governor. "I told you we needed fire hydrants on the capitol grounds. Now you see what happens!"

Governor Roberts was a man of distinguished bearing. His features flushed at the verbal assault. "Talk to these gentlemen," he said, motioning to the gaggle of legislators. "I requested funding and they tabled the bill. They felt it was an unnecessary expenditure."

"Unnecessary!" Burke roared. "Look where your penny-pinching got us. We're gonna lose the capitol."

"Lower your voice," Governor Roberts said coldly. "The fault lies with the legislature, and I will so inform the press. I refuse to debate the matter on a street corner."

Thompson stepped forward. "Governor, there's plenty of time to fix the blame. We've got a bigger problem right now."

"Do we?" Roberts said, staring at him. "What might that be, Marshal?"

"We'd better start worrying about the businesses around the square. We're liable to lose half the town if that fire spreads."

A northwesterly breeze was scattering sparks and firebrands across the southern side of the square. The Governor was silent a moment, assessing the situation with newfound concern. He looked back at Thompson.

"You're absolutely right, Marshal. What do you suggest?"

"Let's get a bucket brigade formed," Thompson said without hesitation. "Start dousing the buildings on the south side of the square. Keep the fire engine where it is for now."

"Excellent idea," Roberts agreed, nodding to the officials gathered around. "Marshal Thompson is acting on my authority, gentlemen. Give him whatever assistance he needs."

Thompson began issuing orders. He told Burke to turn the fire hoses on the buildings at the lower end of the square. Then, after drafting Sheriff Horner and his deputies into service, he sent them off to organize a bucket brigade. He next signaled Dennville, who now had a full complement of police working the crowds. He instructed the sergeant to clear the street around Congress Avenue.

There was something in Thompson's voice that brooked no argument. The men hurried off to their assigned tasks like soldiers rushing into battle. A moment later the dome of the capitol buckled in a screeching, volcanic roar. The oval structure settled inward upon itself, and then collapsed, demolishing the third story. The debris rumbled downward, wiping out the second story, and crashed into the ground floor. Cinders and sparks leaped skyward.

A searing blast of heat shot out around the square. Then, in the next instant, the southern wall of the capitol toppled over in a thunderous firestorm of limestone blocks. Tongues of flame lapped at the rubble, and fiery timbers flashed a brilliant orange, consumed within the smoky pyre. There was one last flare, bright as the sun, then the ruins leveled in a glowing bed of coals. The breeze, stiffening to a wind, quickly fanned the embers.

An eerie hush fell over the square. The crowds jamming the streets stood like rows of sunlit sculpture, shocked beyond speech, staring at the rubble. Thompson's voice abruptly broke the silence, belting out orders in shouted commands. The police and the firemen, as though awakened from a trance, were galvanized to action. Dennville led the police in clearing Congress Avenue, and sheriff's deputies began forming bucket brigades with volunteers from the crowd. Thompson seemed everywhere at once.

Governor Roberts, looking on, nodded in approval.

He turned to Wheeler. "Mr. Mayor, I admire a man who knows how to take charge. I think Austin has found itself a marshal."

"No question about it," Wheeler said proudly. "Ben has a natural gift for leadership. He'll go far."

"I'll depend on you and Marshal Thompson when we start rebuilding the capitol. Once construction begins, the square will require constant policing."

"You can count on us, Governor. Whatever it takes, Ben will handle it."

"After today, I'm confident he will. Just look at how those men jump!"

Thompson barked out a command. The firemen directed their hoses onto the roofs of business concerns at the south end of the square. He then turned his attention to the bucket brigade.

Not a man among them doubted who was in charge.

TWENTY-FIVE

—————

The ruins of the capitol were being cleared by workmen. A crew of some fifty laborers loaded rubble onto wagons, which carted the debris to a site outside town. The cleanup operation was now into its fifth day.

Thompson stepped off the streetcar at Mesquite and Congress Avenue. A two-story frame structure occupied the southwest corner of the state house grounds. Hurriedly constructed, the building had been hammered together and whitewashed over the previous weekend. For the immediate future, it would serve as the capitol.

Pete O'Rourke, foreman of the work crew, stood at the southern end of the square. He motioned a wagon loaded with rubble onto the street, and started to turn away. Then, spotting Thompson, he walked forward with a broad smile. He knuckled the brim of his hat.

"Mornin' to you, Marshal," he said pleasantly. "Looks to be a fair day."

"That it does," Thompson replied. "How's it going, Pete?"

"I'd have to say we're makin' headway. 'Course, as you can see, it's a terrible mess. We'll be at it awhile."

"How long before you'll have it cleared?"

"Couple o' weeks or thereabouts," O'Rourke said, gesturing to the charred skeleton of the capitol. "We still hafta raze them walls and haul off all that gawd-damn limestone. It's a ball-buster, Marshal."

"You'll earn your pay," Thompson agreed. "I can't say I envy you the job."

"Well, somebody's gotta tear it down before they build it back. That's the way of things."

The governor had convened an emergency session of the legislature on Saturday, the day after the fire. The lawmakers met in the Knights of Pythias Building, and shortly before sundown they had put together a deal for a new capitol. By Monday, the governor had contracted with a syndicate of construction companies to build an even grander state house. The syndicate, in exchange for three million acres of state land, would construct an edifice of quarried granite. The capitol, like a mythical phoenix, would rise from the ashes.

"Imagine," O'Rourke said with wonder. "A year from now we'll have ourselves a brand new capitol. Granite, no less!"

"Pete, I just suspect it'll be a sight."

Thompson nodded, about to walk on, when he saw Governor Roberts emerge from the temporary state house. The governor was accompanied by Enoch Langley, the leading architect in Austin. They started toward the ruins of the capitol, and then Roberts caught sight of Thompson on the street corner. He turned with a friendly wave.

"Good morning, Marshal," he called out. "Always on the job, I see."

Thompson laughed. "Governor, you caught me playing hooky. I'm running late today."

"You don't fool anyone. I'll wager you were on the streets till the wee hours."

"Yes, sir, that's the safest bet in town."

"Keep up the good work, Marshal."

Roberts and the architect moved off across the square. Thompson nodded to O'Rourke and proceeded east on Mesquite, toward City Hall. The friendly exchange was yet another indication of how his stock had risen since the day of the fire. The governor had praised his actions in both the *Statesman* and the *Republican,* calling him "Austin's indispensable man." He secretly savored the label, though he tried to downplay it with others. There was talk that he had a promising future in politics.

A few minutes later he entered the squad room. The change of shifts had just taken place, and some of the day patrol were still collecting their gear. Last night, shortly after midnight, Thompson had led a raid on a parlor house, and he nodded to the men on the graveyard shift. Dennville, who looked fresh as a daisy, was seated at his desk. He got to his feet.

"Marshal," he said with a wry smile. "Those whores are set for court at ten o'clock. You want me to handle it?"

"Good idea, Sergeant," Thompson observed. "You're looking perky this morning. How the devil do you do it?"

"Lots of strong black coffee. Works everytime."

"I'll have to remember that."

"There's a telegram on your desk. The boy delivered it just after I came on duty."

"Thanks, Lon."

Thompson walked to his office. He hooked his cap on a coatrack and took a seat in the oxblood chair behind his desk. He tore open the telegram and glanced at the bottom of the form. The message was from Allan Pinkerton, head of the Pinkerton Detective Agency. He quickly scanned the contents.

Urgently request your assistance. Carl Wilson, fugitive on murder warrant Kansas City, believed hiding in San Antonio. Reliable reports indicate Wilson under protection of San Antonio authorities. Fugitive white male, age twenty-nine, dark hair, height five seven, weight one hundred forty. Offer one thousand dollars for apprehension. Please confirm acceptance of assignment by telegraph.

Thompson's immediate reaction was one of surprise. Then, unable to suppress a surge of pride, he felt highly flattered. The Pinkertons, headquartered in Chicago, were renowned manhunters, retained by government agencies and private corporations. Allan Pinkerton, founder of the agency, had devised the original "Rogues' Gallery," with detailed descriptions of criminals throughout America. Among their celebrated cases, the Pinkertons had been retained to apprehend such outlaws as Jesse James and Sam Bass. The agency routinely worked with enforcement officers across the country.

Thompson stuffed the telegram in his pocket. He moved through the squad room, letting himself out the door, and walked down the hall. Sueann Mabry looked up from her desk as he entered the waiting room of the mayor's office. He motioned her down, and without being announced, proceeded directly to the mayor's inner sanctum. Wheeler, who was poring over a stack of correspondence, glanced up with a curious expression. He put the letters aside.

"Good morning, Ben," he said. "I've been expecting you."

"Then you're a first-class mind reader. I only just decided to come talk with you."

"Something important, is it?"

"See for yourself."

Thompson handed him the telegram. Wheeler read it through, nodding slowly to himself. His mouth pursed in thought, and he looked up with a sober gaze. He returned the telegram to Thompson.

"I received one myself."

"From Allan Pinkerton?"

"None other."

Wheeler took a telegraph form from his desk. He passed it across to Thompson and sat back in his chair. His eyes narrowed as Thompson scanned the contents, then read it again. The message spoke for itself.

We are most impressed with law enforcement record of City Marshal Ben Thompson. Request you authorize his assistance in apprehension of fugitive last reported in San Antonio. Your cooperation in this matter highly appreciated.

"I'll be damned," Thompson said in a bemused voice. "Wonder how they found out about me, anyway? I've only been on the job a couple of months."

"How about that article in the *Police Gazette*?"

Wheeler asked. "Those two cowboys being killed attracted quite a bit of attention."

"It's not exactly the first time I made the *Police Gazette*."

"Yes, but you're a law officer now."

"Well, maybe that's the difference."

"I'm a little at a loss," Wheeler remarked. "How would Pinkerton know the San Antonio police are protecting this man Wilson? Where would he get that information?"

"No big secret there," Thompson said. "The city marshal and the sheriff are both crooked as a dog's hind leg. Have been for years."

"You know that for a personal fact?"

"Let's just say I know San Antonio. I spent some time there when I was a gambling man."

"All the same—" Wheeler hesitated, considering. "Why wouldn't Pinkerton contact the Rangers? They have statewide arrest powers."

"Think about it a minute," Thompson said. "The Rangers aren't much on cooperating with detective agencies. They got pretty well singed over that Sam Bass business. Pinkerton almost stole their thunder."

"You mean they were working at odds on the same case?"

"Yeah, it was nip and tuck for a while. The Texas & Pacific hired the Pinkertons to hunt down Bass, and they almost pulled it off. You might say the Rangers took offense at being bypassed."

"Even so," Wheeler wondered aloud. "Why doesn't Pinkerton send his own agents after this Wilson fellow?"

"I wouldn't hazard a guess," Thompson said. "Maybe

they don't feel welcome in Texas anymore. Fact is, he offered me the assignment."

"You couldn't accept it in your capacity as city marshal."

"Then I'll do it on my own. I'm due some time off anyhow."

"I don't understand," Wheeler said with a puzzled frown. "Why would you want to get involved with the Pinkertons? You've made your name as a lawman."

Thompson nodded. "Tom, I guess it's nothing but asinine pride. I'd like to catch myself a murderer."

"That's it, another feather in your cap?"

"I didn't say it made sense. I'm just keen for the idea."

"What about the police department? You have obligations here."

"Things are pretty quiet these days. Lon Dennville's a good man. He can handle it."

"How long will you be gone?"

"I figure a couple of days at the most. Either I'll catch the fellow or I won't."

"What if I ordered you not to go?"

"Are you?"

"No," Wheeler said with an air of resignation. "You never were one for taking orders. But I still think it's a foolish stunt. You've got nothing to gain."

Thompson smiled. "There's always the reward."

"You're not doing it for the money."

"I won't tell anybody if you don't."

"When do you plan to leave?"

"I'll catch the evening train."

"Well, for whatever it's worth, I wish you luck."

Not quite an hour later Thompson walked into the house on University Avenue. Cathcrine hurried into the parlor from the sewing room, clearly amazed to find him home in the middle of the morning. She knew from the look on his face that he was bursting with news. Her smile was quizzical.

"You look like you just swallowed the canary. What's going on?"

"I got a wire from the Pinkertons. Allan Pinkerton himself."

"The detective agency?" she said, now thoroughly bewildered. "Why would they contact you?"

"Pinkerton offered me an assignment," Thompson said. "He wants me to locate a man in San Antonio."

"I assume you're talking about a criminal."

"The wire said he's a fugitive."

"A fugitive from what?"

"Not too many details," Thompson said casually. "Way it sounds, he murdered somebody in Kansas City."

"Oh, is that all?" she said with a mocking laugh. "A fugitive murderer who's visiting San Antonio. And you're supposed to locate him."

"And take him into custody."

"Yes, of course, that too."

"Katie, don't make too much of it. Lawmen take people into custody all the time."

"Honestly!" she said in exasperation. "You are the marshal of Austin, Ben Thompson. What earthly business do you have running off to San Antonio?"

Thompson shrugged. "Tom Wheeler wanted to know the same thing. I told him it was dumb pride, and that's the best answer I've got. Pinkerton asked and I'm going."

Catherine sensed that it was something more than

pride. In two months, he had all but tamed Guy Town, and forcibly persuaded the sporting crowd to walk the straight and narrow. He was bored and looking for excitement, some greater challenge. A new world to conquer.

And yet . . .

The thought of San Antonio bothered her for another reason. Her voice took on a note of concern. "I want you to promise me something."

"I'll try," Thompson said. "What've you got in mind?"

"I want your promise you'll stay away from Jack Harris. Will you do that for me?"

"Katie, I'm going there to arrest a fugitive. I've got no business with Harris."

"I asked for your promise."

Thompson was reluctant to give his word. His dispute with Harris was a long-standing one. In late 1880, while visiting San Antonio, he'd spent an evening in Harris's establishment. A faro game turned ugly when he accused the dealer of cheating and Harris took it as a personal affront. For a moment, gunplay seemed inevitable.

City Marshal Phil Shardon hastily intervened. Thompson was wary of trouble with the law, and he agreed to leave the club. Still, he'd denounced Harris for operating crooked games, and their antagonism lingered on following the incident. Even now, over a year later, he was leery of making promises about Jack Harris. He was accountable for himself, but not his enemies.

"Tell you what," he said lightly, looking at Catherine. "You've got my word I won't go hunting trouble. How's that?"

"I suppose it's better than nothing. I just wish you weren't going to San Antonio."

"You worry too much about things. I'll be fine."

She had some dark premonition it wasn't true.

TWENTY-SIX

—⚬—

The train arrived late in San Antonio. Thompson stepped off the lead coach shortly before midnight, carrying a small valise. He was dressed in civilian clothes, with his badge tucked into his vest pocket. He took a hired carriage uptown.

The Menger Hotel was located on a broad plaza. The night clerk assigned him a room on the second floor, and he crossed the lobby to the stairs. By the time he got undressed, he was bushed, weary from a long day and a long train ride. Yet, after turning down the lamp, he paused a moment by the window. The Alamo was visible beneath the silvery light of a sky brilliant with stars.

Thompson, like all Texans, felt the emotional tug of the Alamo. There, in 1836, a small band of dauntless men had fallen before the might of Santa Anna's army. But for their sacrifice, all of Texas might yet be the northern province of Mexico. Staring out the window, he was reminded that honorable men often found immortality in an honorable death. He went to sleep thinking about the defenders of the Alamo. And honor.

The next morning Thompson crossed the plaza at about ten o'clock. He was rested from a night's sleep, and felt his vigor restored by a leisurely breakfast. The town was situated along the San Antonio River, and with the advent of the railroad, it had become a center of commerce and trade. The plaza was bustling with activity, but even so, the pace was somehow slower, almost indolent, compared to Austin. He often thought there was still a good bit of Old Mexico in the town by the river.

Across the way, he entered the city marshal's office. Another time, under different circumstances, he would have avoided paying a call on the marshal. All lawmen in San Antonio were obligated to Jack Harris, who controlled the vote in the sporting district. The bad blood that existed between him and Harris virtually assured an adversarial relationship with local officers. Yet he needed the marshal's cooperation, rather than interference and meddling. He cautioned himself to play the cards as dealt.

Phil Shardon was a fleshy man with a bristly mustache. His sullen manner indicated that he still remembered Thompson's last visit to town. "Heard you got elected marshal," he said. "Not too choosy up Austin way, are they?"

Thompson ignored the jibe. "I'm not here to swap insults. I have official business in San Antonio."

"What sort of business is that?"

"The Pinkertons retained me to apprehend a fugitive. He's wanted for murder."

"This fugitive got a name?"

"Carl Wilson."

Shardon blinked, a telltale giveaway. "Never heard of him," he said. "'Fraid I can't help you, Thompson."

"I don't want your help," Thompson informed him. "I want to give you some advice."

"Advice about what?"

"Take care that Wilson's not warned I'm in town. I'd be sorely troubled to hear he'd skipped out."

"Told you I don't know him," Shardon said in a surly tone. "You tryin' to call me a liar?"

Thompson stared at him. "I'm telling you to sit on your thumb till I have Wilson in custody. Otherwise you'll answer to me."

"Your badge don't mean shit here."

"I'm not talking about the law."

"That sounds like a threat."

"It is."

Shardon started out of his chair. Then, looking closer, he saw something in Thompson's eyes that gave him pause. He sat back.

"Do whatever you gotta do and get the hell out of my town. I don't take kindly to threats."

"Just remember what I said about Wilson. No tipoffs."

"I heard you the first time."

"Thanks for your cooperation, Marshal."

Thompson walked out of the office. He preferred persuasion to threats, but there'd been no choice. On the street, he told himself that the price of Shardon's silence had been fear. He knew he'd won when the lawman's look betrayed a loss of nerve. Satisfied, he turned toward the sporting district.

The Vaudeville Theater & Gaming Parlor was on the corner of Commerce and Soledad. Jack Harris was the proprietor, but he rarely put in an appearance before noontime. Thompson went there instead looking for Will Simms, an old friend who owed him a favor. Some years ago he'd hired Simms as a dealer at the Iron Front and taught him the trade. Simms later moved to San Antonio and caught on as house manager at the Vaudeville Theater. Their friendship had survived the altercation with Harris.

Simms, like all house managers, was responsible for getting the club into operation by late morning. When Thompson came in, he was checking liquor stock with one of the bartenders. He happened to glance in the backbar mirror, and his face suddenly went chalky. He dropped his inventory pad on the bar and hurried across the room. His eyes were round as marbles.

"Ben!" he said in a shaky voice. "What the hell are you doing here?"

"I'm here to see you," Thompson replied. "Something wrong with that?"

"Damn right there is! I thought you would've heard by now. Jack posted you out of this place."

"You mean Harris won't allow me in the club?"

"It's worse than that," Simms said. "He swore he'd shoot you if you ever came in here again. He keeps a shotgun behind the bar."

Thompson's eyes went hard. "Nobody tells me how to come and go. That includes Jack Harris."

"For old time's sake, I'm asking you to take your trade elsewhere. I don't want to see either of you shot."

"I'll tend to Harris later. All I want now is some information."

"What sort of information?"

"I'm tracking a man wanted for murder. His name is Carl Wilson."

Simms looked blank. "Doesn't ring any bells."

"Maybe he's using an alias," Thompson said. "He's about your height, muscular build, dark hair, late twenties. Someone new to town."

"Well, I'm not—"

"Someone eager to buy drinks for Phil Shardon."

A flicker of recognition passed over Simms's features. Then just as quickly, it was replaced by a guarded look. "I don't want any trouble with the law, Ben. Don't put me on the spot."

"Shardon won't bother you," Thompson said with conviction. "I came to an understanding with him not ten minutes ago. He took himself out of the game."

"You're sure about that?"

"It's the straight goods, Will."

"Charlie White," Simms said. "That's the name your man's using. He hit town sometime last week. Likes the dice table."

"Any idea where he's staying?"

"A dump just down the street. The Commerce Hotel."

"I owe you one, Will."

"Ben."

"Yeah?"

"Don't come back here again and we'll be square. Okay?"

"I'll think about it."

"I'd sooner have your word."

"See you around, Will."

"Sweet Jesus."

* * *

The Commerce Hotel was halfway down the block. The lobby was spartan—creaky wood floors and one tattered sofa placed before the front window. Thompson closed the door behind him and crossed to the registration desk. He nodded to the clerk.

"I'm looking for a friend of mine. I believe he's staying with you."

"Yes, sir, and the name?"

"Charles White."

"You're in luck," the clerk said, glancing past him. "There's Mr. White now."

Thompson turned from the desk. He saw a man in a rumpled suit descend the stairs and move toward the door. The description was a match for the one supplied by the Pinkertons, but he wanted to be certain. He quickly crossed the lobby.

"Hello, Carl."

The man broke stride. His shoulders stiffened and he looked around. "You talking to me?"

"Police officer." Thompson flashed his badge with his left hand. "I have an outstanding warrant on you, Mr. Wilson. You're under arrest."

"There's been some sort of mistake. My name's White. Charles White."

"Save it for the judge, Carl. Put your hands behind your head."

"I'm telling you—"

Wilson, like a magician, tried for misdirection. He broke off in midsentence and his hand snaked inside his coat. Thompson was a beat faster, popping the Colt from his shoulder holster. He thumbed the hammer.

"Don't get yourself killed, Carl. Bring that gun out real slow—and drop it."

A frozen moment slipped past as Wilson debated his chances. Then, careful of any sudden movement, he eased a stubby bulldog revolver from his waistband. He dropped it on the floor.

"Turn around," Thompson ordered. "Hands behind your head."

"How'd you find me?"

"A tip from the Pinkertons."

"Dirty bastards!"

"Walk ahead of me, Carl. No monkey business."

Thompson marched him uptown. On the plaza, bypassers hurriedly moved aside as they turned into the marshal's office. Shardon was seated behind his desk, his expression glum. He avoided Wilson's eyes.

"Got a prisoner for you," Thompson said. "Lock him up nice and tight till the extradition hearing. He's headed back to Kansas."

"You don't have to tell me my business."

"I'm wiring the Pinkertons he's now in your custody. Take care he doesn't escape."

"What the hell's that mean?" Shardon demanded. "I've never yet lost a prisoner."

"A word to the wise," Thompson said flatly. "You turn him loose and I'll come looking for you. Got it?"

"Don't try to bullyrag me, Thompson. I'm tired of your goddamn threats!"

"Think of it as a prophecy."

"You playing God now?"

"No, just the messenger."

Thompson walked out of the office. He crossed the plaza to his hotel, where he borrowed pen and paper from the desk clerk. After composing a wire to Allan Pinkerton, he tipped a bellman to take it to the telegraph operator at the depot. He thought the wise thing would be to send it himself, and catch the next train out of town. Instead, he went up to his room.

The Alamo was awash in sunlight. He stood at the window, reflecting again on honor and honorable men. The smart move, he told himself, would be to forget Jack Harris, ignore the insult. But then, almost certainly, the word would spread that he'd tucked tail and run, lost his nerve. Honor dictated that he at least make an appearance at the Vaudeville Theater. A couple of drinks, no more, then leave. A quick in and out.

Just long enough to thumb his nose at Harris.

The Vaudeville Theater & Gaming Parlor was ablaze with light. A crescent-shaped bar occupied the center of the main room, with gaming tables along the walls. The theater was at the rear, through an arched doorway, footlights spilling out over the stage. The first show of the evening opened with a team of acrobats.

There were two doors into the establishment. One was just off the corner of Commerce, and the other off the corner of Soledad. Thompson walked through the Commerce Street door shortly after seven o'clock. He'd waited until evening, when the place was packed, to make his appearance. He moved directly to the bar.

A bartender nodded a greeting. "What's your pleasure?"

"Whiskey," Thompson said, glancing at the gaming tables. "Jack Harris around?"

"Haven't seen him tonight."

"Doesn't he usually show up before now?"

"Ask Mr. Simms. He'll know."

Will Simms rushed forward from the entrance to the theater. He appeared agitated, his features flushed. "Ben, for chrissake! I thought you'd left town."

"Not yet," Thompson said. "Where's Harris?"

"I talked him into staying home till later. Word's out you turned that Wilson fellow over to the marshal. I figured you would've caught a train by now."

"Will, here's the way it works. I'll have a drink and wait for Harris to show. He has to understand I won't be barred from a public place. His or anyone else's."

"You're asking for trouble," Simms said earnestly. "The minute he walks in here and sees you, he'll start a fight. You've got to believe me."

"I'm not looking for a fight," Thompson assured him. "I just won't be barred by the likes of Jack Harris."

"Listen, let me try to smooth things over. You go wait outside and I'll collar Jack the second he walks in. Maybe we can patch things up some way or another."

"You think there's any chance he'll listen to reason?"

"Hell, Ben, it's worth a try. Just give me a little time."

Thompson was silent a moment. "All right," he finally said. "We'll play it your way. But I won't wait all night."

Simms walked him to the Commerce Street door. "I'll come get you as quick as I can. Jack ought to be here any minute."

"Tell him what I said, Will. I won't be barred."

"I'll do my damnedest."

Thompson went out the door. Simms walked to the opposite door, moving onto the sidewalk. He hoped to intercept Harris, who lived west of the club and usually came to work by way of Soledad Street. He kept darting glances back through the barroom to the door on Commerce. He wasn't sure how long Thompson would wait.

Outside, Thompson tossed the stub of a cheroot into the gutter. He patted his pockets, surprised to find he was out of smokes, and turned downstreet. A few doors down, he entered a cigar store, which stayed open during the evening hours. He bought a half-dozen cheroots, a brand imported from Mexico, and stuffed all but one into the inside pocket of his suit jacket. He lit up as he went through the door.

On the street again, he walked back toward the vaudeville house. As he approached, he noted a crush of men shouldering their way out the door onto Commerce. Their features were apprehensive, oddly alarmed, and he heard one of them say, "Harris has got a gun." He dropped the cheroot, blocked a moment by men rushing past, and then hurried forward. The door was open and he saw most of the crowd in the barroom scattering for cover. Jack Harris rounded the far end of the bar with a double-barreled shotgun.

Simms tried to stop him. "Jack, I'm begging you," he pleaded. "We can settle it if you'll just talk to Ben. Don't do this!"

"Out of my way," Harris shouted in a rough voice. "I'm through talking with that son-of-a-bitch. He wants a fight, he'll get it."

"I'm telling you he doesn't want a fight."

"Then he should've stayed out of my place!"

Thompson stepped into the doorway, his pistol drawn. "Ditch the shotgun, Harris. I'm not looking for trouble."

"You've found it!" Harris yelled, his features contorted. "Nobody calls me a sharper."

"Then you shouldn't run crooked games."

"Goddamn you to hell!"

Harris brushed Simms aside. He raised the shotgun, earing back both hammers, and brought it to his shoulder. Thompson leveled his Colt, staring over the sights, and fired. Harris staggered, a starburst of blood dotting his shirtfront, and tried to right the scattergun. His eyes were crazed.

Thompson fired two shots in quick succession. The slugs struck Harris just over the sternum, not a handspan apart. He reeled sideways in a nerveless dance, dropping the shotgun, and slammed into the bar. His legs gave way and he collapsed, overturning a spittoon. His foot drummed the floor in an afterspasm of death.

A sudden pall of silence fell over the room. The crowd waited in a stilled tableau, their eyes locked on Thompson. He moved just inside the doorway, placing his back to the wall. His gaze swept the startled faces, the Colt at his side. He looked at Simms.

"Will, go get the sheriff. Tell him I won't surrender to Shardon."

"I got it," Simms said in a rattled voice. "You'll surrender to him but not the marshal."

"Tell him to come right along."

"I'll tell him, Ben."

Simms took off running for the plaza.

TWENTY-SEVEN

The courtroom was mobbed. Friends of the deceased, most of them members of the sporting crowd, turned out in force. They were in an ugly mood, and extra sheriff's deputies were stationed by the doors. The atmosphere was electric with tension.

The benches were jammed as well by the general public. The sensational nature of the killing drew people who had never before entered a courtroom. They were there for a look at the most famous shootist in the state of Texas. The fact that he was now a lawman merely whetted their curiosity.

Three days ago, on Friday afternoon, a coroner's jury had been impaneled. Thompson, who was being held in the county jail, had testified in his own behalf. He was represented by John Walton, who had been summoned from Austin the night of the shooting. The coroner's jury had ruled death by homicide in the demise of Jack Harris.

By Monday morning, the newspapers were demanding a speedy trial. For some years, Harris had been a power in local politics, routinely delivering the vote of the sporting crowd in any election. He was a popular figure as well, operating a vaudeville house that was all but an institution in San Antonio. The newspapers urged the swift and certain conviction of his killer.

Shortly before ten o'clock, Thompson entered the courtroom from a door behind the jury box. He was escorted by Sheriff Dave McCall, and his appearance brought a restive murmur from the crowd. A weekend in jail had left his suit in need of pressing, but he was freshly shaved, his eyes alert and confident. He joined Walton at the defense table.

"Good morning, Ben," Walton said. "Are they treating you all right?"

"Well enough," Thompson replied as the sheriff walked off. "I wouldn't recommend the accommodations."

"No guarantees, but I think you've spent your last night in jail. Our case has improved over the weekend."

"What happened?"

"I had a long talk with Will Simms last night. He's come around to our way of thinking."

On Friday, at the coroner's inquest, Simms had been the state's chief witness. He testified that Thompson had provoked the shooting, ignoring repeated warnings to stay away from the vaudeville house. Under cross-examination, he proved to be a hostile witness, evasive in his answers as to details about the actual gunfight. His testimony virtually assured a ruling of homicide.

"That's a switch," Thompson said. "What changed his mind?"

Walton chuckled. "Well, first, I appealed to friendship. You might say that got me nowhere fast. He really does blame you for Harris's death."

"So what brought him around?"

"I told him there was no guarantee you would be convicted. Then, not all that subtly, I suggested he didn't want you as an enemy."

Thompson smiled. "You're a shifty one, John. Doesn't the law frown on threatening witnesses?"

"Who threatened anyone?" Walton said wryly. "I prefer to think of it as the carrot and the stick. Simms opted for the carrot."

"Let's hope he's got the gumption for it. Lots of people in this town would like to see my neck stretched. They'll put the heat on him to stick with his story."

"I suspect he fears you more than he does them. That's always an inducement to tell the truth."

"We'll find out," Thompson allowed. "Did you send my wire to Catherine?"

"Just as you instructed." Walton took a telegram from his briefcase. "Hers came in early this morning."

Sheriff McCall refused to permit delivery of telegrams to the jail. Thompson's only means of communication with Catherine was through his attorney. Over the last three days they had exchanged several messages. He quickly scanned today's reply.

My Dearest, trust in God during your ordeal. Bobby and I are with you in spirit, and we know you will return home safely. We await your good news.

Your loving wife,
Catherine

Thompson folded the telegram. As he tucked it into his pocket, he told himself God could always use a little help. He trusted Walton's veiled threat to Will Simms far more than he did divine intervention. There was something to be said for the persuasive effects of fear.

"All rise!"

The bailiff's command brought the spectators to their feet. Judge George Noonan, who presided over the District court, entered from his chambers at the rear of the room. He mounted the bench, seated himself in a high-backed chair, and took out his spectacles. He nodded to the bailiff.

"This court is now in session," the bailiff dutifully responded. "The docket concerns the matter of the State versus Benjamin F. Thompson. Be seated!"

The crowd resumed their seats. Judge Noonan adjusted his spectacles, waiting for everyone to get settled. He was an imposing man, with salt-and-pepper hair and sharp features. His eyes were magnified behind the glasses, and his look left no doubt as to who was in charge. He addressed the courtroom in an orotund voice.

"This is a preliminary hearing to determine if Mr. Thompson will be bound over for trial. Are you gentlemen ready to proceed?"

Fred Cocke, the prosecutor for Bexar County, got to his feet. "The State is prepared, Your Honor."

"The defense is prepared," Walton echoed. "And may I say it's an honor to be in your courtroom, Judge Noonan."

"Save it for your closing argument, counselor. Call your first witness, Mr. Cocke."

Sheriff McCall was the lead witness. Under Cocke's

guidance, he testified that he'd arrived at the vaudeville house some twenty minutes after the shooting. He went on to relate that Jack Harris—"dead as a doornail"— was found on the floor beside the bar. Thompson, he noted, was still on the premises and readily admitted to the killing. He concluded by stating he had taken Thompson into custody.

Walton rose for cross-examination. "Sheriff McCall, did Mr. Thompson attempt to flee the scene—at any time?"

"No, he was there when I got there."

"As a matter of fact, he sent someone to fetch you. Isn't that correct?"

"That's right."

"And he voluntarily surrendered his gun to you— didn't he?"

"Yes, he did."

"And he voluntarily surrendered *himself* to you didn't he?"

McCall shrugged. "Yeah, I suppose he did."

"No further questions, Your Honor."

Thompson watched the sheriff walk to the other side of the room. His attention was diverted when he saw City Marshal Phil Shardon seated in the front row of spectators. He idly wondered if extradition papers had been filed on Carl Wilson, alias Charles White. But then, on second thought, he decided that was a matter for the Pinkertons. He had problems of his own.

Doctor Anton Herff, the county coroner, was called to the stand. Upon arriving at the vaudeville house, he testified, he had examined the deceased. The cause of death was gunshot wounds, one high on the breastbone and two through the heart. He offered the opinion that death was almost instantaneous and remarked again on the massive damage to the heart. He seemed impressed with Thompson's accuracy.

Walton kept his chair. "We have no questions of this witness, Your Honor."

Leo Sneed, one of the bartenders at the vaudeville house, next took the oath. His hair was freshly greased and parted in the middle, and his handlebar mustache appeared coated with wax. Prosecutor Cocke approached the stand.

"You were tending bar January thirteenth, the night of the shooting?"

"Yessir."

"You served the defendant a drink, isn't that so?"

"Yessir, I surely did."

"In the course of which," Cocke elaborated, "you overheard a conversation between the defendant and one Will Simms, an employee of the establishment. Would you kindly relate the gist of that conversation for the court?"

Sneed cleared his throat. "Mr. Simms all but begged Thompson to leave the place. Told him just being there was bound to cause trouble."

"What was Thompson's response?"

"Well, he got real hot under the collar. Said he wouldn't be banned by anybody—especially Mr. Harris."

"What happened then?"

"Thompson went out and directly Mr. Harris come in the other door. Mr. Simms told him Thompson was outside and Mr. Harris looked scared for his life. He grabbed a shotgun from behind the bar."

Cocke led him through the sequence of events. Sneed testified that Thompson burst into the barroom without warning and shot Harris dead. He stated that he had no recollection of an exchange of words before Thompson opened fire. He went on to say that Harris never fired the shotgun. Cocke walked away with a smug look.

"I have nothing more, Your Honor."

"Mr. Sneed," Walton said, moving to the stand. "Where were you when the shooting started? When the shots were actually fired?"

"Well—"

"Isn't it true that you ducked beneath the bar?"

"Yeah, I reckon I did."

"And you didn't see who shot whom or when, did you?"

"No, not just exactly."

"Nor did you hear the warning issued by Mr. Thompson to Mr. Harris. You were too frightened to hear anything—weren't you?"

Sneed swallowed hard. "I was mighty scared, that's a fact."

"Thank you for your candor, Mr. Sneed."

The state's final witness was Will Simms. After swearing the oath, he seated himself, clearly uncomfortable. Cocke prompted him through a recitation of events immediately prior to the shooting. Then, pausing for dramatic effect, Cocke shook his finger in the air.

"You *pleaded* with the defendant to leave in peace. Not to provoke an altercation. Correct?"

"Yes."

"You warned the deceased that Thompson would not accept being barred from the establishment. That he would force the issue. Isn't that so?"

"I tried my best."

"And yet the defendant stormed back into the barroom—acting in cold blood!—and shot Jack Harris dead. Isn't that what happened?"

"No."

"What?" Cocke thought he'd heard wrong. "What did you say?"

Simms fidgeted nervously. He was all too aware of the puzzled stares directed his way from the sporting crowd. "I said 'no.' "

"No? No what?"

"Thompson warned Harris to drop the shotgun. He told him plain as anything he didn't want a fight."

"Well, Mr. Simms, that's patently ridiculous. You testified in the coroner's inquest that no such thing happened."

"I didn't testify one way or the other. I just didn't say it."

"And now—suddenly!—you're changing your story?"

"I'm not changing anything," Simms said, squirming in his chair. "I'm telling you the way it was."

"Your Honor!" Cocke exploded, turning to the bench. "This man has impeached *himself.* He's lying!"

Judge Noonan frowned querulously. "He's your witness, Mr. Cocke."

"I demand that he be charged with perjury. I demand it!"

"Another day, another time," Judge Noonan informed him. "Get on with your questions."

Cocke stalked back to the prosecution table. "I'm through with this—this perjurer."

"I have a couple of questions," Walton said, crossing to the witness stand. "Mr. Simms, did Jack Harris raise his shotgun and point it with deadly intent at Ben Thompson?"

"I'm sorry to say he did," Simms admitted. "He swore he'd kill Ben if he ever set foot in the place again."

"And did Mr. Thompson attempt to avoid a fight? Did he try to talk Harris out of it—before he fired?"

"Yes, he did."

"So to put a point on it, Mr. Thompson acted in defense of his own life. Is that correct?"

"I wish he'd never come back to the club. But, yeah, that's the way it worked out."

Fred Cocke, his eyes rimmed with disgust, rested the case for the prosecution. Under the law, there was no obligation for Thompson to testify in his own defense. Walton nonetheless called him to the stand. He went straight to the point.

"Mr. Thompson, did you seek an altercation with Jack Harris?"

"No, I did not."

"Was it your intent to provoke him when you went to the vaudeville house on the night of January thirteenth?"

"I went there because no man can be barred from a public place. I wasn't looking for trouble."

"And you didn't draw your gun until he started toward the door with a shotgun. Isn't that true?"

"That's the whole truth of it."

"And as a last resort—when all else failed—you fired in protection of your own life . . . didn't you?"

Thompson nodded. "I regret there was no other way."

"Thank you." Walton turned from the stand. "Your witness, Mr. Cocke."

Cocke snorted derisively. "I have no questions for your mankiller."

"The defense rests, Your Honor."

Judge Noonan ordered closing arguments. Cocke railed on, his voice an octave too high, damning perjurers and holier-than-thou mankillers, and slick defense lawyers. Walton reviewed the case in a calm, dispassionate manner, and asked that the facts be allowed to speak for themselves. After he finished, the judge announced that it would serve no purpose to delay his decision. He ruled it a case of justifiable homicide.

The courtroom went from shocked silence to a drumming uproar. Harsh mutters of protest turned to angry catcalls and shouts of outrage. Several members of the sporting crowd surged toward the balustrade separating the spectator section from the front of the courtroom. Deputies waded into the throng, and Sheriff McCall moved to block the center aisle. The situation seemed on the verge of riot.

Judge Noonan rose from his chair. He furiously wielded his gavel, every whack resounding with the report of a cannon. He finally hammered the jostling crowd into silence. His eyes were fierce.

"You men stand back!" he thundered. "I will not tolerate disruption in my courtroom. Anyone who opens his mouth will be held in contempt and thrown in jail. Clear that aisle!"

The men mobbed around the balustrade slowly backed off. Deputies bulled a path through the crowd, and formed a tight wedge blocking the center aisle. Sheriff McCall turned and walked quickly to the defense table. Will Simms, terrified for his own life, vaulted the railing and followed along. The lawman glowered at Thompson.

"You'd best clear out," he said. "That bunch would as soon lynch you as not. I won't have it in my town."

Thompson nodded. "What time's the next train?"

"Half past two. I'll put you on it myself."

"I want my pistol back."

"You'll have your damned gun." McCall jerked a

thumb at Simms. "Take your weasel with you. His life's not worth a plugged nickel around here."

"How about it, Will?" Thompson asked. "Want to come along?"

Simms grinned weakly. "Austin sounds mighty good to me."

Sheriff McCall led them to the door at the back of the courtroom. Walton and Simms brought up the rear, and a fresh outburst of angered curses followed them through the door. Thompson appeared stoic, but he was inwardly saddened, at odds with himself. A thought persisted in some dark corner of his mind.

He'd won the battle but lost the war.

TWENTY-EIGHT

The train chuffed to a halt shortly after ten o'clock. Austin lay cloaked in mealy darkness, the depot lights like a beacon in the night. A bitter wind whipped down out of the northwest.

Thompson stepped off the observation deck of the rear passenger coach. Walton and Simms followed him across the platform and through the deserted stationhouse. Outside, on Cypress Street, one carriage for hire waited at curbside. After Thompson gave the driver instructions, they climbed aboard. The carriage rolled off toward the center of town.

The men sat wrapped in brittle silence. All the way from San Antonio, Thompson had been moody and withdrawn, his thoughts turned inward. He stared out of the carriage now, his features dappled in the glow of streetlights along Congress Avenue. He seemed singularly downcast for a man who had escaped from the shadow of the gallows. He was clearly brooding on something too personal for words.

Uptown, the carriage stopped at the Austin Hotel. Simms, who had fled San Antonio with the clothes on his back, opened the door. His mood was no less bleak than Thompson's, for he'd left behind a good job and a future full of promise. His face was squinched and tight as he stepped down from the carriage. He looked back at Thompson.

"Hope you've got a job for me at the Iron Front. I'd hate to wind up at some joint in Guy Town."

"Don't concern yourself," Thompson assured him. "You put your neck on the line, and I'm not one to forget a friend. We'll work something out."

"I'll see you tomorrow, then?"

"You can bank on it, Will."

The carriage pulled away from the curb. Thompson was silent a moment, staring out the window as the driver circled around to Congress Avenue. Then, his mood seemingly broken, he turned to Walton. His mouth quirked in a faint smile.

"John, you saved my bacon," he said. "I want you to know I'm grateful. Damned grateful."

Walton waved it off. "What the hell, that's what lawyers are for. I was just doing my job."

"No, it was more than that. If you hadn't turned Simms around, I would've been shaking hands with the Devil. They had me slated for the hangman."

"All's well that ends well. I'm glad things went our way."

Thompson merely nodded. "You send me a stiff bill for services rendered. You earned it."

"Any lawyer appreciates a generous client."

"Just put me at the head of your list."

Thompson dropped him off at his home on Chestnut Street. A few minutes later the carriage drew to a halt outside the house on Elm. After paying the driver, Thompson started up the walkway to the porch. He'd wired Catherine before departing San Antonio, and he wasn't surprised by the light burning in the parlor window. He knew she would be waiting.

Catherine met him at the door. "Oh God, Ben!" she cried, slipping into his embrace. "Don't you ever go away again!"

"I think I'm home to stay awhile."

"Are you all right? I practically fainted when I got your telegram. They won't bring any more charges?"

"No, it's over," Thompson said. "I'm a free man."

"I prayed and prayed. You can't imagine how hard I prayed."

"Somebody up there must have heard you. Where's Bobby?"

"I sent him to bed." She waited while he hooked his coat and hat on the halltree. "He tried to stay awake, but he kept dozing off. He's wild to see you."

"Tomorrow's time enough."

Something in his voice seemed to her strangely subdued. She followed him into the parlor, seating herself on the sofa as he slumped into his chair. In the light of the lamp, she saw that his features were gaunt, oddly morose. He appeared anything but a man who had been exonerated just that day of murder. She searched his face with a quizzical expression.

"What's wrong?" she said softly. "You look so—I don't know—so down in the dumps. Shouldn't we be celebrating?"

"There's nothing to celebrate." Thompson scrubbed

his whiskery jawline. "I went to San Antonio and damn near got myself hanged. I'm not exactly proud of it."

"Yes, but you were freed. You weren't at fault."

"Katie, don't you see, I killed a man. A sworn law officer and I killed a man in a personal fight. I'm just not cut out to wear a badge."

"That's not true," she said quickly. "You've done a marvelous job. Everyone says so."

"No," Thompson said in a weary voice. "I shouldn't have run for marshal. It was the biggest mistake of my life."

"Why on earth would you think that?"

"I haven't thought about anything else. All the way back from San Antonio it kept eating at me. I am who I am, Katie. Nothing's going to change."

"You're talking about yourself . . . aren't you?"

"On the train tonight I figured it out. A lawman has to put personal things aside. But I've never been able to overlook an insult. You can't teach an old dog new tricks."

She sensed he felt he'd dishonored the badge, his oath of office. "You've made up your mind, haven't you?"

"Yeah, I have," Thompson said flatly. "What happened with Jack Harris just proved it could happen again. I'm going to resign as marshal."

She leaned forward, touched his arm. "Why not sleep on it? You might feel different in the morning."

"Tomorrow or the next day wouldn't matter. The fact is, I wasn't meant to be a lawman. I know that now."

She desperately wanted to believe he was wrong. But in her heart she knew he'd looked deep within himself and found the truth. The only truth.

His personal code of honor was more important than the badge.

Dear Mr. Mayor,
    I hereby tender my resignation as marshal of the City of Austin. Consider the resignation effective immediately, or as soon as a successor can be appointed. I endorse Sergeant Lon Dennville most highly for the position of city marshal. He is an honorable man and a distinguished peace officer.

                    Your obedient servant,
                    Ben Thompson

Thompson delivered his resignation to the mayor early the next morning. Tom Wheeler was at first stunned, and then argued strenuously that the resignation was not acceptable. He finally persuaded Thompson to hold off until the city council be convened in emergency session. The aldermen began trooping into City Hall late that morning.

Lon Dennville was flabbergasted. Like everyone else in Austin, he'd read the newspaper reports of Thompson's problems in San Antonio. He knew something was seriously wrong when Thompson walked into the squad room dressed in civilian clothes. Yet he was shocked to learn that only moments before Thompson had tendered his resignation. He was even more amazed that Thompson had recommended him for the job.

"I don't want it," Dennville protested. "I couldn't' fill your shoes and we both know it. The whole thing's crazy."

"You underestimate yourself," Thompson informed him. "You've played second fiddle long enough, and now's the time to move up. You'll make a fine marshal."

"Dammit, Ben, you're the one that was elected. Nobody wants me in the job."

"Take the appointment and make the most of it. Next time they'll elect you."

"I still think it's nuts."

"Life's a lot like poker, Lon. Play the cards you're dealt."

Their discussion ended shortly before eleven o'clock. Thompson was summoned to the City Council conference room, down the hall from the mayor's office. He found Wheeler and the aldermen seated around a long table, all of them solemn as owls. They eyed his Prince Albert suit with looks of trepidation.

Earlier that morning, when he was dressing, Thompson had considered donning his police uniform. But then, with hardly a moment's thought, he'd left it hanging in the armoire. He felt it only fitting to retire the uniform with the badge. What was past was past.

"Listen to me now, Ben," Wheeler said, motioning him to a chair. "We've put it to a vote, and it's unanimous. We refuse to accept your resignation."

Thompson knuckled his mustache. "Tom, it's not like you've got a choice in the matter. I've resigned and that's that. It's official."

"Let me put in a word." Wayne Latham, the alderman for Guy Town, sat forward in his chair. "Marshal Thompson, as you'll recall, I opposed your election to office. But today, I've voted with these gentlemen." He nodded around the table. "We want you to stay on."

"Damn right!" Wally Peterman, who represented the First Ward, waved his arms. "So you killed some no-account in San Antonio. So what? Who cares!"

"I do," Thompson said soberly. "Alexander Wooldridge got it right during the election. He told the voters a 'shootist' shouldn't be allowed to wear a badge. I'm sorry to say I proved his point."

"That's old hat," Peterman countered. "You were cleared of that business in San Antonio. We need you here in Austin."

Thompson wagged his head. "What you need is a professional peace officer. Lon Dennville's the man for the job."

"You're wrong," Wheeler persisted. "Everybody in this room—the people of Austin!—want you. We're asking you to stay."

"Gentlemen, I appreciate your vote of confidence. But I guess I'll have to decline. Some things just aren't in the cards."

Thompson shook hands around the table. Then, with a final nod to Wheeler, he walked out of the room. He felt a momentary sense of pride that Wheeler and the aldermen had tried to argue him into staying on. But in the next instant, he knew he'd done the right thing— Austin would get the marshal it deserved.

On the way out of City Hall, he met Ed Creary coming through the door. The man he'd defeated in the election seemed more presentable than usual. He was dressed in a freshly pressed suit and he radiated confidence. His mouth creased in a sardonic grin.

"Well, Thompson," he said in a gloating voice. "The word's out you were forced to resign. Good news travels fast."

"I wasn't forced into anything," Thompson said. "I resigned for my own reasons."

"Likely story! You shouldn't go around shooting

people. Not on your own time, anyway. Doesn't look good."

"What's it to you one way or another?"

"What else?" Creary retorted. "Austin has to have a new marshal and I'm here to present my case. I've got an idea the city council will jump at the chance."

Thompson grunted. "They'd probably get railroaded out of town. You're too crooked for the job."

"You ought to learn to watch your mouth. I might just call you out."

"Go ahead, call me out."

Creary's hand edged toward the inside of his suit jacket. The move was hesitant, somehow tentative, but all the excuse Thompson needed. He popped the Colt from his shoulder holster and lashed out in a shadowy blur. The barrel struck Creary across the forehead in a splatt of blood and his hat went flying. His eyes rolled back in his head and he wilted at the knees. He dropped in a bloodied heap on the sidewalk.

A woman rounded the corner and stopped with a gasp. She looked from Thompson to the fallen man, and back again. "Ma'am," Thompson said, tipping his top hat. "You'll have to excuse the disturbance. I've been wanting to do that for a long time."

She glanced down at the sidewalk. "Isn't that Ed Creary?"

"Yes, ma'am, it is for a fact."

"Well, then, I say high time, Marshal Thompson."

"Former marshal, ma'am, but you're exactly right. High time."

Some ten minutes later Thompson walked through the door of the Iron Front. The noon hour was approaching and the bartenders were busy stocking shelves. Joe

Richter stood talking at the bar with Will Simms. The bartenders paused, greeting Thompson, and Richter hurried forward. He pumped Thompson's arm.

"By God, it's good to see you, Ben. You gave us a scare what with that business down in San Antonio."

Thompson laughed. "Had a good lawyer and an eyewitness. Will, here, was my ace in the hole."

"We were just talking about it," Richter said. "Will tells me you offered to put him back on the payroll."

"Joe, that's not the half of it."

Thompson briefly explained that he'd resigned as marshal. Before they could recover from the shock, he launched into a whole new plan for the future. He intended to buy the building next door, an older mercantile that was rapidly losing ground to the stores uptown. The building would be gutted and refurbished, and transformed into a variety theater. Will Simms would manage the operation.

"Last night it came to me," he went on. "There's money to be made in the show business, and Will's the perfect man for the job. Not to mention it'll draw even bigger crowds to the Iron Front."

"We'll be swamped!" Richter agreed heartily. "After the show, where else would they go? Right here!"

"Joe, that's the whole idea. We'll corner the market in Austin."

Richter and Simms fell to discussing how the Iron Front and the variety theater would work in tandem. Simms was wild-eyed with enthusiasm, already planning how he would stage the hottest vaudeville extravaganza in Texas. He'd bring in Eddie Foy, the great comedian, and Lola Montana, the exotic dancer. Maybe even Lillie Langtry, the toast of New York!

Thompson listened with appreciative interest. They

were both good men, and he knew they would make it a resounding success. Yet, even as they rambled on, his gaze was drawn to the poker tables at the rear of the room. A vagrant thought surfaced in his mind, and he wondered that he'd ever run for public office. For a time, goaded by some wayward ambition, he had pretended to be a lawman. The folly of it seemed to him now beyond reason.

There was, in the end, a sense of having come full circle. He was who he was—a gambler—and a damned good one. Perhaps the best who ever traveled the cowtowns and mining camps of the frontier. A sporting man with the nerve to bet it all on a single card.

One thought triggered another. He turned to Richter. "Spread the word to the high rollers. I'm open for business."

Richter appeared surprised. "You want a game tonight?"

"Tonight and every night, Joe. I'm back in action."

Thompson laughed with the wonder of it all. Old times or new times, it was the best of times. For he was where he belonged.

A gambling man with the world to win.